Black City
Tales From the Edge of the Abyss

By

Jane Grey

Black City

A HellBound Books LLC Publication

DEDICATION

For my co-conspirator…

See you in the Black City.

Jane Grey

INFERIS

CHAPTER ONE.

FRIDAY NIGHT, DECEMBER 2010.

"Trident" has always been the most popular bookshop at Ashbridge College. The building itself used to be a small, traditional Boston home on the edge of the campus, but sometime in the 1970's it was converted into a European-style coffee house. As the clientele were almost entirely students and faculty who would come there to read, one of the owners got the idea to convert one of the side rooms into a used bookstore, which did a brisk trade buying and selling various textbooks, monographs, and novels from Trident's small but bustling community. Sometimes the bookshop hosted poetry readings, author's nights, and even the occasional art exhibit in the former garage adjacent to the house proper. The coffee was good, the owners were friendly, and on a Friday night in December, there was really no better place to be, especially for those on a student budget.

On this particular night, I remember that it was cold, even for New England in December. I was meeting Jade and Reagan to study for the final exam of our common "Art and Myth" course. There was no question in my mind that I was absolutely doomed to fail the course, as weekend debauchery was pretty much the only subject I excelled at, but the same could not be said of my two friends. Jade was herself an art major and seemed to intuitively understand almost every nuance and brush-stroke of each sculpture and painting the instructor presented. She'd stare intensely at the image of some renaissance portrait for five minutes, without breathing, and then she'd write a detailed review of the artist, their state of mind, the meaning, the materials, and the exact technique used to create the painting. She would even, on a good day, tell you exactly what kind of rock, wood, or parchment had been used, and why the artist had picked that exact media. Reagan was a history major who usually couldn't tell an engraving from a print but made up for it with an uncanny grasp of dead cultures and their symbols. Put it this way: on the midterm exam, when I saw a three-bodied giant wrestling some dude in a lion-skin, Jade saw a second century CE carving in Italian limestone, while Reagan saw a Roman interpretation of Hercules wrestling the monster Geryon. They each got "A+" and I failed the midterm. Needless to say, I was hoping that studying with them would help with finals.

We'd been studying for a few hours when Jade announced it was break time. Trident was relatively quiet, as most students were studying in their rooms or in the campus library. The salon we were seated in had small radiators which kept the place warm, while the large windows were fogged up from the icy cold outside. Trident had a very friendly 'browsing' policy, and so you could pick several books out of the bookstore room and read them while you sipped your drink of choice. Consequently, the other tables had piles of books and magazines scattered across them, and so Reagan began thumbing through some of the stacks on the tables nearest to us. Most of them were used textbooks from students who were cramming for exams, like us, with the occasional very dated copy of Vogue magazine, or the rare copy of National Geographic or even Soldier of Fortune. Students (and a couple of faculty) sometimes wrote graffiti in the margins of books or magazines, so you might actually see running conversations between two or more people who were debating a point through competing annotations in various shades of red, blue, and black ink.

There was a sharp *thud* – a book had slipped off the table as Reagan momentarily fumbled with a pile of badly sorted textbooks on the table next to us. At first glance, it appeared to be a medium sized book with bits of newspaper and bookmarks sticking out, and I assumed it was someone's textbook with exam notes stuck inside. Cursing under his breath, Reagan stooped to pick it up so we could get a better look. It was a strange volume, medium sized and bound in grey cloth, with no title or author immediately evident on the front cover. When Reagan flipped through it, it appeared to be a journal of some kind, with a mix of handwritten essays and personal entries, together with newspaper clippings and other photos that had been glued and stapled into the book's pages. The back page of the book was blank, except for the word *INFERIS* written in very large black letters. The author had then scrawled what looked like a spiral below this title, and all of this in a very clean hand, as if by someone from that generation that had studied and learned penmanship at school.

Jade returned from the barista, carrying three steaming mugs of java. She saw us leafing through the newfound book.

"What's that?" she asked, putting the coffee mugs down on our table.

"Not sure," said Reagan, "I think someone left it behind, it must be someone's journal." He and I took our mugs of hot coffee, and I began putting a decent helping of sugar into mine.

"Well, maybe we should turn it to the barista instead of reading it?" she suggested pointedly.

"Sure, we can do that," I nodded, "but this isn't someone's daily confessions, it's more like someone's scrapbook of history."

"Or a manifesto," Reagan looked up from the notebook. "This thing is really odd."

"Odd how?" asked Jade. She eased herself into her chair, and we too took our seats at the table.

"Take a look," the history major handed her the tattered book. As he passed it to her, I got a better look at the thing. For a moment I thought it looked grimy, but then realized it was not so much dirty as it was just extremely well worn, with more pages dog-eared than not.

Jade took the notebook and started to thumb through it. She was a slow reader, not because she was slow to read, but because she was incapable of seeing the words and not the page. She glanced through several pages, turning two, three, four folios and then she paused.

"What is that?" she muttered, and she lifted the book to her nose to take its scent.

Her nose wrinkled. "It smells like rusted metal, I think iron, or maybe copper. And some of the pages have been stained with alcohol, probably whiskey."

I hadn't noticed that at first, but now that she had said it, some of the pages did seem stained with water, or whiskey, or something similar. The pages were off-white, but some sections had faint splash marks, which you don't get from tinted drinks like coffee or tea.

"Also, look here," she pointed to a particular page, with very clean, evenly handwritten lines. "This is very good writing. But look here," and she turned forward several pages, where there was a jagged newspaper clipping that had been badly stapled into the book.

There were dark, smudgy circles around several sections of the clipping in what looked like a thick blue crayon; the number '11' seemed to feature prominently in whatever newspaper story it came from.

"Or here," she turned to the front of the book, where several of the pages looked to be typed with an old typewriter, in a brownish-red ink, so old that it was almost black. "Who puts together a book with beautiful penmanship, badly inserted newspaper clippings, and uses wax crayons to highlight things?"

Admittedly, it was an odd combination. I reached to take the book from her, and she passed it to me. I started flipping through it, trying to look through it with something passing for a detective's eye. Most of the entries were in English, but a couple pages had texts or clippings in Greek, Latin, and something that looked like Arabic or Persian. The numbers '11' and the shape of a dark spiral were scrawled frequently throughout the entire text, sometimes in that same blue crayon, other times in the neat handwriting, and sometimes in messy, almost angry black pencil marks. Some of the sections had weird title names, like "Annunaki," "Irkalla," and "Chthonic Devotion". Some pages had weird, esoteric diagrams of circles inside of other circles, triangles with eyes, and some strange characters that looked hieroglyphic. Other pages had photos of deep holes in the ground, either manmade or sinkholes. There were also images of politicians and military figures, some of whom I recognized, like Kennedy and Hitler. Some of the newspaper stories mentioned these leaders by name, and in the margins, the book's maker had scribbled 'DO THEY SERVE IT?"

"Sort of a strange book for someone to leave here," I mused out loud, "it looks like it took a while to piece that thing together. Do you see a name anywhere on it?"

"Well there's no name – but maybe the title means something," remarked Jade, "the one on the back page, it reads '*Inferis*.' Does that mean anything to either of you?"

We both looked at Reagan, of course. He looked intrigued.

"It could be Latin for 'below,' or 'the darkness,' or 'the underworld.'" he mused. "It's more a question of which particular symbology to use – dark places come up in so many different cultures. It's a really common symbol, I mean the 'darkness' is literally everywhere as a concept.”

“Semiotics,” I pointed out sagely.

“What’s that?” he asked?

“Symbology isn’t a real word,” I observed with feigned patience, and with the studied air of someone who is trying to parody an expert. “The term you’re looking for is *semiotics*.”

Reagan chuckled. “Well done, grasshopper, and if you can remember that for the final exam, you might actually pass.”

The final exam. I felt a sudden cold feeling in the pit of my stomach and remembered the reason I was meeting my friends.

At that point, my interest in the book began to wane very quickly, and so I waved a hand dismissively and reached for the course textbook, and my badly cribbed study notes.

Jade, however, folded her arms and leaned back in the chair.

“*Inferis*. Deep places. Dark places. Caves? Well, I

remember from my 'Mediterranean Archaeology' class that most Near Eastern cultures depicted the underworld as a black pit, and a couple university teams have actually found these bottomless pits when doing digs in Lebanon and Turkey. Maybe it's someone's archaeology journal?"

Reagan shrugged.

"I guess it's possible," he replied, "because there are some dead language fragments in there, but the majority of the collection sure doesn't look like it has anything to do with archaeology at all."

"What do you make of it then?" Jade pressed him. Her eyes were narrowed, indicating that she was challenging him to see who was the better art critic. Sometimes I wanted to punch them both for being so smug.

"Well, how can I tell? I've only seen it for a few minutes," he shot back, "but at a glance, I'd say the author has serious mental issues and is given to conspiracy theories involving dark, square shaped objects, and a phobia of digits that add up to nine."

"Lame," retorted Jade, "that kind of mental weakness will get you zero on the exam."

"Think you can do better?" he shot back.

"Even Tom can do better," she indicated me across the table. I made a face and buried my nose deeper in my art history textbook. This was not a game I intended to play.

"But I'll tell you what," she steepled her hands and leaned forward. "We'll take turns. The owner won't miss it for one or two more nights, so I'll keep it tonight and give it a read through, then you do the same tomorrow night. We each draft a list of key details, then compare notes. Tom will cross-check and keep score. Whoever has the most information wins free coffee for a month."

"Oh, you're on," Reagan smiled widely, his eyes glinting.

"You're stealing the book?" I asked with some concern.

"It's lost and found," Reagan said, "we're really just borrowing it, so we can figure out to whom it needs to be returned."

"But what about the exam on Monday – are you seriously going to waste the weekend on this?" I asked curiously.

"Come on," Jade retorted, "if you actually understood art, you wouldn't need to *study* to pass the exam."

"Some would say," Reagan interjected, "if you had actually studied, you wouldn't need to *understand* art to pass the exam."

Jade glared at him across the table.

"Give me the damn book."

Reagan passed it back to her. She glanced around the room to see if anyone was watching and stuffed the book into her backpack. Jade locked eyes with the historian and raised her mug of coffee. There was a soft *chink* as Reagan's mug brushed against it, as if one lance had glanced off another.

The game was on.

SATURDAY MORNING

After drinking several mugs of coffee, and struggling to study as late as possible, it would not be fair to say that I slept well. After exchanging a series of texts with Jade and Reagan, I made my way to the college cafeteria for Saturday morning brunch. The morning air was cold, much as the night before, and my shoes crunched on the snow and ice that covered the walkway from my dormitory to the college restaurant. Ashbridge College had one of the better university cafeterias in the New England region, and though I realize that is pretty back-handed praise, we did eat well. My usual Saturday brunch was a mix of sausages, bacon, fried tomatoes, and home-fries, all covered in a generous dose of steak sauce. That particular day, I helped myself to a slightly healthier breakfast of fruit salad and coffee, as I felt I needed the vitamins to be in better shape for the exam.

As usual, Reagan was there before me. He was a chronic early riser, and he was also not a big breakfast eater, preferring a hot coffee and a muffin. I joined him at the table, and as I was ravenous from studying all night, I started right away without waiting for Jade.

Eventually Jade showed up, looking tired with heavy, dark circles under her eyes. She tended to be fair-skinned, and winter didn't usually help, but she seemed even paler than normal. She came to our table with her cafeteria try largely empty, except for a glass of apple juice and some cereal. Slumping into the chair beside me, Jade mumbled good morning and started mechanically eating. I just assumed she'd stayed up late reading the book, until she said:

"I had really, *really* fucked up dreams last night." She actually shuddered in her chair.

"Yeah? Maybe it was too much coffee before bed?" I suggested.

"No," she shook her head, "it was reading that scrapbook before bed. I spent the entire night having nightmares about painting these big black canvases, with spirals, and sigils, and eyes. Whenever I'd finish a painting, the eyes would start following me around the rooms. I know it doesn't sound scary when I say it out loud, but in the dream, it was terrifying. What was worse was the shadows. In my dream, these shadowy figures kept coming out of the spirals and into the room where I was working. Then when I'd wake up from the dream, I kept seeing them in the room. I rubbed my eyes until they went away, but then it was hard to fall back asleep. When I feel back asleep, I was painting more of those black canvases."

She paused and rubbed her eyes. "God damned night terrors, I guess. That, and way, way too much coffee before bed. That is one messed up scrapbook, belonging to a truly disturbed individual."

"Sorry you didn't sleep well. Then I guess you didn't take any notes from the book?" Reagan asked. He seemed concerned, but I could sense the competitive tone underneath the sympathy.

"Fuck that noise," she snapped, "I took notes. You don't get to see them until you take your own turn with the book." She reached into her backpack and pulled out the grey journal. Just for a moment, I could smell a hint of rusted copper as she slid the text across the table to Reagan. He took the book, nodding to her in acknowledgement, and place it in his own satchel.

"I'll read it tonight and write up my list of notes. We can meet after the exam on Monday, in the Library, and Tom can decide which of us has the better set of notes. Then it goes back to Trident, or to the owner if we can figure out who it might be."

Jade nodded. "Sure, whatever. God, I'm tired, I think I'm going to finish breakfast and go back to bed for a few hours. I'm really feeling drained – can't afford to get sick before the exam."

"You should definitely sleep," I said, "even a few hours will make a big difference. We can meet up at suppertime, if you guys are feeling like taking a break for food."

Jade and Reagan agreed, and we parted ways to

study. I actually spent several hours, productively cramming information that I'd ignored for most of the semester. I was pleasantly surprised at my own progress. When I met my friends at dinner time, Jade looked a lot better rested, and the three of us spent a good hour seriously discussing what might and might not be on the exam, and how we planned to spend the Christmas break. They each planned to go to their respective homes, while I was going to stay on campus, as my parents were themselves wintering in Florida, and I did not relish being at home alone for the vacation. As it grew dark, Reagan indicated that he was heading to the Library to read the scrapbook, while Jade and I decided to study at Trident.

SUNDAY.

If Friday evening was weird, and Saturday more so for Jade's reports of nightmares, Sunday is when things began to feel somewhat surreal.

When we three met again on Sunday for breakfast the cafeteria was pretty quiet. Most students had finished their exams already, and the upcoming Art History final on Monday was literally one of the last exams of the semester. So in a room that served breakfast to usually 300 people at a time, there were probably fifty students at most.

Jade looked worse than the day before. She was tired and short tempered and ignored our polite questions about whether she'd slept better than the previous night. We passed breakfast mostly in silence. Eventually, though, at the end of the meal, Jade confessed that she'd experienced the same nightmare, except this time it was worse. She was not only painting black canvases with strange symbols, but also painting weird symbols on the walls of, as if the paintings were exceeding the limit of the canvas and growing outward into the space itself. Again and again she'd tried to wake up, but failed, and when she finally had awoken, she had a perverse urge to go to the campus art studio and actually recreate one of the paintings from the dream. She sometimes painted things that she dreamed about – all artists do – but she felt that in this case, it would not be a wise idea.

"It wouldn't even be hard to do it," she said, "but it would be creepy and weird. I need less nightmares, not more."

I am not by nature a superstitious person, and don't normally believe in psychic phenomena of any kind. But this all seemed pretty obvious.

"It's that insane conspiracy notebook," I stated in a matter-of-fact tone of voice. "It was written by someone who was clearly deranged, you read it while you're in a state of stress from exams, and some of the author's craziness has managed to transmit itself to your subconscious. Let's just return the creepy thing, or throw it out, or whatever. I think your competition is just going to cause you more stress than it's worth."

"Well for my part," chimed in Reagan, "I read it straight through all last night, and I made my list of notes, but I didn't have any weird dreams, or visions, or anything creepy. I didn't sleep much, granted, but I feel completely fine today. Sorry Jade, I think Tom is right – you're just stressed out from exams. Maybe sleep a few hours after lunch, that seemed to perk you up yesterday."

Jade rubbed at her eyes and yawned. She nodded. "You're both right, I'm clearly just tired. But that journal is still completely fucked up."

Reagan nodded. "Yeah, I can't argue there. What is with the author's obsession with the number 11? It's funny, I didn't mind reading the clippings or the weird messy notes, but the red typewriter pages were just – I dunno – they just felt cold somehow. Who uses a typewriter today, anyway?”

Jade drew her scarf tighter around her throat and shivered from the cold. The cafeteria was normally warm, even uncomfortably so from the heat of the kitchens, but today the warmth seemed to have been swallowed up by the frosty windows.

“Plans for the weekend?” I asked, eager to discuss something that did not involve red typewriters, or other abnormal scrapbooking fetishes.

“What, besides studying for finals?” returned Reagan. “Just hitting the books. I think I’ll keep working in the Library today, it’s really empty since almost everyone has finished exams and left. You guys should join me there, if you like, then maybe we can hit Trident later for a break.”

That sounded good to me. “I’m in,” I said. We both looked at Jade.

“I think I’ll stay in and draft some black spirals on my walls,” she said in a strangely quiet voice.

“Are you serious?” I asked, surprised.

She laughed sharply. “Are you fucking insane? Hell no, the Library sounds good. I’m going to crash for an hour, then I’ll meet you guys there.”

We finished breakfast, cleared our trays, and Jade headed back to her room to rest, while Reagan and I went straight to the Library to start the final review session. The air outside was chilly, but not unpleasantly cold, and we crossed the small campus briskly. With Jade gone to her room, Reagan confessed he was intrigued by the journal.

"I didn't want to wax poetic while Jade was complaining of nightmares," he started, "but that book is such a mystery! I really have no idea who would have put it together, but they've managed to stitch together their own very complex neurosis and conspiracy theories, together with some bizarre occult and astrology concepts I've never read about before."

"What, so it's some kind of Scientology manifesto?" I asked, trying to sound like I understood him.

"Ahhh, no, not quite." He smirked. "That's not an entirely bad parallel though. No, it's more like some very intelligent and well-read person has taken it into their head that there is some kind of death-worshipping movement which is secretly working to take control of planet earth. That's the abridged version in thirty words or less. The scary thing is that whoever put together the text has managed to find evidence of underworld cults in about ten different cultures, which are not remotely connected in terms of their geography, but they all seem to have held the same basic ideas, even the same semiotics."

"And what would those be?"

"Well, in two words, 'the underworld.' Some religions or myths personify it as an entire universe made up of this seething blackness, like these cold liquid shadows that are expanding and contracting all at once. It pops up in different cultures under different names. The Greeks called it "Erebus," and Romans called it "Inferis," the Babylonians called it "Irkalla" or "Kur" but the basic idea of this weird living darkness is pretty much universal."

"So what's the connection with the number 11, or the spiral?" I asked. Despite my aversion to anything involving art, or history, Reagan was making this interesting.

"Well that's trickier. Before I read the scrapbook, I wouldn't have had any ideas. But having read it, there's a few answers that the book's compiler seems to advance. To start with, take the number 11 – there is this old Buddhist king that has many problems with his people, like rebels and famine and plagues, all the thing a ruler worries about. So he petitions the bodhisattvas to help him save his kingdom, but they don't answer. Next he entreats the Mara, the personification of darkness, and the Mara appears and gives him the means to summon these 11 demons to assist in the political issues. Things get weird at that point. So, if you focus on the number of spirits, which is 11, and then you look at Babylonian mythology, the goddess Tiamat also has 11 companions. That's not a coincidence, there's obviously a connection between those stories."

"So the Buddhists borrowed it from Babylon?" I asked.

Reagan shrugged. "Honestly, I have no idea. Maybe?"

We were nearing the library. The sun shone dully off the frost and ice near the walkway, crunching under our shoes. I wanted to reach the building and get out of the cold. Reagan continued his description of the book.

"Then there's the symbolism of the black spiral. That thing is everywhere, like literally everywhere on the planet. I did a Google search for "black spiral" or "underworld + spiral" the stuff you find is nuts. There are artistic installations of giant black spirals all over the planet. Seriously, look it up yourself. The Kaaba in Mecca is black, and what do people do? They circumambulate the thing. The Kaaba even has a black meteorite in its side that used to be a cult object of the underworld goddess Allat, and the Moslems still kiss the thing today when they circumambulate on pilgrimage."

"What's circum – ah – circumambulance?" I asked cautiously.

"Oh, it means to circle something, again and again," he explained, "You can see it on YouTube. The notebook claims that it's mirroring the rings of Saturn, which circulate the planet itself. And that's another thing – there's this storm at the north pole of Saturn, in a hexagonal shape, which is a two-dimensional interpretation of a spiral."

"You're saying that there is a black spiral on Saturn?" I asked.

"No," he corrected, "I'm saying that there is this perpetual storm at Saturn's north pole, and NASA has no real explanation for it. It just keeps going around, and around, and around in the shape of a hexagon."

"Weird," I said.

"It gets even more weird. You should read the descriptions of what people thought the underworld looked like. I mean, some mystics just thought the actual entity was this monstrous black ocean. Any other shape was just an avatar for dealing with people."

"How else did it appear?" I asked, somewhat intrigued.

"Well," Reagan paused, "it's different in every mythology. Take the Romans – they believed that "Inferis" wasn't just a place, it was an entity. The Assyrians called it 'Irklla,' and they had the same idea, like it was a place *and* a god, and it's the reason for all the evil in their understanding of the universe. There are some weird Arab texts where the Islamic underworld, al-Gehennam, is described as a hostile presence that pre-dates the cosmos. Like Allah didn't make it, he *found* it, crawling through space when he started creation. Anyway, call it the underworld, or living darkness, or hell – it's all the same, and no one loved it, everyone feared it, but this notebook says that a few people are crazy enough to worship it."

"Why would anyone do that?" I asked.

"Despair, I guess?" Reagan mused. "Or a love of black chaos and death. If someone got to the point where they had absolutely no faith in the status quo, and they'd just given up on the gods and on their fellow humans to do anything positive, the underworld would be the kind of being that might make a really interesting master."

"You mean ally, don't you?" I suggested.

"No, there's absolutely no culture that ever approached the underworld as an equal. The journal has a couple examples of spells and rituals from the different cultures, and they're all the same. The words *"Master"* *"Sovereign"* and *"Please don't eat me,"* all seem to occur frequently."

I laughed, and Reagan chuckled too.

"So you actually read some *real* spells?" I asked.

"Yes a few," he said, "though I didn't understand all the words. I mean, the Latin and Greek stuff is easy enough, and the Arabic material is a lot harder, but I can read all of that. It's the Etruscan that is just gibberish to me."

"What's Etruscan?" I asked.

Reagan frowned. "Well no one is totally sure, but they're the indigenous people of Italy, before the Italians came. They had a really nihilistic religious system, pretty much all demons, and no gods at all. They believed that the underworld was alive, like some kind of unending black storm. Weird, eh?"

***

We reached the Library and climbed up the short flight of stairs to the entrance. God, it was getting cold. I reached for the door handle. The Library was clearly open and the entryway lights all should have been on, but we found that the foyer was quite dark. Assuming that the entryway bulbs had just been shut off by accident, I motioned for Reagan to enter the dimly lit library.

There was a blur that began in the darkness and shot out towards the unsuspecting Reagan. A furious shadow obscured his face, screaming hideously at him, and then it darted away. A crow, I realized. Reagan stood in the doorway in shock, blood running down from a very nasty gash over his eye. The sound of the crow receded rapidly.

"What the fuck," Reagan breathed, his eyes wide in shock. I let go of the door and moved to help him.

An actual storm of crows (a *murder*, my subconscious whispered) erupted from the Library's closing door, hammering into us as they streamed past. Instinctively, I shut my eyes and threw up my arms to cover my face as best as I could. Caught off balance, Reagan lurched backwards away from the door and ploughed hard into me, knocking me to the ground. Hundreds (it felt like) of beaks and claws scraped at my hands, hair and neck, pecking and biting, and I was sure that small bits of flesh were being excised with each bite. I screamed again and again, wanting to flail at the mass of birds, but terrified to let them get at my undefended face. The birds shrieked and cawed with the most hateful aggression I'd ever seen. It was like being buffeted like a hurricane.

The sudden silence around us was deafening. Cautiously, I opened my eyes just enough to peak out. The birds were gone. Gingerly, I sat up, feeling at my face and looking at my hands. Oddly, there was no blood. In fact, as I surveyed my hands, there were no marks at all. The skin hurt in places, but there was no evidence at all that I'd been swarmed by a murder of crows. The same could not entirely be said of Reagan, who was still bleeding from the same initial gash over his eye. But even this was not a deep cut, on inspection, and he too had no visible evidence of assault.

We struggled to our feet, careful not to slip on the ice.

"What the hell was that?" I asked aloud. "Where did those birds come from?"

"Or where did they go?" Reagan answered, looking around, still with the air of someone in shock. "Jesus, let's get inside before they come back."

He moved to the entrance of the Library, and hesitantly opened the door. This time, the light of the Library interior shone brightly and warmly. No sudden shadows or movements flicked inside, in fact there was no evidence that anything strange had happened at all. We made our way into the building. It felt warm, and more importantly, safe.

"Did I just imagine that?" Reagen asked cautiously. His eyes looked understandably haunted.

"You're bleeding from just over your eye, so I would say not," I offered.

In the absence of any further strange phenomena, we found a quiet corner in which to work. The Library was still open through to tomorrow, the final exam day, so I was comforted that we were not alone. Small clusters of students were busy cramming for their finals, and several librarians moved through the stacks. I found the presence of other people reassuring. Reagan went to the restroom to wash the blood off his face, and I took a moment to get the attention of one of the librarians.

"Have there been any birds in the Library?" I asked her cautiously.

The librarian looked puzzled. "No, there's no animals of any kind allowed. You can't bring birds, cats, or dogs into the building, sorry."

I shook my head. "My friend and I just got attacked by a flock of blackbirds in the entryway. You must have heard them."

The librarian pursed her lips. "Sorry, I definitely didn't hear or see anything like that. If there were a flock of birds in the Library, someone would definitely have reported it."

"We were *attacked*," I insisted.

"Oh, well, were you injured?" she asked cautiously. She was looking around now, as if for someone to jump out with a candid camera.

"No, but another student was, and he's just in the washroom washing the blood off his face."

The librarian didn't seem impressed. "Look, if you're trying to get out of a final exam, you're going to need a note from the campus medical center, and I don't think we can help you with that. We haven't had any bird sightings, or attacks, or anything like that, and the Library doesn't have any animal issues, we keep the space very clean. Now if you'll excuse me, I have to get back to work." And with that, she turned to help some desperate graduate student who couldn't find a misfiled book.

Very aware that I had no cuts, scrapes, or other signs of having been rushed by an angry swarm of crows, I decided to let it drop. Somehow, it seemed to me that it was better to ignore weird events like what we'd just experienced, and just to focus on the day-to-day reality that governed things like exams and grades.

I took my textbooks out of my backpack and began to stack them onto the wooden desk. Among them, impossibly, was the grey scrapbook.

My skin began to crawl. *What the hell was going on?* I knew for sure that I had not packed that book, and

I had absolutely no interest in reading it. Whatever its contents, they had nothing to do with passing my upcoming final exam, and Jade and Reagan's weird competition just did not interest me – in fact, I felt a surge of distaste even looking at it. I knew that Reagan ought to have had it, and I began to wonder if somehow he'd managed to put it in my bag during the confusion with the crows.

At that moment, he returned from the washroom. With the blood washed off his face, it was plain that he had a nasty cut, but it didn't appear to be bleeding any further. The gash ran across his eye, but mercifully seemed to have avoided doing any serious damage, apart from leaving a cut that would probably heal into a fairly livid scar if he didn't get stitches.

Reagan sat down across the table from me and began to open his own backpack. He paused as he saw me holding the grey scrapbook. "How did you get that?" he asked in surprise. "I thought it was in my bag."

"No idea," I replied, and held it out to him. "Here, take the damn thing. It's creepy, I don't even like to look at it."

He took it from me. "You know, it's odd," he said, "I was just thinking about one of the passages in the book, about the way that the underworld manifests in the material world. Here, I think the compiler had a page that lists its traits in different cultures... yes, here it is! Ok, so just to give you some context –"

I cut him off.

"You were just attacked by a swarm of crows in the entry of the library, and you're thinking about that book?"

He nodded, "Yes, it's all connected. So the compiler notes that there is this famous Arabic alchemist named Al-Majriti, and he might or might not have authored this famous grimoire called the 'Death of the Soul,' or *Mawt al'Ruh*, if you use the Arabic name. Crazy stuff, spells for controlling the weather, destroying cities, talking to gods from outer space, it's totally Lovecraftian."

"Who's Lovecraft?" I asked in a puzzled voice. It sounded like the stage name of a second-rate porn star.

"Lovecraft, famous author, early forerunner of American sci-fi and horror. He was totally insane and wrote about horrible star gods and entities that want to consume us all. He invented some terrible book called the Necronomicon, which is really borrowed from al-Majriti's supposed manuscript, which is said to be in three pieces in Leiden, Paris, and London."

"You are making this shit up," I accused.

"I swear I'm not," he replied, "and more importantly, there is an actual complete manuscript called the *Mawt al'Ruh*, totally famous in the medieval period, and it has these spells for calling down spirits from the stars, or up from the darkness beyond space."

"Like Inferis?" I guessed.

"Exactly," he nodded. "So this book, the *Mawt al'Ruh*, it has all kinds of crazy rites to summon these spirits, and I kid you not, some of the rituals are really psychotic stuff. Blood sacrifices, narcotic incenses, fasting – I mean, if you actually did any of the rituals, the opiates in the incenses would give you visions for sure, whether or not any kind of spirit actually showed up."

"You are suggesting," I said hesitantly, "that some Arabic book has actual spells for calling up spirits, and that they work."

"Of course not," he said in an exasperated tone, "but I'm saying that there were hundreds of people who tried this stuff out in the medieval period, and they swore that it worked. Like even devout Muslims, like Ibn Khaldun, admitted to successfully experimenting with some of these rites.”

“Who’s Ibn Khal-doom? Some wizard from ‘Conan the Barbarian’?” I asked. I really liked Reagan, but the guy was a walking encyclopedia who seemed genuinely unaware that not everyone else had occult Wikipedia downloaded into their brain.

“Ibn Khal-*doon*” he emphasized the pronunciation, “Not a wizard, he was the social scientist who invented sociology. He wrote in his major work that he experimented with the *Mawt al’Ruh* and had some very real shit happen to him.”

“Reagan, how did we go from raven attacks to some Arab sociology guy?”

Reagan made this gesture with his hands like re-winding a tape. “Sorry, Tom. Ok, so there are books, like the *Mawt al’Ruh* and the fictional Necronomicon, and they describe all these ancient gods and spirits. Anyway, the crazy person who compiled the scrapbook has a ton of passages in Arabic and Latin, and a couple of them are talking about these really bad entities that serves the powers of underworld. Like, they believed they manifested as ravens, snakes, even as people, and that very bad people could summon them to do some really awful stuff, if they performed these rituals, which the book explains in really clear detail.”

“So you are saying that the scrapbook has these ancient Arabic spells and rituals for summoning malevolent spirits, because some ancient death cult actually did that, and that the scrapbook compiler actually believed in this shit.”

“Yes, that’s pretty much it.”

I shook my head. “Seriously, I’m starting to think that this is all some elaborate joke that you and Jade are playing on me. I bet you’re making up the entire thing – the Arabic *Mawt*-al-whatever-you-call-it, this underworld cult, evil spirits, Jade pretending to have bad dreams, this is just some stupid joke. Look, you guys might not have to study, but some of us actually need to work to pass Art History. Enough is enough."

Reagen looked taken aback. "You can't honestly believe that. Did you not just see the raven claw open my face?"

"I don't know what I saw, and I honestly don't care."

Reagen flipped open the book, turned a few pages, running his fingers across several pages and newspaper clippings as he searched for something. He found it and turned the book around.

"Read this" he said.

"No," I retorted, "I've had enough of your stupid game. Get that thing out of my face."

"Tom, I'm not making this up. Seriously, we can get the library to find some essays on the *Mawt al'Ruh* in the stacks or online. The *Mawt al'Ruh* is an entirely real book, I am not inventing it, and it really does seem to have some pretty fucked up stuff about the underworld cult."

"Fine," I folded my arms. "If you want me to take this seriously at all, you get me a serious article or essay on the *Mawt al'Ruh*. If it's even a real book, I will consider taking this scrapbook thing seriously. Otherwise, you and Jade are just wasting my time."

Reagan raised his hand, as if in class, and one of the librarians came to our table. It was, I noticed, the young woman who had spoken to me earlier. She looked suspiciously at me for a moment, but then nodded appreciatively when Reagan made his research request. She led us over to one of the Library research kiosks and typed in several keywords to the search panel. Over her shoulder, I could see her enter the search terms "Darkness + underworld + manuscript + occult +

history" into the library's system. At least a dozen entries popped up, and she sent the top ranked essays to the printer, which was next to the research kiosk. Reagan used his student card to pay for them, and the printer began to spit out several pages on this supposed "*Mawt al'Ruh*" book. When the printer stopped, he passed me a small mountain of documents. I confess, the titles alone were intimidating – things like "Feeding Hell: a study in Proto-Semitic Linguistics", "Sacrifices to al-Gehennam: Motifs in Islamic Art," "Erebus, Irkalla, and the Netherworld as Magical Deities." I skimmed several, and as best as I could tell, Reagan was right – these different ancient cultures really did seem to think the underworld wasn't just a place, it was a living thing. Moreover, the various essays all seemed to refer to the Arabian *Mawt al'Ruh* as one of the key texts in understanding that particular theory.

"Ok," I conceded, "Clearly this *Mawt al'Ruh* thing is a real book. Those were actual spells the professor was discussing?"

Reagan gestured. "That's what I'm trying to tell you – it's what the whole scrapbook is kinda about. It's like there is this weird esoteric fascination with Darkness, and it runs through a lot of cultures. Not all of them, maybe, but a lot of them."

This constant repetition of the underworld was beginning to feel really creepy. I'd been mad when I thought momentarily that this was some ridiculous exam-time hoax, but it had also been comforting. Equally, where Jade and Reagan seemed fascinated by reading that occult journal, I considered it as enlightening as reading the scribbles on the wall in someone's cell in an insane asylum. Like, there might be a few lines worthy of Facebook, but the rest of it would be total nonsense.

But this new idea – that the book was not entirely

crazy – that did not sit well with me, not at all.

"You said before," I asked slowly, trying to digest this all, "that this ancient Arabic text talks about evil gods, and spirals, and ravens? I don't mean the journal," I gestured to the weird, metallic scented scrapbook on the table, "I mean that *Mawt al'Ruh* thing. The real occult book."

Reagan looked thoughtful for a moment. I knew that look, he did it whenever I asked him something that I thought was simple and was actually a real headache for him to answer, because it was complex. Lucky for me, he was not one to give up easily on missing the chance to look smart.

"Think of it like this," he said, "there are a lot of books, I mean entire libraries of weird, nasty occult books written in Arabic, Persian, Turkish, Coptic, Greek, other eastern languages like that, and we've only translated a handful of them. The ones that have been translated, I know some of them. The *Mawt al'Ruh* is the one that was really popular in the west, probably the most popular, so you can find it in a lot of places. What the scrapbook is saying is that ALL of those cultures had their own weird deviant underworld cult. But whoever compiled the journal, they were definitely fascinated with the Arabic materials – you can tell because they included a lot of examples from the text."

"This *Mawt al'Ruh* book is only one example of a larger set of manuscripts then?" I asked, trying to understand how big this picture was.

"Yes, exactly," he nodded, "it's the most popular one in Western scholarship, but we don't know if the Arabs themselves prized it that much. What is more relevant is that there are a number of Arabic texts that are all death-obsessed, and they all describe this underground spiritual movement that worshipped "living death" as some kind of literal black entity that they believed was outside the entire solar system."

"Like a god?"

"They use the term, but I don't know what they mean by that."

"Were the Arabs Muslims?"

"Sure, some were," he said, "but there's Muslims, and then there's Muslims, right? And some were pagans, or Jews, or Christians, and these are just labels. Like, for example, take those Catholics in Mexico who worship Santa la Muerte – the Vatican does not recognize them as Catholics, but you try and tell them they're not Christian. I think it's the same with these people – they might have worshipped Allah on Friday, but then sacrificed a black ram to the underworld on Saturday. Stuff like that happens."

"And the scrapbook has passages from different Arabic texts that show evidence of this historic underworld cult?" I asked.

"Yes, exactly, and with similar traits, like death, reaping, the cold, ravens, spiral imagery. The compiler has already put together what he claims are passages from different texts. But he's not claiming that it's a historic sect – he's saying this death cult is still entirely operational."

"That's crazy, Reagan." I replied.

"I guess. I dunno about the modern stuff like Kennedy or Oppenheimer. Honestly, at this point, I'm intrigued by the historical sources he's pulled together. There's references to some books I don't even know, like the '*Kitab al-Istimatis*' and the '*Letters of the Brethren of Purity*.' It's going to take weeks to check this stuff all out. Jesus, that's only the Arabic sources, I'm not even thinking of the Hellenistic or Sanskrit materials."

"You're not actually going to waste any more time

on this?" I asked in alarm. This had been interesting, but he seemed a little too enthusiastic with the work of a crazy person, whether or not it had any half-truths to it. I mean, a conspiracy that includes the sun rising every day does not make it any better a conspiracy, just because the sun does happen to rise daily.

"Oh hell yeah!" Reagan exclaimed, "I need to know if there's any truth to it. This is going to take the entire break – maybe the entire semester. I mean, if even half of this checks out, this would make an incredible undergraduate thesis. Heck, I could even use this for doctoral work, I could get a serious grant for this research." This last point seemed to seize his imagination, and he busied himself in cross-checking the *Mawt al' Ruh* essay against the grey scrapbook.

Maybe I should have tried harder to stop Reagan from what sounded like an insane project, but you need to appreciate that as I was only barely passing Art History (and college in general), my hopes of changing Reagan's mind were literally nil. He was a good friend, but he was always terribly pleased with his own academic prowess, and so I just could not bring myself to argue with him further. Besides, if he said it could lead to a scholarship of some kind, maybe it was not a complete waste of his time.

As we seemed to have finished the conversation, I turned my attention to preparing for the Art History exam. Reagan, however, seemed intent on following up on more leads on the scrapbook, and so he made increasing trips to the shelves and the research kiosks. Then he monopolized the small library's printer and photocopier and came back armed with a small mountain of photocopies and printed essays. He made even more notes, got more books, printed more electronic documents, and made more photocopies. Not once did he appear to have any interest in studying for the exam.

After Reagan had continued in this way (searching, printing, copying) for no less than three hours, Jade appeared in the Library entrance, and seeing us, made her way to our table. She looked a lot better rested that she had a few hours earlier in the cafeteria. Our table, of course, now looked like the Battle of Waterloo had been fought in stacks of paper and messy notes. Some of the notes had spilled off the table and onto the floor, and the various piles of books and photocopies vied against each other like a city of leaning towers about to collapse.

"Guys, what happened here?" she asked, pulling up a chair and pointing at the papers scattered about us.

"I'm getting a student research grant, that's what's happening here," Reagan looked up from the scrapbook. His eyes looked harried and his face was flushed, as though he'd had a really, really good cup of coffee. "So many connections, Jade, they're just, I mean, this underworld movement is everywhere. These notes are just the tip of the iceberg."

Jade was staring at the claw mark over his left eye. "Jesus, Reagan, what happened to your face?"

Reagan passed a hand over the scar. Over the time we'd been in the library, the bleeding had stopped entirely, but a nasty pink welt glistened wetly where the raven had scratched him.

"Oh, this? Bird attack, of all things."

"You got attacked by a bird? Shit, was it rabid?"

"I don't think so. Can birds even get rabies?" Reagan glanced at me. I shrugged, having no idea.

"I'm fine, really. It stings a little, but I'll splash some rubbing alcohol on it later. I must have startled it, coming into the library."

Jade looked like she would have pressed the issue further, but at that moment, her phone chimed. She pulled it out and checked to see what the text message was. As she read it, her face darkened.

"Son of a bitch!" she spat. She put the phone back into her jacket a bit forcefully, and folded her arms across her chest.

"What's wrong?" I asked with concern.

She took a deep breath.

"Do you remember that band on campus that had me design some graphics for them?" In addition to being a gifted art student, she was also a much sought after painter and designer, and she paid most of her room and board through her artistic talents. Evenings and weekends even if I could convince Reagan to leave the library, it was much harder to get Jade out of the studio. She would work hours, days even, on the smallest projects, and was an absolute perfectionist. She wasted many a perfect weekend, holed up and brooding over the right paint shade or image to use in a particular piece.

"I think so, the new death metal group, *Shades of Erebus*," I remembered aloud.

"Yeah, exactly right. Well their vocalist just texted me to say that they love the new album cover, but they can't pay for it. The guy had the nerve to say that if I love art, I should actually do it for free. Where the hell does he get off? Can you imagine what would happen if they got hired to perform at venue, then got told they wouldn't get paid because they should perform for the sake of art? I hate, HATE getting hired by people who don't intend to pay. It's dirty, it's just fucking unclean. Why the hell does this happen to artists ALL THE TIME?!"

It was not the first time this had happened, and she was right. Frequently, Jade or her other colleagues in the fine arts faculty would get hired to a job – it could be anything, like music, dance, whatever – and when they'd done the work and it was time to get paid, the client would have some song and dance about not having enough money and promising to pay them extra "next time." Of course, there would never be a next time, because artists hate getting cheated. I felt badly for Jade, especially since it was not the first time she'd been cheated this way. It was unfortunate, but not entirely unusual.

She started texting them back.

"Whatever, I'll reply and just remind them that we have an agreement," she muttered. She didn't seem especially convinced that they were likely to hold to whatever contract.

"I hope you get paid," I offered helpfully. I didn't know what else to possibly say.

After that, understandably Jade said she didn't feel like studying and wanted to head back to the studio, but Reagan wanted to stay band keep reading, so I told her we could go get a coffee together. We did stop at Trident for some coffee, it was nice to not talk about evil cults and living shadows. But I was tired myself and not the best of company, so I told her I needed to rest for a bit. She didn't seem to mind, so I walked her to the studio, and then headed back to my dorm to rest for a bit. We agreed to meet to meet up at 7pm, and she said she'd text Reagan the time.

At 7pm, I was at the restaurant. Jade arrived first, looking in great spirits. We waited for Reagan, and Jade and I both texted him, but he didn't write back. This wasn't abnormal – he was completely obsessive when he worked and tended not even to hear his own phone ringing if he was immersed in a project.

Jade slid into the chair across from me. She'd already filled her tray with a generous portion of pizza (the Sunday night specialty), and she only paused long enough to say "hello" then went straight for the food. She was really ravenous – this was a good sign with her, because when she was angry or depressed or being "artistic" she'd often stop eating entirely.

"Good studio session?" I asked hopefully. She nodded her head. Well that was good, at least – it was bad when creative types weren't able to work. We talked briefly about the final exam, and our plans for the winter break. She promised she'd write from her parents' place in Boston, and we both used Facebook, so we'd definitely keep in touch.

We finished dinner in relative silence after that. Reagan never showed, and Jade was looking full and tired by the end. We said goodnight to each other, and walked back to our respective dorms.

I saw them both at the exam the next morning at 8am. Early exams suck. Reagan had sent a text to apologize for missing dinner the night before, and I caught glimpses of he and Jade in the exam room. It was a three-hour exam, and of course they both finished early, and left the room. I didn't get to say goodbye to them for the Christmas break, but I knew we'd be in touch by email, and I'd be seeing them a few weeks later in January.

CHAPTER TWO.

HRISTMAS BREAK

[9:10pm]

JadePaintz: What are you up to?
ReaganM9: Reading a paper on archaeology from JSTOR, cross-referencing it with the notebook.
JadePaintz: So much for vacation J What's the topic?
ReaganM9: Semiotics of spirals in classical Roman curse tablets.
JadePaintz: IT'S CHRISTMAS EVE, FFS, REAGAN!! TAKE A BREAK!
ReaganM9: It's either this or watch my sister and her fiancé get drunk and make out by the fireplace.
JadePaintz: Ewww. Noted.
JadePaintz:

JadePaintz:
JadePaintz: So what does it say?
ReaganM9: The article?
JadePaintz: Yeah.
ReaganM9: Ummm… basically it's not a common symbol so much, but it shows up in several tablets around the Mediterranean.
JadePaintz: It's certainly showing up in my dreams.
ReaganM9: Shoot, sorry. Are you ok?
JadePaintz: Just tired, I can't seem to sleep without seeing the notebook. It's not nightmares, but I keep waking up feeling really tired.
ReaganM9: Maybe you should lay off reading your copy?
JadePaintz: I tried for a few days, it didn't seem to make any difference. Besides, it is genuinely an interesting read.
ReaganM9: You think? So it's not just me?
JadePaintz: Nah, it's actually a really interesting composition. I'm not so much interested in the history of the thing as I am the images he's included or drawn.
ReaganM9: Tell me more?
JadePaintz: Well the author (?) clearly has very little skill at drawing, but you can see a progression of images from the beginning to the end.
ReaganM9:
ReaganM9: I don't quite follow? You mean he's getting better as he draws?
JadePaintz: Why do you assume it's a male author?
ReaganM9:
ReaganM9: Right, my bad. But I still don't understand what you mean.
JadePaintz: Ummm, it's like in the beginning s/he has these ideas and does not know how to execute them, so it's just spirals. See page 5 in your copy.
ReaganM9: Yes, I can see that here. Glad I made you

that photocopy.

JadePaintz: Yeah, smart choice to make a copy.

ReaganM9: So you were saying on page 5?

JadePaintz: What do you see there?

ReaganM9: You mean the text? Very nice handwriting.

JadePaintz: No, in the margins.

ReaganM9: Spirals, three of them. Looks like someone used crayon.

JadePaintz: Exactly right. So jump ahead to page 27.

ReaganM9: sec.

ReaganM9:

ReaganM9: Ok, I'm there.

ReaganM9: Wait brb need coffee.

JadePaintz:

JadePaintz:

JadePaintz: …

ReaganM9: Back sorry. Coffee is good. Coffee is life.

JadePaintz: Agreed.

ReaganM9: So page 27?

JadePaintz: Same question, what do you see?

ReaganM9: Almost same as page 5. Spirals are more detailed, manuscript is still handwriting. Looks like it was written in haste, there's more smudging of the ink.

JadePaintz: Good, now jump ahead to p.83.

ReaganM9: K.

JadePaintz: You there yet?

ReaganM9: There now. Oh wait. I think I see what you mean…

JadePaintz: What do you see?

ReaganM9: Spirals have evolved into sigils, patterns of some kind. The handwriting is almost illegible though, it's really degraded badly. Maybe the author was drinking?

JadePaintz: The whiskey stains on that page would suggest it.

ReaganM9: You've got the copy, how you can tell from that?

JadePaintz: It's almost invisible, which suggests its alcohol of some kind. Too dark to be whiskey.

ReaganM9: Oh, right, of course.

JadePaintz: "Of course."

ReaganM9: Pray continue.

JadePaintz: You're worse than Tom, you do know that?

ReaganM9: That reminds me, I need to actually write him back. Just been busy with this.

JadePaintz: Yeah me too. I blame sleep deprivation.

JadePaintz:

ReaganM9:

ReaganM9: So page 83?

JadePaintz: You already noted the essentials. Degraded handwriting, but sigils are executed really nicely, together with some new elements not on previous pages.

ReaganM9: Does it mean something?

JadePaintz: Yes I think so. But I don't know what exactly.

ReaganM9: Oh.

JadePaintz: And that's what I've been dreaming about. I'm painting these sigils on the walls in my room at home, or in the basement of my parents' house.

ReaganM9: That's kind of creepy.

JadePaintz: Isn't it?

JadePaintz:

ReaganM9: So anything else?

JadePaintz: I'll give one last example. Jump ahead to page 330, it's near the end.

ReaganM9: K, sec.

JadePaintz:

ReaganM9: Ok, I'm there. Oh yeah, this section is really bizarre. This is where the author is using a type-writer. Who does that?

JadePaintz: Someone who lost the ability to shape letters with their hands.
ReaganM9: But the art in the margins is amazing!
JadePaintz: I can see that.
ReaganM9: So what's your take on it?
JadePaintz: Well this is just a stab in the dark.
JadePaintz: My guess is that there is some really fucked up person out there who starts getting visions or dreams.
JadePaintz: They try putting the notebook together as a way of coping with the weird images there were experiencing. Somehow they started believing that the symbols were significant, like in a religious sense, and connected to the underworld.
ReaganM9: I see…
JadePaintz: You asked.
ReaganM9: Go on.
JadePaintz: The writer becomes convinced that these symbols are connected to a global conspiracy of some kind, which is why the newspaper and encyclopedia clippings are interspersed. The foreign language pages, no idea what that's about.
ReaganM9: What's that?
JadePaintz: Where the text isn't in English, so you need to tell me what it says.
ReaganM9: NP, I'll translate it for you, but it's going to take time. My Latin is good but I read slowly. Arabic will go slower.
JadePaintz: There's no rush, right?
ReaganM9: So your final conclusion?
JadePaintz: My final conclusion is that the author is trying to express something with those symbols, and it gets more and more detailed on every page until the very end.
ReaganM9: So what is the message?

JadePaintz: Well based on the English alone, I think it's instructions for opening a door.
ReaganM9: What?
JadePaintz: I'm just going off the English pages. The book is next to incoherent, you can see for yourself. The Arabic and Latin pages have a lot more symbols, but I don't know the context.
ReaganM9: I know, I know. Ok, I'll try to translate the Arabic and Latin pages.
JadePaintz: Thanks.
JadePaintz: So yeah, the author seems to be talking about creating a door.
ReaganM9: Door to where?
JadePaintz: Dunno.
ReaganM9: K.
JadePaintz: Yep.
ReaganM9: We'll figure it out.
JadePaintz: I need to sleep.
ReaganM9: Yeah me too.
JadePaintz:
ReaganM9: You're worried about the dreams?
JadePaintz: They're not stopping.
ReaganM9: Maybe see your doctor?
JadePaintz: Maybe.
ReaganM9: K get some sleep. Talk tomorrow?
JadePaintz: Yeah for sure.
ReaganM9: Sleep well.
ReaganM9: Sleep well.
ReaganM9: ...
JadePaintz: I'll try.

CHAPTER THREE.

JANUARY.
Sunday morning.

After a three-week winter break with my folks in Rockport, Maine, I could hardly wait to get back to Ashbridge. It was nice to be home, and I did get to reconnect with some friends from my old high school, but we lived in a really small town, and there wasn't much to do, apart from binge-watching stuff on Netflix. I watched literally every Sopranos episode, then moved on to the rebooted X-Files, and gorged myself on Stranger Things. But that only got me through the first week, and then I had two more weeks of boredom. I used the time to start reading ahead for my new courses, since I'd been able to get the reading lists for several of them, and it helped to pass the time.

When the three weeks were done, I was itching to get back to Ashbridge. I didn't realize how much I actually liked my tiny dorm room, the bad cafeteria good, and the coffee at Trident. I knew that I missed my friends, and I hadn't realized how much Jade and Reagan had become part of my daily routine. We'd spoken on Facebook a couple of times, but they both seemed really busy visiting with their friends and family. Truthfully, I was kind of annoyed that they had a busier social life than I did, but it wasn't their fault – they both lived in Boston, where there was a lot more stuff to do. What was more annoying, though, was that they seemed to be online at the same time increasingly, but not answering my messages until a day or more after I'd send them, even though I knew they were seeing them in real time. But I didn't read much into it, and it was nice to have some down time and get caught up on reading too, and not just for coursework – I also got the latest Game of Thrones novel, which made for some really excellent afternoons and evenings when I didn't feel like studying or watching television.

In any case, the break passed quickly enough, and soon my parents were driving me back to Ashbridge. We left in the early morning, and it was a two-hour drive from our Rockport to Ashbridge. The trip was decent, and despite the icy roads and the generally inclement New England winter weather, we made good time. It was just after 10am when we arrived, and Mom wanted to visit Boston to do some shopping. Dad helped me get my bags out of the trunk of the car, then I hugged my mother and father and promised to Skype with them the following day to say how the first day of Spring courses was. Then I was dragging my suitcases up the steps of the dorm, watching the family car receding into the distance.

I hauled my luggage into my dorm room; it was tiny, but it was all mine. I'd had a roommate earlier the previous semester, but he'd been expelled for writing papers for other students. The administration seemed to have forgotten to assign me another roommate, and I wasn't about to remind them. It took me about an hour to get settled, which involved unpacking my clothes, books, and setting up my laptop at the small wooden desk. There were no messages on my phone. I called Reagan's room, but no answer, then I called Jade, also no answer. I wasn't surprised, because they said they'd probably be arriving either later tonight or the next morning, depending on the train from Boston. So I sent them both text messages to say I'd gotten to campus, and then I decided to take my Game of Thrones novel and head to Trident to enjoy my last lazy morning before classes began.

It was a fifteen minute walk from the dormitory, across campus, and across the street into what passed for downtown Ashbridge. It was still early in the day, but I could see the chimney of Trident puffing smoke into the air, and through the frosted windows I could see the silhouettes of other students, like me, who had decided to spend the remains of the morning with friends or curled up with a good book.

When I opened the door of the coffee house, I could feel the rush of warm air pushing past me, and smell the mix of freshly baked goods, as well as the scent of freshly brewed coffee. I made my way to the counter and surveyed the range of muffins and cookies and decided to order a mug of the signature "Irish Cream" flavored coffee, which was the house special. The owner (a nice older lady, who'd served coffee to college students for longer than I'd been alive) poured the coffee with a practiced hand and slid the cup across the counter towards me with a smile. I paid for my coffee and turned to head towards my usual table. It would be nice to spend a few hours by myself, with a really good book, without any interruptions.

You can imagine my surprise when I found Jade and Reagan at our usual table, bent over a pile of notes and that familiar notebook that had been the cause of some unease prior to the break. The notebook lay open before them atop the pile of papers, and their food appeared to be untouched – Reagan's half-empty mug of tea looked as though it had long gone cold, while Jade had a plate with an uneaten donut, sitting to the side. They were facing away from the me, and so they evidently weren't aware that I was there. I made my way towards them slowly – part of me was happy to see them, but I felt weirdly angry and out of place, like I was interrupting something private. Jade was hunched over the table and strangely immobile, staring intently at some images in the notebook. Her left hand was absentmindedly tracing a spiral, over and over again, while she listened to Reagan, who was speaking quite insistently in a hushed tone. Reagan might not have actually drank any of his coffee, but he was so animated that he clearly didn't need the caffeine. He probably thought he was being quiet, but Jade had to keep telling him to keep it down. He kept gesturing at his notes, flipping through the notebook to point at a particular passage when it was relevant.

Not wanting to disturb them yet, I moved to the table nearest them. They were both so absorbed in their conversation that they didn't seem to notice me sitting down, let alone anyone else in general part of the shop.

"So here, this page in Arabic, I'm partially through it," Reagan said to Jade, pointing at a particular worn page of the notebook, "and it's some sort of description for a particular incense to be made. It's almost like a grocery list: opium, dried grass, apple, sandalwood, hairs of a black cat. Weird. I guess the point is to produce some sort of hallucinatory effect, what with the opium in there."

He paused, checking his notes.

"So anyway, this page here," he flipped forward, "is in Persian, I had a hard time with it, but it's definitely talking about making a doorway to the other place."

Jade stirred momentarily.

"There's been a door in my dreams a lot this week."

Reagan looked sideways at her.

"Really? How often?"

"A lot. Too much." She rubbed her eyes. I couldn't see her face, but she sounded tired.

"Jesus. What did it look like?"

"Different in each dream. Sometimes it's an actual doorway that looks out of place in the dream, like the frame is crooked, or it's the wrong color. Other times, there's this light coming out of the cracks in the frame that seems really frightening."

"And are you doing anything with the door?" Reagan asked.

"Yeah, sometimes I'm trying to open it. Two nights ago, I was trying to force it open, but it was locked tight from the other side. I was hitting it so hard in my sleep that my hands hurt when I woke up. Other times, I'm painting stuff on it or the frame."

"Painting what?"

"Words, but I can't remember them when I wake up. Symbols too, I think." Jade shrugged.

"Black spirals?" he asked.

"I think so," she answered, "but it's hazy."

"Maybe," he paused, "you know… I really think there's something here, you know?"

"Of course there is," she agreed, "and I want to figure it out as much as you. I'm just really tired of not getting a good night's sleep without seeing weird symbols in my dreams or waking up and seeing fucked up shadows creeping around my room."

"So it's really not stopped at all since you stopped reading the notebook?"

Jade paused, thinking.

"I haven't actually looked at my copy of the notebook in over ten days, and it's literally the only thing I've dreamed about since, in one form or another."

Her head tilted slightly, as she looked at him across the table.

"Reagan, your nose, it's bleeding a bit."

He wiped his sleeve across his face absentmindedly.

Jade's phone buzzed in her pocket. They both jumped. She reached inside her jacket and pulled it out. She looked and the screen for a moment, then cursed.

"Son of a bitch," she spat.

"What is it?" Reagan asked in a surprised tone.

"Shades of Erebus, *again*. Fuckers!"

"They didn't like the album cover?"

"No, they do. I sent them a digital sample image, and they're saying that they like it, but they'll pay me later in the semester. I put a lot of time into that, they owe me several hundred dollars. What is it with fucking musicians?"

"Not sure," said Reagan, "I don't normally fuck musicians, they're all narcissists."

She punched him, making him flinch. "Not what I meant."

"Sorry, just trying to make a joke."

"Whatever." She stood abruptly and started to

stretch. As she did, she turned slightly, and caught sight of me.

"Tom! When did you get here?" she pushed her chair aside and came over, arms open to hug me. She had the presence of mind to smile.

I stood up to return the embrace. Reagan hugged me next, though he looked flushed, clearly embarrassed not to have seen me sooner. He had a trace of blood at his nostrils, where he'd wiped the blood off with his coat sleeve.

"Merry Christmas," I murmured as I hugged him.

"Yeah, you too." He patted me on the back, then motioned for me to join them at the table. Reagan began to stack his papers and pile them atop the notebook, attempting to make it look very nonchalant. "So when did you get back? We didn't even notice you come in."

"Just got back now," I lied, "but I didn't see you guys, so I just grabbed a table and had just started to read." I waved my Game of Thrones novel.

"So good to see you," Jade beamed. "How was the break?"

"Boring, there was nothing to do," I complained, "and my friends didn't keep in touch like they promised."

They both had the decency to look uncomfortable.

"Shit, sorry Tom," Reagan apologized, "it was just really chaotic at my place. My sister had her fiancé over, my cousins were there too. I just didn't get online much."

"Yeah, same here, just busy, and I think I was sick with a flu for most of the trip. Didn't spent much time online, sorry Tom," Jade added. She looked away, rubbing her eyes. To be fair, she really did look slightly under the weather.

"I see you guys haven't given up the quest for the

grail," I said, gesturing at the pile of notes and stained pages.

"Oh that, yeah, that's been quite the project," said Reagan. He looked a little sheepish.

"I expect so, you made so much about having a competition to find the owner," I reminded him, maybe a bit sharper than I intended to do. "Figure out who the owner is yet?"

He looked at Jade, who shook her head.

"No luck there," he admitted, "but this is a really, really interesting notebook."

"Interesting how?" I asked.

Reagan paused, and I could see the wheels in his head turning. He made that face, the one that signified he was about to go into lecture more.

"Interesting, meaning–" he began, but Jade cut him off.

"Interesting like it's giving me chronic fucking nightmares," she spoke in a suddenly vehement tone. "Interesting like its make me see shit at night, stuff that isn't even there. Interesting like I'm jumping at shadows at all hours of the day, and I'm dreaming about crazy symbols and runes covering walls and entire buildings."

She stood up, leaving Reagan and I looking at her in surprise. Even Reagan seemed taken aback, despite their complicity in the project.

"Fuck this," she muttered to herself, "to hell with these images. Meditating isn't working, exercise isn't working, and sleeping pills just make it harder to wake up when I'm dreaming black dreams. I'm getting out of here. This is what happens when you read the journal of a crazy person for several days during exam stress." She pulled on her hat and mitts and wrapped her scarf around her neck. She pushed back from the table and stood to go. She did not look ok, not in any sense of the word. Now I could really see how dark the circles under her eyes really were.

"Jade, hang on," Reagan began, but she pushed past him and hurried out of the coffee shop.

"Reagan, what the heck is going on?" I asked.

Reagan was staring after her, a mix of confusion and alarm on his face. "Honestly, Tom, I don't really know."

"Well, what do you think is happening?"

"I think," he swallowed, "I think Jade is really sleep deprived. She's been under a lot of stress.

"Stop lying to me, damn it!" I was struggling not to yell at him. I started to get to my feet, unwilling to put up with his secrecy any longer.

"It's hard to explain, Tom, and you wouldn't believe me if I told you." he said to me, his eyes watching Jade as she hurried down the sidewalk, and back towards campus.

"Try me," I insisted, "it's that notebook, isn't it?"

He nodded. "Look, I can try to explain, but you need to keep an open mind, ok?" He looked at me, and I could see he was genuinely embarrassed about this whole situation.

I shrugged but moved to sit down again.

"Reagan, in the last two months since you found that journal, Jade hasn't slept well for fear of shadow men in her room, and we were attacked by a murder of crows trying to get into the library. We're well past me needing to keep an open mind. Just stop making this some weird secret between the two of you and tell me what you're working on."

He sagged into his chair, running his hands through his hair.

"Ok," he said, "you already know how we found this book. I genuinely thought it was a harmless puzzle, a sort of treasure hunt mystery put together by one of the faculty, and it really seemed like someone had put a lot of work into it. I just wanted to solve the puzzle and figure out who. But after I started looking into it, it really started to seem like someone actually believed in this thing, like it wasn't just a harmless prank. Like, a lot of work went into putting this together, it must have taken someone a couple of years, maybe a decade to find all the scraps and stitch them together."

"None of this is news to me, you said this all during exams week," I reminded him.

"I know, I know," he muttered. "Well, the weird thing is the effects it's had on both of us. Jade hasn't slept in weeks, not properly, unless it's during the day. I think she went almost nocturnal during the Christmas break, 'cause she keeps having nightmares about things tied to the book, or thinking she's being attacked by shadows at night in her room. I can't explain it, I mean, she loves horror books, but she's never complained about nightmares before."

This much was true – she was a rabid fan of horror films too, much more resilient than Reagan or I were.

"What about you?" I asked, "Are you having freaky dreams, or hallucinating at all?"

He shook his head. "No, I've had some vivid dreams in the last month, but none of them like her, and I'm not even sure they're any weirder than normal. My only complaint is that I've been getting some bad headaches and stomach cramps, like I have a flu or something. I went to midnight mass with my folks, and when I got home I was violently ill, spent the entire night over on the toilet. But when I read the notebook, or work it, I feel great, like not sick at all."

I shook my head. "Look, just get rid of it, throw the thing out."

He frowned. "No, I honestly thought about it, but I feel like I'm really close to solving the mystery. This thing is a puzzle, and I've already translated half the non-English passages, and a lot of the stuff I thought was non-English turned out to be English written in cipher. Like the author is using Arabic script, but it's English words entirely. Really, a few more days, and I think I'll have this thing solved."

I stared at him. "Reagan, who cares?! It's just someone's idea of a sick joke, and it's really got Jade messed up. I don't know if I believe in the occult, or magic, or conspiracies, but I can tell that you're not yourself, and Jade is really not doing ok. Just throw it out and be done with it."

For a moment, I think he actually considered it. But this wasn't Lord of the Rings, and Reagan was definitely not Frodo Baggins.

"I'm really touched that you care, seriously," he said, his eyes warm. "Look, I'm fine, and Jade is clearly not, but this is just a book, there's no way that it's the root cause of whatever she is going through. I'm not having nightmares, or seeing monsters, and I've put WAY too much time into this to quit now."

"Ok, well can I at least ask a favor?" I said, with more worry on my face than I wanted to show.

"Sure, anything."

"Take one more week to try to solve this thing, but if you can't crack it in a week, then promise me you'll burn it. There's no certainty it even can be solved – it could just be a malicious goose chase by someone with enough knowledge of psychology and subliminal messages to give a sensitive artist like Jade a complete nervous breakdown. And besides, nausea and vomiting?"

He blushed. I could tell he knew I was right, but he was too arrogant to admit that he should quit, after all this time.

"You got it – and I won't even need the week, you'll see."

"Shake on it?" I offered my hand.

He took it. We shook.

"You have my word, Tom. But seriously, this will be done in another day or two."

I wasn't as reassured as I'd hoped to be, but I'd take any win at this point. And frankly, it was nice not to feel like they were hiding anything from me. It had hurt to find them huddled together like that, knowing that they were keeping something from me.

We spent the rest of the morning reading – me with Game of Thrones, Reagan with the notebook. I bought us a fresh round of hot chocolate, and this time his mug was drained properly before it went cold.

CHAPTER FOUR.

JANUARY.
Monday morning.

It was the first day of classes, and I had a great schedule that semester: nothing earlier than 10 am, and no classes that ran later than 7pm. I'd texted Jade and Reagan to say that I'd be having breakfast in the cafeteria around eight o'clock. Despite the awkwardness of my run-in with Reagan and Jade, I had slept really well and woken early. I took a long shower, checked my class schedule repeatedly, and made sure that my backpack had all the books I'd need for my first day of classes. I keyed my classroom locations into my phone (like "English Novel at 10am in Building 32 room 5," "World History at noon in Auditorium 5"). On reflection, I wish I'd read less Game of Thrones and more of the Spring required reading list, but no one was perfect.

It was January, and a cold morning at that. At 7:50am, I pulled on my coat and boots, wrapped my scarf tightly around my neck, and put on my gloves. Making my way into the hallway and down the stairs, I exited the dormitory and made my way to the cafeteria building. Other students, early risers like me, were making their way across the frozen ground, and I waved to a couple that I recognized. Steam was pouring from the chimney on the cafeteria building, and my stomach growled with hunger as I could smell the fresh cinnamon rolls baking all the way from the dormitory. It was only a five minute walk to the cafeteria, but it seemed longer since my stomach was rumbling.

I made it into the cafeteria and looked around. Reagan was there ahead of me, already seated at one of our usual breakfast tables with a plate of French toast. I helped myself to scrambled eggs and sausage and walked over to him. He looked up as I approached and waved at me.

"Good morning, right on time," he called out.

"Good morning to you too," I returned the greeting. I took a seat at the table.

"Did you see Jade this morning?" he asked.

"Not yet, did you speak to her yesterday after we left Trident?" I replied.

"No, she turned off her phone. Hopefully she was able to sleep, poor kid."

I shrugged. "I guess we'll find out shortly, assuming she makes it for breakfast. When's your first class?"

Reagan took a bit of his French toast, chewed, and swallowed. "Nine o'clock, so I'll finish breakfast up and head over. It's the Archaeology Field Seminar course, should be good. I think the summer dig is in Tunis this year."

Reagan *loved* digging. This was his senior year, and it was no secret that he was hoping to get into Chicago for their graduate program in ancient near eastern archaeology. Ashbridge was a small college, but it was able to field a summer archaeology camp almost every year.

"What about you – what's your first class?" he asked, taking a sip of his coffee.

I had finished my mouthful of food, and was about to answer, when Jade appeared with a huge tray of pancakes, bacon, sausage, and orange juice. She put it down at our table, pulled out a chair, and seated herself next to us. She brushed a tangle of unruly hair out of her eyes and smiled.

"Morning, boys. Sleep ok? Man, I'm starving!" She didn't wait for an answer but launched into her food like she hadn't eaten in days.

Jade didn't look ok – she looked amazing. Gone were the dark circles under her eyes. Her skin had its usual, healthy tone, and she smelled faintly of perfume, like sandalwood or some eastern fragrance. Her hair looked freshly washed, and even her outfit of dark grey jacket over black cargo pants had a very professional look to it. If my eyes weren't wrong, she'd even put kohl on her eyes. Reagan and I stared at her for a second, then back at each other. He mouthed *wow* to me.

"How are you this morning?" I asked.

"You know, I feel great. I slept great, got up early, already hit the gym, and I'm psyched to hit the studio. I have Mass Communications at 10am, should be a solid course." She took a bite of her pancakes, slathered in syrup.

Reagan arched an eyebrow in surprise at her energy level.

"What happened to you? A whole month of

insomnia and fatigue, and today you look like a new person. Don't take me wrong, you look good. Better than good even."

She nodded appreciatively. "Thanks," she said through a mouthful of pancake, "I feel good too."

She swallowed. "You know, after I got back to the studio yesterday, I thought long and hard about all this stuff. If I keep having dreams about painting a sunrise, then I paint a sunrise. If I'm daydreaming about painting a pink elephant, I paint a pink elephant, you know? So for a month, I've been dreaming about giant black spirals, so I decided to finally paint a giant black spiral."

She took a sip of her orange juice, thinking for a moment.

"And you know what?" she asked rhetorically, "it felt amazing to do it. Normally I'd sketch the thing first, but I didn't even need to trace. Hell, it was like my hands were freaking possessed, I just put the canvass on the board, and I started painting on instinct, or memory, or whatever the hell it was. It just – I dunno how to say it – it just came out of me, it was like giving birth to an image. I painted straight for six, maybe seven hours."

She took a bite of her pancakes, next the sausage. She chewed, swallowed, then continued.

"Anyway, when I'd finished, I just felt – Christ – I felt alive for the first time in weeks. It was like I'd had this fever, a virus or something, and the act of projecting it onto the canvas just transferred that virus out of me. Sort of like how vomiting makes you feel better by getting the poison out. That's – that's not what I mean, exactly, but you get what I'm saying?"

Reagan and I nodded silently, but neither of us painted, so we really didn't know what she was talking about, apart from understanding that it had clearly been a good experience for her. It actually sounded sort of horrible as she described it, but she was so enthusiastic about it that I think we were both trying to be happy for her.

She turned her attention to her food, apparently being done with her explanation of the process.

Reagan, of course, was intrigued.

"So you actually painted a black spiral, and then you felt better after? No dreams, no nightmares, just a good sleep?"

She nodded, her mouth too full to answer.

"How's the painting? Is it good? Do you like it?" he asked.

She swallowed. "Yeah, it's good. I mean, it's really good. You guys should come and see it after breakfast, if you have time."

It was only 8:15am, and I didn't have class until ten o'clock.

"Sure, would love to see it," I replied.

Reagan nodded. "I have class at nine, but sure, if you're almost done eating."

Between the three of us, we finished breakfast another ten minutes later. So with just thirty minutes until Reagan's class, we made our way across campus towards the large, rectangular building that housed the fine arts program, the campus gallery, and the studios for the arts majors like Jade. We passed a few more familiar people, who called out greetings or else waved as we passed them.

Ashbridge was a well-endowed college with wealthy donors and a very competent team of instructors. One of the donors had been a family with some notion of being patrons of the arts, and so they'd left a small fortune to make sure that Ashbridge never lacked for the fine arts program. This meant in concrete terms that Jade had her own small studio to work in, insofar as the room itself was gigantic, but had been divided with artificial walls into ten smaller studio spaces. She also never complained about materials, since the grant that funded the fine arts program ensured that the students were provided with the requisite material to really explore and grow as artists, without worrying about how to pay for whatever paints, metals, or glasses that they might need after graduation.

Jade's studio space always felt to me like something of another world, where I was an obvious barbarian treading on holy ground. Nevertheless, I allowed myself to be lead through the maze of smaller rooms, until we stood inside her own small studio. A series of her Fall semester works still hung on the walls, and in the center of the room stood her easel, with a large painting covered with a drape of cloth. Jade planted herself next to it and stood facing the two of us. She grinned, and just for a moment, there was an almost feral quality to her eyes.

"Ready to see it?"

We both nodded. She pulled the cloth off the easel.

At first, as the cloth fell to the floor, it seemed to me that she had painted the entire canvass with a black oil paint. But as Reagan and I stepped closer to examine Jade's work, I realized that this was a trick of the light. The canvas was entirely black, but not uniformly so. I'm not an artist, and so I don't have the technical vocabulary to describe her process, but it seemed that she had mixed ashes together with oil, pressed the brush to the center of the canvas, and then spiraled slowly outwards in a counter-clockwise pattern. I could see the black oil paint – a paste, almost – thickest at the innermost core of the painting and getting slightly thinner as the strokes worked their way towards the edges of the canvas. It seemed to me that there was more in the spiral, bits of resin or strands of some foreign material that Jade had worked into the paint mixture. And when I got close enough to really study the painting, it didn't seem that the color of the paste was totally consistent – it was darker in some places, lighter (if only faintly) in others. There were traces of other colors, so fleeting that I almost missed them – hints of brown and red, and darker shades of black than the base of the oil-and-ashes she'd chosen for her main tone. It had clearly taken hours to paint, and it was difficult to see where an earlier layer ended, and the subsequent layer began.

Without question it was an impressive painting, beautiful even. It had a sort of fluid, seductive quality, in that it drew you into the composition and made you want to study it. It was an easy piece to lose yourself in, at least for several long minutes. Still, there was also something almost repulsive about the painting. It was certainly not caused by any technical flaws, since the painting appeared to be executed very competently, but still I found the painting uneasy to look at. My stomach tightened when I looked into the heart of the spiral.

Jade was looking expectantly at us, waiting to hear our reaction. I forced myself to smile.

"Wow, Jade, it's amazing!" I said. It was true that she'd done an amazing job, and I was hardly an art critic to understand what the unsettling element could possibly be.

I looked back at the painting, and Christ, I would have sworn that the center of the spiral had shifted slightly. Reagan was studying it intently as well.

"I really like the eyes at the center," he remarked, "very subtle."

Jade looked surprised. "What's that?"

Reagan gestured to the center of the spiral. "The eyes, here, at the heart of the storm. Right here."

I looked closer, but for the life of me, I didn't see any eyes.

Jade was looking suspicious at Reagan, then stared at her own painting. She blinked several times.

"Oh, ha, I see what you mean. Funny, I didn't even see that when I painted it. Just goes to show, the creative power of the subconscious, you know?"

I felt like an idiot, but I absolutely couldn't see any eyes. If anything, the paint seemed to have shifted again, as if it hadn't hardened onto the canvas.

Reagan suddenly looked down at his watch.

"Shoot, I need to run, I've got class in ten minutes. Jade, it's fantastic, you really did a great job."

Jade smiled warmly, and I patted her on the shoulder. "Yeah, you did a superb job. It's creepy, but it looks really impressive."

She nodded. "It's not my most cheerful work, but it really does seem to have a life of its own, right?"

She bent to retrieve the cloth and covered the easel again. I confess, I felt a momentary twitch of relief in my stomach when she veiled the painting.

Reagan and I both hugged her before leaving, and we three made plans to meet again at supper time. I tried to be happy for her, despite the very alien direction that her painting had taken. I hoped that it was not indicative of where her work would lead her in the upcoming semester.

CHAPTER FIVE

The first month of classes went really well. I had "American Novel" "Applied Social Sciences" some "Critical Theory" and "Modern World History" all which seemed like interesting enough courses. I didn't especially like anything I was studying, but I knew that I needed a certain number of courses to graduate and had an instinct for avoiding the tougher instructors and their classes. On most days, I even managed to take an afternoon nap, which felt positively luxurious compared to my previous semesters. Regan had been characteristically morose – he tended to get obsessive about his studies and various projects, and he had a scholarship that depended on a high GPA, so I couldn't fault him. Jade, on the other hand, had been in excellent spirits the entire week. Whatever she'd done with that weird painting, it had clearly exorcised the demons that were plaguing her.

By now, it was the first Wednesday of February. I hadn't seen either of my two best friends since the weekend, and I was starting to think that I should check in with them. By 7:30pm, I was getting ready to head to the cafeteria building. So I called Jade to see where she was.

Her phone rang. She answered.

"Hello?"

"Hey, it's Tom. Are you heading to get supper soon?"

"Definitely, I'm starving. Meet me at the gallery and we can walk over."

"Sounds good," I said, "I'll call Reagan."

"No need, I'll let him know. See you soon," and she hung up.

I pulled on my coat and scarf, locked my dorm room, and headed into the night air. It was cold and windy, but February could be a lot worse in Massachusetts. I almost slipped twice on the ice, heading towards the gallery, but my reflexes were generally pretty good, and so I managed to avoid any bad falls. The campus grounds staff did a really good job of keeping the walkways clear of ice, as much as anyone could, but it had rained and frozen several times while we'd been away on break, and it's really hard to clear ice without using heavy amounts of salt. Ashbridge wasn't a big campus, but in the winter, travel speed was greatly reduced, so a five-minute walk became something closer to ten, or even fifteen minutes at night. But I was happy to meet Jade in the studio and see what she'd been up to.

The fine arts building was well lit both inside and out, and it was really a constant hive of activity at all hours of day and night. I passed a few friends in the architecture program, who I knew pretty much lived in their studio and not in their dorm rooms. Jade could be like that at times, but usually the fine arts majors were a little better balanced that the architecture kids – though exceptions did happen. I made my way into the building and began to thread through the large factory room that housed the smaller studio segments. As I passed the studio space immediately prior to Jade's, another resident artist ran into me in the hall. He clearly hadn't seen me coming, and he jumped as if badly startled when I bumped into him, his eyes flashing as if I were a sudden predator. *Sensitive fucking artist*, I thought to myself. He shot me a dark look, but I murmured an apology and moved past him in the corridor, so I could get into Jade's studio as quickly as possible.

For a moment, I wondered if I'd stepped into the right room, because the colors were all wrong. Gone were the white walls, or at least obscured, because almost every inch of space was covered with either painted canvases, large sketches, or mirrors. There were a lot of mirrors – multiple mirrors on all four walls. In fact, on closer inspection, I think that most of what I'd initially thought to be painted canvasses was actually mirrors covered in paint, in which case a lot of the room must have initially been glass. The central easel had been moved off to the side and it was still covered, but the large black spiral had been moved to the north wall. Now, however, it was flanked by several other paintings which seemed to contain the black spiral which had somehow overflowed from the original canvas. Now the spiral dominated an entire wall; the central piece served as the heart of the mass, but it literally looked as though it had grown. I couldn't really even see a spiral anymore – it had grown to become a black hole. Whatever technique she'd used to make that oily, clotted paste, she'd made a lot more of it, and then covered other canvases. On the one hand, the effect was really impressive – especially with the other mirrors around the studio space, which reflected the image so that you felt that it was surrounding you. I felt a momentary pain in my stomach, as a wash of vertigo swept over me. For a fleeting second, I imagined that I was not in a studio, but cast to some terrible place without light and sound, with a sharp wind that cut to the bone as it howled past me, into the grinding darkness of that terrible maw. I shuddered, despite the relative warmth of the room.

As expected, Jade was in her studio. She was still painting, and her jeans and smock were stained with various darker hued paints. She was working on the detail of one of the smaller pieces, and complaining to Reagan, who, to my surprise; was there also. He was standing next to her, holding that weird notebook, and consulting it as she was painting. She was speaking while she painted.

"It's all too small," she was saying to him, "I just feel fucking trapped in here. Like the room is too small, and so the void looks constricted, even with the mirrors."

"But how could you possibly go bigger?" he asked. "Oh, you misspelled that word there," and he pointed at something that looked like an obscure squiggle in the paint – I realized then it was text."

"How's it read?" she asked.

"I – R – K –A – L – L – A" he read slowly, checking his notes, "at least, that's what I think it says. The handwriting is almost illegible. So frustrating – just when the author was getting some real answers, they couldn't even write any longer."

"K – A – L," she intoned as she painted the letters carefully into the canvas. "I feel like I'm painting a cave, but not a door. Does this feel like a door? It doesn't feel like a door to me. Are you sure you're reading the book correctly?"

I cleared my throat. Reagan spun around – he clearly hadn't expected to see me here. Jade continued painting but raised her paint brush in a salute.

"Hi, Tom, almost done. Sorry Reagan, I forgot to tell you he was coming to pick us up."

Reagan looked annoyed, as if I was interrupting something private. It felt like shades of that awkward meeting two weeks earlier in Trident.

"Hey there," I greeted him.

"Hey," he replied, and turned his nose back to the notebook.

I stepped carefully across the room, not wanting to brush against anything wet or drying. Standing next to them, I could see that Jade was detailing some very fine text into one of the mirrors. I couldn't quite make it out, but it looked like lines of calligraphy that repeated themselves over and over. Again, my stomach twisted, this time more violently. Right then, there was a soft wet sound, like a water droplet, and Reagan cursed and wiped his nose with his sleeve.

"Stupid nosebleed," he complained.

Oddly, he'd gotten them a few times that week, usually first in the morning, or else late at night.

"So, what's all this?" I asked Jade.

She lowered the brush and took a step back.

"This is me trying to prepare a gallery showing, but I'm not liking it very much."

I was surprised, because despite the fact that the entire thing felt weird and sickening in some way, it was a brilliant series of connected paintings.

I made a show of looking around the room.

"I like the use of mirrors, that's a neat effect."

She nodded appreciatively.

"Yeah, that was one of my better ideas. I got the idea

from this architecture classes, where the prof was talking about using glass to create a false sense of depth in confined spaces. It's working partially, but walls are walls, and there isn't much I can do to change the laws of physics in here."

Reagan was inspecting another painting off to the side. "Jade, you misspelled this line here too," he commented. "It's supposed to read N – E – R – G – A – L not L – A – G – R – E – N."

I chuckled at the absurdity, and he glared at me.

"Oh come on, Reagan, who cares what ancient script she's painted into the walls? You're the only one that will know."

He looked at me for a moment as if I'd said something about his mother and clutched the notebook so that his knuckles turned white. Then he frowned suddenly, snorted (blood flecked his nostrils), and he started to chuckle.

"Sorry, Tom, you're completely right. I dunno what came over me there. Literally no one will notice except me."

He closed the notebook and wiped his nose again with the back of his hand. I could see the red sheen on his hand as he did so.

"Kleenex?" I offered, reaching into my backpack to pull out a tissue.

"Thanks," he said, taking one. He wiped his hand clean, then dabbed his nose. "I think it's the dryness from winter."

"Ok, I think I'm done here," said Jade. She had finished whatever characters she had been working on and was putting her brush into a jar of water. She wiped her hands on a towel that rested on a chair near the easel.

"This is amazing, Jade," I gestured at the walls around me, "how did you paint so much so fast?"

"You know, you can get a lot done when you cut

back on sleep," she said with a wry smile. "You know me, I get obsessive when I work on a big project."

"So is this for an exhibit?" I asked.

She shook her head.

"No, I don't know what this is. I started working on the central piece, and it just all kinda grew out from there."

"It's really something else," I ventured, "I mean, it's kind of menacing, if you know what I mean. It feels kind of alive, in a really dark, nihilistic kind of way."

Jade smiled and nodded.

"You know Tom, the funny thing is that once I started painting the spiral, I stopped having the nightmares. No more dreams, no more freaky shadows in my room at night. In fact, I feel focused, you know? Like I painted this entire room, and I've already completed all my portfolio work for the month on top."

"So you're really feeling better? You were having a bad couple of weeks." I asked.

"Oh, there's no comparison. Don't I look better?" She turned to face me.

Truthfully, she did look a lot better. Her face was pale, but there was a healthy glow to her cheeks, and her eyes looked sharp. Even the way she stood had none of the slouch from before Christmas – there was a vibrancy to her stance that looked like she'd spent the day working out. Even her smile, crooked as it was, seemed relaxed and stress free.

"Yeah, you look a lot better rested, that's for sure," I agreed.

I gestured at the covered easel.

"So… what's under the hood?"

Jade snorted. "It's the album cover for *Shades of Erebus*. I told the vocalist that they either pay me in full, or else lose their deposit and get nothing in return. It's not finished yet, and it's also a commission, otherwise I'd show it to you."

That made sense – she usually showed her own works to Reagan and me, but she worked in absolute confidence when she worked on commissions. There was no sense in pressing her on this – she'd show us when she was ready, or not at all.

Jade took offer her smock and rolled down her sleeves. She took her coat and cap off a hook just outside the door and put them both on. Reagan stuffed the notebook back in his own backpack. Jade grabbed her bag, and together the three of us walked to the entrance of her studio and stepped into the hallway.

The lights overhead flickered, and there was a sharp clattering sound behind us in the studio. I turned with my friends to see the source of the noise.

The easel had fallen to the floor, and the covered piece had tumbled face-down to the ground.

"That's the third time today, fuck!" she muttered. She went back inside and stood the easel upright. "Piece of shit carpentry, I should probably just make a new one myself." She put the covered painting back on the stand and tested to make sure that the easel was planted well on the floor. Having assured herself that it was, she turned back to join us in the corridor.

We began to thread our way through the maze-like halls that threaded the various studios within the giant room. When we were two or three studio-spaces closer to the exit, the lights overhead flickered again. There was a muffled shriek from ahead, and the weird, frantic artist darted into view.

His eyes were wide, and he had an angry, suspicious look on his face. He stared at us for a moment, and he looked like he was going to say something, but he bit his lip and vanished around the corner again.

"Jesus Christ," Jade muttered, "He's been acting

insane this past week." Reagan and I glanced at each other.

"What's his problem?" Reagan asked.

"Well he claims that someone has been into his studio at night, but I haven't seen anyone coming or going, and he's just down the hallway from me. He's been crazy skittish too. I actually wonder if he's been drinking on site, or using, or something along those lines, but it's rude to ask. But he has got to chill out – he seems on the verge of having a stroke or something."

Ashbridge had a tolerant stance about alcohol in the dorms, but there was a strict zero-tolerance policy for drinking or drug use in the academic buildings. Still, a lot of the architecture and fine art students were known for using chemical methods to work 50 hour shifts, but that was not really common, and it definitely wasn't encouraged even among peers.

We left the building without further incident and began to make our way towards the cafeteria.

"So, how's your work coming along?" I asked Reagan.

"Good man, good. I really need to get on top of the student research grant stuff this week, if I want to get any money before the semester is out."

"How does that work exactly? I've never had the grades to get anything like that, so it's all kind of a mystery to me," I admitted.

He shrugged sympathetically. "Well, basically outline a research proposal, and you show how you're going to use the money to further your research, and eventually the idea is that you finish your bachelor's degree with an undergraduate project that can become a master's thesis."

"What's the project you're going to pitch then?" I asked.

He considered for a moment. "Well, you know I've been studying this notebook."

"Studying? I think you've been having sexual fantasies about that notebook… but sure, whatever."

He grinned.

"Ok, so the author's basic premise is that there is another entire reality, like an absolute state of being, and that through the correct experiments, an ordinary person can access that absolute state. And throughout history, different people have formed cults or secret societies, and tried to do this."

"You mean like a quest for God?" I asked.

"Not quite. But kind of. Like, take the Nazis in the Indiana Jones movies – they're always hunting for relics, right?"

"Yeah, or the Russians sometimes too." I pointed out.

"Right, yes. So the Nazis are hunting for the Spear of Destiny, or the Holy Grail, or the Lost Ark, not because those relics are important by themselves, but because their symbols of something outside this world. They're not magical, they're alien."

"Alien like UFOs?" I asked.

"No, 'alien' like they represent another reality altogether."

"You're making my head hurt," I complained.

"Take an aspirin," he snorted. "Anyway, the notebook says that there is another reality, and that if you could figure out the right combination of symbols and acts, you could open a door to that place."

"Is it a good place?" I asked.

"Ummm, well it's not good or bad, I mean those are Christian terms," he explained. "It's a pure place, like it doesn't have any discriminating features."

"Like no racism?" I asked, trying to understand.

"No, I mean that in that other reality, there hasn't

even been a Big Bang, there's no me, no you, no God, it's all unity. Everything's connected."

"Oh, like that text you showed me before – not dead, not alive, not existing, not non-existence, is that right?"

"Yes," he nodded, "that's exactly right."

"Do you not find that description a bit horrifying? Like how can something be not-alive and not-dead? It sounds undead," I said.

Reagan made a face.

"Well, I guess I can see what you're saying. Most cultures didn't exactly think of it as a positive state either. But when I read the texts that talk about it, there's something that just really resonates with me, I can't explain it."

"And just *why* would anyone want to try to see this, or experience this thing?"

"Enlightenment," he said without pause, "because experiencing that would be experiencing everything. It's like the ultimate answer to every spiritual question. Like once you'd experience this, you'd never need God again, because you'd know God, or the gods, or whatever. Total enlightenment, like the Buddha."

"Ok, and according to your research, how does a secret society experience this thing, this enlightenment?"

Jade made a rectangular tracing motion in the air with her two hands.

"You build a door," she said, in a slightly dreamy voice.

"Exactly," said Reagan, "you construct a door."

"How do you build the door? Is it like the Stargate movie?" I ventured.

"Not far off," he replied, "the manuscript says you need to construct a large physical frame, and it needs to have certain keys to open it."

"What kind of keys?" I asked.

"Well, it's a tall order, and the book gives different keys in different places. Opiates, symbols, the right words in the right places, and animal sacrifices."

"Then you go through the door, I guess?" I asked.

"You know, the book isn't clear on that part," Reagan admitted, "I mean, it seems pretty clear that the person who wrote the journal wanted to build a doorway, but I don't think that they managed to do it."

"Why not?" I asked.

"Well, the manuscript kind of trails off at the end. You'd think if they actually achieved perfect enlightenment that they'd have said so explicitly." He paused. "Also, they might have had better handwriting, and not have included all the morbid warnings."

"So tell me again how you're going to get a grant for all this?" I asked.

"Probably I won't if I explain it that way," he admitted, "but what I'll put on paper is that I'm going to research the history of the secret enlightenment societies in early modern USA. The journal identifies several prominent Americans who were allegedly involved with the cult, so I'll access the Library of Congress in DC to pull the records on these fine gentlemen and their occult activities."

"Like the Illuminati and the Freemasons?" I asked?

"Well the Illuminati are fiction, but the Freemasons, sure," he agreed.

"Jade, are you actually on board with this?" I asked.

She nodded. "I think Reagan's really got something there, and I think that it's worth seeing what happens."

I was starting to put two and two together.

"So your gallery – that's a doorway?" I asked.

She shook her head. "No way, I just borrowed inspiration from Reagan's research. I have some elements in my gallery that are door-like – the symbols, the texts, that kind of thing, but an actual door would need a lot more, if Reagan's anywhere near right."

I was surprised that she was on board with this.

"You actually think that you guys can make a sci-fi portal to deep space, and walk through it, and get enlightened?"

"How is that any different than any other religious system," she asked, raising an eyebrow. "Like, on a certain level, I actually think the notebook makes sense. Why were all those politicians and military people spending so much time and energy on hunting for those "keys" if it's all just make believe? And so far, the limited contact I've had with the notebook has lead me to believe that it's got some energy to it that I can't explain otherwise. Didn't you guys get attacked by ravens? This stuff isn't normal. So, yeah, I want to see where this goes."

This was so far beyond normal that I wanted to scream or shake them. My friends – my sane, normal friends – were talking like nerds who'd watched far too much science fiction.

"You do realize how this sounds, don't you Reagan? The university is definitely not going to give you funding to chase some sort of global conspiracy. Besides, you can't tell them that you're going to create some sort of portal to outer darkness, they'll call counselling services, and have you put on medical leave."

"You're totally right, Tom," he acknowledged, "which is why I'll frame the project outline as a study of American secret societies, which is a legitimate field of study. And besides, no one is talking about creating an actual portal to whatever, it's… what's the word, Jade?"

"Symbolic," she said, raising a hand, mimicking Reagan's usual pedantic style. "The door is a symbolic space, which symbolizes the artist's mind opening to new psychological plateaus, where only the subconscious roamed prior." She was smiling faintly, and I got the impression that she was quoting him from some earlier conversation, from which I'd also been excluded. Charming, my two best friends.

Still, what she was saying did sound a little more sane.

"So this entire experiment, it's a symbolic act? It's not a ritual that opens a literal door into outer space then?"

"Of course not," Reagan sounded disgusted, "I know it sounds all weird, but it's not like I'm crazy or something. Honestly, Tom, you make it sound so dramatic. Look, the incense that you fumigate the site with has high concentrations of opium. Clearly there are psychoactive properties, which admittedly I don't fully understand, and these things stimulate parts of the mind which experience the whole process as an 'opening' of the subconscious."

He sounded convinced of himself. I thought he sounded insane.

"It's normal," Jade said, "like early modern artists couldn't work unless they were stoned off their asses on laudanum, for crying out loud. This is just a more refined, liturgical version of the process. Well, it would be, if Reagan could figure out the liturgy."

I threw up my hands.

"Ok guys, if you say you're both good, and it's all symbolic, and no one is going to drink Jade's paint thinner, I guess you should just have at, and get this thing out of your system. I just wish you wouldn't make such a big deal with the sneaking around."

They both winced. I know they weren't trying to be hurtful, but it was pissing me off that they weren't including me. I know I didn't have the same aptitudes for creating, or scholastics, but no one likes being left behind.

The night was cold and dry, and the smell of the cafeteria reached us well before we were near it. It had the usual student late-night food.

"God, I'm starving," Jade muttered, as we entered the building. The food did smell good. It was surreal to watch her eat, not in a messy sense, but because she could put away as much as one of the football team, and somehow stay as lean and muscled as a dancer. Reagan and I each took some pizza, while Jade took pizza, a salad, and was trying to choose between steak or lasagna for her main course. She opted for the steak.

We seated ourselves in the usual section of tables. The cafeteria was packed tonight, so we didn't get our preferred table, but that's college life for you. Overhead, the lights flickered, once, twice, three times. Across the room, another light bulb shorted out with a sharp crackling sound.

"What is it with the college lighting?" Jade grumbled between mouthfuls of pizza.

"Is there something with the lighting?" I asked. Certainly there hadn't been any issues in my dorm or classrooms.

"Well the lighting in the studio sucks, the bulbs have been burning out faster than they can replace them this week. Makes it next to impossible to paint when you can't see the canvass, you know?"

It made sense. Reagan nodded sympathetically.

Jade's phone beeped. She mumbled under her breath and took out her phone. Another text message. She didn't say anything, but her face tightened into a scowl.

Wordlessly, she jammed her phone back into her jacket.

"Let me guess, Picasso wants his brushes back," Reagan joked, oblivious to the annoyance that was radiating off her.

"No, it was the fucking band. They said that they're coming over tomorrow to get the painting, or their deposit. How dense are they? I swear, I'm going to call campus police and have them booted out."

"Do you want us to be there when they show up?" I asked.

Jade glared at me.

"What, do I look like I need help fighting my battles?" she said, her tone angry. I knew she was mad at the band, and we both felt badly for her.

"Just trying to help," I muttered and busied myself in my pizza.

Reagan, however, looked at her a bit strangely. He thumbed through the notebook as if searching for something. "Do you think there's any chance at all of getting paid by these jokers?"

"No," said Jade, shaking her head. "The text was pretty clear. I mean, hell, if the guy is messaging me and plans to bring his entire band to pick up the piece, he's not going to pay. And I was just about to give them the scans too. Fucking hell, I thought since we went to school together that they'd have some decency."

"Ok." Reagan began fishing around in his backpack and pulled out the notebook. "Are you open to some creative problem solving?"

"What did you have in mind?" she replied. "We're not picking a fight with those guys, there's six of them in the band."

"No, no, nothing like that," Reagan shook his head dismissively. "You alter the album cover, so that the thing is hexed."

Jade looked in the same suspicious way that the

librarian had stared at me early. "What was that?"

Reagan glanced again at the scrapbook, then sorted quickly through one of his several piles of photocopies. "Bear with me," he said, "let me read some of this thing to you." He found his page. "Ok, this is a bit long. Bear with me," he repeated again. "It's from the *Mawt al'Ruh*."

"The what?" she asked, frowning.

I did my best to look incredibly knowing. "Yes, the *Death of the Soul*, 12th century Arabian occult text on planetary magic. A real cult favorite with the Black Spiral movement." I brushed my hair out of my eyes, and glanced modestly around the room

Reagan chuckled. "Tom's a quick study. OK, listen up." He started to read.

Jade was looking back and forth between the two of us, clearly wondering if she was on the receiving end of an elaborate joke. I definitely knew that feeling.

"So you read the scrapbook, I did too. How is that even remotely relevant?" she queried.

Reagan stared off into space for a moment, while his mind worked. He looked again back at Jade.

"This scrapbook, we both read it. Let's assume for a moment that there is a chance that this journal is describing an actual force, the Black Spiral, and it's MORE than just a doorway to some other reality. Assume for a moment that it really does get channeled by these different secret societies. Assume it's sentient, or alive, or whatever, and it really does like to intervene in matters of betrayal, grievances, disputes, and money. Isn't that totally your case right now?" he asked in a very earnest voice.

"I guess," she admitted, "but how is this practical? I'm an artist who has been robed, and I don't see how this creepy journal will help me in any practical way, except by giving me recurring nightmares which I've just managed to kick." She shuddered, and I felt badly for her.

"It's practical because the book includes some tools for channeling the Spiral's power. Like, you could actually use the Spiral's power to fuck with those idiots who won't pay you."

"How? Be specific."

"I don't know," he admitted, "I'm just picking up bits and pieces. But some of the rites are pretty simple. A lot of this stuff is all art and symbols – maybe you could find a way to make them suffer through the painting alone."

Reagan flipped through several dirty yellow pages, then his finger came to rest on a particular line. "Here, look."

The text was in Arabic, but on the facing page, the compiler had included what was presumably the translation, carefully typed out in red typewriter ink. It showed a series of squiggles, together with instructions for ink that required some dyes, the blood of a raven, and some collyrium.

"What is it with the ravens?" I exclaimed aloud, but no one seemed to hear me. Jade seemed fascinated by the page.

"Hmmm, interesting patterns," she murmured, her finger tracing the designs. I also wondered what an intuitive mind would make out of foreign alphabets, and I guess that occult squiggles and sigils must equally provoke in someone such as her a process that was just beyond my own limited frame of mind.

That, by the way, was the single biggest difference between my two friends. Reagan saw script, but Jade saw symmetry.

Jade thought, and thought, then thought some more.

"You know, maybe I haven't totally finished the

album cover," she mused aloud. "Maybe I could add those sigils to the album cover, with the intent that it's like a gift to the Spiral entity, and give it to them, asking for the original terms. If they pay me, good, if they don't, then who knows. Karma, maybe."

I looked carefully at the text of the short ritual.

"What about your nightmares? Are you not afraid it's going to seriously fuck with your sleep patterns?"

Jade looked bemused. "You know, at this point, I do want the sleep, but I really need the cash from the album. Worst case scenario, they get the cover, nothing happens, I'm broke. Best case scenario, maybe I get paid something."

"And the raven sacrifice?" I asked.

"Hell no, I'm not killing some raven," she retorted. She paused. "Well objectively, I don't think this is likely to work, but I may as well give it a shot. I'll head back to finish the album. Do you guys want to come study in the studio for a change?"

Reagan shook his head. "No, I'm heading back to the library. I want to print a few more articles so I have some serious research materials to work on the grant proposal."

Reagan was actually kind of freaking me out, so I was fine with leaving.

"I think I'm going to head home to sleep like *a normal person who doesn't believe in occult conspiracies*," I said with exasperated patience.

They both looked at me a bit sharply, and I raised my hands defensively.

"You guys sound nuts. I'm just saying. Do you honestly not hear yourselves? It's the twenty-first century, for crying out loud."

The lights overhead flickered and went out. Reagan looked up.

"Man, you're not wrong about the lighting in this place," he acknowledged.

Jade shrugged.

"Look, they're coming to my studio, I may as well have something to give them, whether or not I get paid. If it gives them bad dreams, that's awesome. If not, whatever." she said, in a tone that was more tired and frustrated that anything else.

On reflection, it didn't seem worth arguing about. If she felt that giving them a commission with some subliminal graffiti would make her feel better, that was the important thing.

"You know what?" I said, "you're absolutely right. I'm being a dick. You should mess with their album cover. It's poetic justice, right?"

She seemed relieved to hear I wasn't against it, and she reached over and squeezed my shoulder.

"Thanks, I need to do something. I appreciate you being understanding. I know it's weird, but what the hell, right?"

"You do whatever you need to do," I said as warmly and sincerely as I could. She did not need a guilt trip from me. That would have been needlessly unkind and judgmental.

We finished up dinner, making small talk about classes and our plans for the weekend. Midterm exams were coming up, and studying would be the smart thing to do, but there was a fraternity party that weekend that I wanted to attend. Ashbridge was a small college, but I don't think any New England schools didn't have fraternities, they were part of the usual life of the college. Fraternities at Ashbridge were loud, but not insane (or criminal) like in Boston proper. Reagan started griping about the usual out of control drinking and drug use at these events, but Jade said she might be up for going. We agreed to speak again on Saturday afternoon to see if we both felt like hitting the party.

After dinner, Reagan left for the Library, Jade headed back to the studio to work on the album cover. True to my word, I headed back to my dorm room, because unlike my friends, I did not believe in secret societies, alien abductions, or weird books written by crazy people who believed in the mystic power of symbols.

CHAPTER SIX.

**hursday night 2011**

[3:20am]
JadePaintz: Are you awake?
ReaganM9:
ReaganM9: I am now
JadePaintz: Finished it.
ReaganM9: Finished what?
JadePaintz: The album cover.
ReaganM9: Jesus, J, it's like 3 in the morning.
JadePaintz: So go back to sleep then.
ReaganM9: No I'm here. Go on. Sorry just sleepy.
JadePaintz: I was trying to tell you. I finished it. And you know what, it felt great! I was so angry when I got to the studio, but I just got into the zone, and it was poetry.

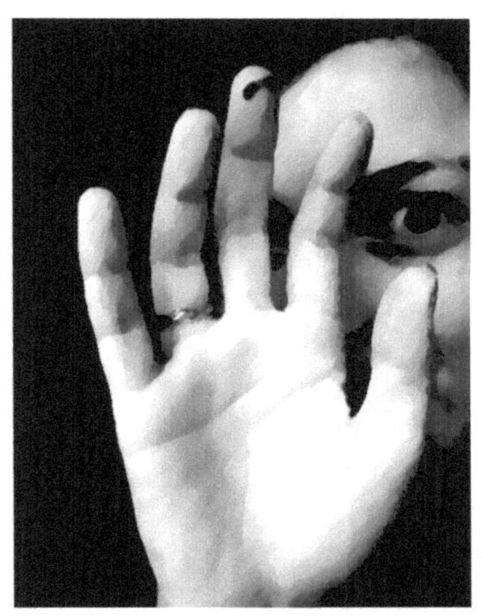

JadePaintz: I edited the album cover, it's really slight, but I managed to place those different black sigils around the piece.
JadePaintz: They're black on black, so you really can't see them if you don't know to look for them.
ReaganM9: You mean like they're subliminal.
JadePaintz: Yeah, I guess so, something like that. Anyway, I finished it, and then I had an accident.
JadePaintz: Cut myself.
JadePaintz sent an image:
ReaganM9: "Shit, are you ok? What happened?"
JadePaintz: Yeah it's not bad.
JadePaintz: I was using a box cutter to get some fresh supplies out of their packaging, and somehow I ended up stabbing myself. There was blood everywhere.

JadePaintz: And then, it was weird, I got this kind of feeling.
JadePaintz: I can't describe it without sounding creepy, but I just felt really inspired, like in a good way. So I took some of the blood, and I rubbed it onto the sigils.
JadePaintz: You can't even see it because of the black on black effect, but I'll know it's there, and you will too."
ReaganM9: So you rubbed your own blood into the painting? Is that a Van Gough thing?"

JadePaintz: No. I dunno, I mean some painters do use their own blood, it totally happens.
JadePaintz: I never have before.
JadePaintz: But fuck – I got such a rush doing it.
ReaganM9: What did it feel like?
JadePaintz: Like – this will sound weird – like the force that was in my nightmares was really aware of what I was doing. I know it sounds crazy.
JadePaintz: Anyway, maybe that's the cost of doing some of this stuff without sacrificing ravens."
ReaganM9: I guess we'll find out, right?
ReaganM9: So what happens now?
JadePaintz: What do you mean?
ReaganM9: The album cover.
JadePaintz: Well, I scanned the piece and sent it to them. I told them I expect to be paid tomorrow.
JadePaintz: If they don't pay me, to hell with them.
JadePaintz: Kaaaaaarma.
ReaganM9: That sounds right to me.
ReaganM9: Can I please sleep now?
ReaganM9:
ReaganM9:
JadePaintz: Yes go sleep.
ReaganM9: See you tomorrow.
ReaganM9: Happy for you.
JadePaintz: Thanks. Sleep well.
ReaganM9: zzzzzzzzzzzzzzz

CHAPTER SEVEN.

Sunday afternoon.

espite a really, really bad hangover from the fraternity party the night before, that morning I went to see Reagan in his dorm. He hadn't shown up for lunch or dinner on Friday, and I didn't see him all Saturday. This worried me, and when I tried to call, his phone was shut off, and so I went to his room. Reagan's dormitory was right next door to mine, so it was not even a five-minute walk from my door to his, though I didn't go often, mainly because he didn't like to have people inside his personal space. It's not that he was territorial or anything, it's more like I got the impression that he needed to feel like he had some privacy. He even allocated a large part of his annual honors scholarship to get a private room. I had a room to myself, but only because my roommate had dropped out at the beginning of the semester.

I knocked at his door. There was a faint rustling inside the room. I knocked again, this time a little more insistently.

The door swung open, and Reagan stood there in his faded jeans and a dark turtleneck. His eyes looked tired and bloodshot, as though he'd been asleep, or maybe drinking. I expected him to smell stale, but he smelled as though he'd been working near burning incense, and it had saturated his clothes. He was clutching his left hand, which was wrapped in a cloth bandage. The bandage showed blood slowly oozing through.

Reagan squinted at me in surprise.

"What time is it?" he asked.

"Nearly noon, and you haven't surfaced since Thursday. What happened to your hand?" I asked, pointing at the blood stains on the cloth.

"Why didn't you just call? I've been busy," he said awkwardly.

"Your phone is turned off. Christ, it's been off since yesterday, would it hurt you to at least check in once in a while?"

"Sorry, I didn't realize. Is it Saturday already?" He seemed somewhat befuddled, and it irritated me.

"Reagan, for fucks sake, it's Sunday. SUNDAY. Put on a clean shirt, we're going for breakfast at Trident."

"Yeah, ok. Just wait out here, I'll get dressed?"

He tried to close the door on me.

"Jackass. I'll wait inside," I insisted, and pushed past into his room. He was startled by my abruptness, and I was angry enough at his weird appearance that I didn't allow politeness to keep me outside.

His apartment, however, was in such a state that I wished I had waited in the hallway. It's not that the room was messy, exactly, at least not in the traditional sense. In fact, the room was immaculate, and while it was poorly lit, it smelled of freshly burned incense. I expected to see piles of paper, plates of uneaten food stacked messily, and dirty bedsheets and laundry tossed haphazardly. However, there was none of that in evidence. The disturbing aspect was that Reagan had very obviously converted his entire living quarters into some kind of a shrine.

Reagan's apartment was a large, single loft, with a tiny bathroom and a closet. In the main room, he'd neatly moved everything to fit against the walls, which left the majority of the room a bare floor. Even the rugs which came with the room had been neatly piled and set aside near the closet. The curtains were blackout fabric, and had been pulled tightly against the window, which allowed in only a very weak illumination. The majority of the light came from candles in empty jars, which were placed around the room at what appeared to be specific intervals. The candle-jars were placed within small chalk circles, around which Reagan had written characters and symbols that I did not recognize from any particular alphabet.

"I wish you'd stayed outside. And for Christ's sakes, don't step on any of the lines," he muttered, as he crossed the room carefully to retrieve his coat, which had been folded and placed on his desk chair. The desk itself was against the wall and had on it a small mountain of books and photocopied pages that he'd obviously taken from the library. There was also a mortar and pestle atop his desk, with what I think was home-made incense being ground inside – the smell was overpowering but otherwise pleasant, when I neared the desk for a closer look.

As my eyes adjusted to the gloom and the faint trails of smoke from the incense, I could see that in the center of the room, there was a triangle which appeared to be facing north (I think). That was my guess, because the sun was shining still in the east, and its light filtered in weakly from a window that faced that direction. The triangle seemed to dominate the center of the room, and there was a meditation cushion in the center, which suggested he'd been sitting there.

But the main feature of the shrine was the northern wall, which had neither furniture nor objects of any kind piled against it. Instead, Reagan appeared to have traced a rough doorway in thick chalk. It was obvious that he was no artist, if the doorposts were intended to be straight, he'd done a bad job. The white chalk was stained with blood in several places, and there was bloody handprints in the center of the door itself, pressed on top of the image of a large chalk spiral. Candles were clustered around the base of the door, giving a bizarre illumination to the entire seen. A box cutter was lying outside the triangle, with a wet red stain along the cutting edge.

"Not a good time to come", Reagan repeated, "I'm busy working on the research project." His voice seemed hoarse and strained. He kept glancing at me as I surveyed the room. The scene was so bizarre that I was really at a loss for words.

"What… what the hell are you trying to do?" I managed to rasp out loud.

He shook his head glumly.

"Nothing, it didn't work, doesn't matter."

I was starting to really, truly worry if he was ill in some way. "Reagan, what's going on here? Why are you *bleeding*?" I said, stressing the last word especially.

Having gotten his coat off the chair, he was putting his arms through the sleeves. This done, he began to slowly make his way around the room – walking backwards and counter clockwise, I noted – and taking the mason jars, he blew out each candle one at a time. He paused at the chalk door, as if trying to decide whether or not to leave the candles burning. Ultimately he must have decided that they were something of a fire hazard, because he stooped to snuff them out also.

"I hoped," he began, "that I had solved the riddle. I was hoping to see what would happen if I made the door, but it didn't work. I must be missing something. Maybe it was the blood, maybe I needed more blood? Could it be?"

He looked off into space, as if he was oblivious to the fact that I was even there. His mouth was working, as if he was speaking to himself, but no sound was coming out. I was wondering if he had taken drugs, when suddenly a dark, thin flow of blood began to trickle out from his nose.

Then he turned to me, and seemed to actually see me in, as if for the first time. He smiled.

"Tom, hi! Did you just get here?" He paused, as if disoriented. He looked around. "Man, I need to clean this stuff up, I must have dozed off again."

"Are you feeling ok?" I asked cautiously.

"Oh yeah. You know, I must have dozed off or been sleepwalking again. You see all this," and he gestured around the room, "I was doing a recreation of the secret society rites, to better understand their process. Absolutely fascinating, it's all symbolic, you know. The actual practice of drawing the circles, the triangle, lighting the lamps, all indicative of deep psychological processes that the ritual is meant to unlock."

"Uh-huh. And what's that?" I asked directly, pointing an accusing finger at the chalk doorway with the bloodstains.

"Yes, very good that you noticed. Well the door symbolizes the transitory state of ignorance to wisdom, and the candles represent the gnosis that flows from the door."

"Ok, but why are there bloodstains on the doorway?" I asked with increasing insistence.

"Well the ritual calls for the death of an animal, but obviously its symbolic of the death of innocence. So I cut myself, hoping that the pain and blood flow would stimulate nerve centers of the brain, and simulate the alchemy that an actual sacrifice would unlock. No success though, obviously, as I'm not enlightened!" and he chuckled as though this was all obviously funny.

His explanation did make a certain amount of sense. Literal sorcery was obviously unreal, but some weird kind of psychodrama – well it was weird, but I could appreciate his mental process, at least. I mean, it was fucked up even, but he explained it so rationally that I was no longer freaked out. The neat, orderly arrangement of the room did seem more or less the product of an orderly mind, as opposed to finding stained needles, or empty bottles of whiskey on the ground.

He straightened his coat.

"You know, it's good you came, and I'm sorry about my phone – battery must have died, and I was meditating for so long, I think I literally fell asleep. Must have been sleepwalking when you came to the door, so I'm glad you brought me back inside. So, we're getting some lunch, right?"

He pulled a glove over his bandaged hand, and one over the other as well.

"Yeah, that's the plan," I agreed. We left his room together, entered the hallway, and began to make our way to Trident to get our morning coffee.

e walked together across the campus, ice and snow crunching under our shoes. I told him about the party the night before, which had been really wild. At the end of the night I was really drunk, and I think I was trying to hook up with this hot girl from my "Introduction to Psychology" course, but I blacked out and came to while heaving over the toilet. Jade had come with me to the party, and I think she'd had a good time dancing with some of her friends. The only weird memory I had was seeing her paying one of the guys that was there dealing chemicals – I don't remember her taking anything, and if she did it must have been *really* mild, but whatever. She'd been a lot more sober than me, and she'd practically carried me home to my dorm. I only partially remembered making the walk back, and she'd helped me into my room and tucked me under the covers, leaving only after she was sure I'd had some water to drink.

Reagan laughed.

"Well it sounds like I should have come to the party, because I didn't get a lot done on my own. But I did file the research grant proposal on Friday, so fingers crossed for that."

I wished him luck on the grant – I knew how much that stuff mattered to him.

We made our way across the campus. The student newspaper, Ashbridge Gazette, had just been stocked, and I grabbed a copy from the dispensary box as we went by it. The cover line caught my eye:

AUTO ACCIDENT RESULTS IN TRAGEDY

'The Rector's Office at Ashbridge College released a statement today that six Ashbridge students died in a tragic car accident, while driving home on Saturday night after attending a fraternity social event. The car appears to have deviated from the road, rolled, and caught fire. The coroner's office report indicates that the students were under the influence of alcohol and an unidentified hallucinogenic substance. The six members belong to the Ashbridge College musical group, 'Shades of

"Fucking hell," I breathed aloud, and showed the paper to Reagan. His expression was curious to watch – at first, he was shocked as me. But his eyes grew, well, crafty almost.

"Wow, that's too bad," he sighed, passing me back the paper.

"Isn't that the group that tried to stiff Jade on the painting?" I asked.

"I think so. It said that they were at the party too – did you see them drinking heavily?"

It was embarrassing to admit, but I'd drank so much at the party that I was honestly unable to remember much of anything. I shook my head.

"Nah, there were a lot of people there, but I don't remember seeing a lot of sober people."

Reagan nodded.

"It's too bad, but it's not unexpected – people drink and drive, accidents will happen. I guess Jade will never get her cash now." He paused. "You know, maybe it's better that she doesn't hear about this from us."

On the one hand, telling her seemed like it might be a good idea. But on the other hand, it could not possibly make her feel anything but sad, and sometimes it just didn't pay to be the bearers of bad news. I agreed with him that she would find out in time on her own, and that there was no sense in being the ones to tell her.

Our morning went well otherwise, with coffee and freshly baked muffins at Trident. It was good to hang out with Reagan, and we spent at least two hours after breakfast in browsing the bookstore section of the coffee shop. After, he headed to the Library to study, and we promised to meet for supper at the end of the day.

I actually don't know if he told Jade about the deaths

of the band members, but I know for certain that she never learned about it from me, and I'm happy to think that maybe she never learned it at all. It was definitely karmic justice, I told myself, and hoped that it was that, and not something else.

CHAPTER EIGHT

February 20. Thursday night

[3:06 pm]
ReaganM9: OMG I got it!
JadePaintz: What's that?
ReaganM9: The grant, they're giving me $20,000 to work on the project. I got the first part of the cash this week, I get 7K to start.
JadePaintz: That's really nice, I'm happy for you.
ReaganM9: Thanks, I appreciate it.
JadePaintz: Well things are not as good on my end.
ReaganM9: How so?
JadePaintz: Well my studio space is full to bursting
ReaganM9: That's better than being empty, right?
JadePaintz: In a manner of speaking, sure you could say that.

JadePaintz: but it's also not ideal. No room to grow there.

ReaganM9: Yeah that's not ideal.

JadePaintz: On the other hand, I think we have everything we need for the ceremony.

ReaganM9: No we still need opium for the incense.

JadePaintz: Got it.

ReaganM9: How?

JadePaintz: The fraternity party you skipped, I managed to get some there.

ReaganM9: For real?

JadePaintz: Yes for real.

JadePaintz: But it doesn't matter because we don't have the space for the installation.

ReaganM9: Can't you book the university gallery?

JadePaintz: Too small. I need a LOT of space. Corridors, smaller rooms.

ReaganM9: Is there anything like that on campus?

JadePaintz: No way.

ReaganM9: So?

JadePaintz: There's an old factory available for rent in town, but it's way too expensive.

ReaganM9: How much is "expensive"?

JadePaintz: It's $1250 monthly, I can't afford even close to that.

ReaganM9: I can cover it.

JadePaintz: No you can't, you're poorer than me.

ReaganM9: I just got $7000 from my grant!

JadePaintz: Ooooooo!

ReaganM9: And this is kind of research, I mean it's directly related to the book, so it kind of counts as grant spending.

JadePaintz: We'd just need to rent it for a month or two.

ReaganM9: I know, that's what I'm thinking too.

JadePaintz: Ok I'll speak to the owner and see if we can get it for…. When?
ReaganM9: March and April, I guess.
JadePaintz: Ok, sounds good, let's aim to open the installation in April.
JadePaintz: EXCITED.
ReaganM9: YESSSS
JadePaintz: Wait.
ReaganM9: ???
JadePaintz: We need to tell Tom.
ReaganM9: Why?
JadePaintz: Because we keep cutting him out of the loop, and he's not stupid.
ReaganM9: He wouldn't understand anyway.
JadePaintz: FFS REAGAN.
ReaganM9: Sorry ok ok ok
JadePaintz: Jesus Christ. I'll tell him myself.
ReaganM9: What will you say?
JadePaintz: I'll tell him I'm using the factory for a gallery showing. I'll say I rented it for cheap cause it was in bad shape.
ReaganM9: Sounds believable.
JadePaintz: I think so too.
ReaganM9: My notes are way too scattered.
JadePaintz: Your place looks clean though, how is that even possible?
ReaganM9: The piles are neat, but it's a lot of dead ends. I need to compile into a single volume. Like put all the translations together, pictures, instructions, so it's actually carriable.
JadePaintz: You're making another notebook?
ReaganM9: Yes, I guess so. Haha.
JadePaintz: Creepy.
ReaganM9: I want to add some photos from your studio.
JadePaintz: Sure, I can send some over, if you think it

will help.

ReaganM9: Definitely. A lot of the art in the notebook is flawed, I think you've captured the Spiral better than the original author.

JadePaintz: It's weird to think so, but I agree completely on that point.

ReaganM9: So I'll write up the Ceremony, and we can go over it next week.

JadePaintz: K but after that I'm going to be busy working offsite at the factory. A LOT of work to do.

ReaganM9: Do you need help?

JadePaintz: I'll let you know.

ReaganM9: K sounds good.

JadePaintz: I'm having coffee with Tom, so I can tell him about my new installation.

ReaganM9: Sounds good. K so I'll see you guys at supper time.

JadePaintz: Ok see you later.

ReaganM9: Bye for now.

CHAPTER NINE

April

It was the last week of April, and Jade was finally about to open her installation to the public. For a good six, maybe seven weeks, she'd hardly been on campus, except for classes and the occasional meal. Reagan and I were really excited for her – she told us that she was able to rent a vacant factory on the edge of Ashbridge for a really decent rate. I didn't want to embarrass her by asking about the numbers, but I think she said that the owner was a college alumnus or donor, and so he must have must have given her a break. I'd been out to the site right at the very beginning, when she asked Reagan and I to help bring over all her work and supplies from her studio on campus. It was strange seeing her studio go from being covered in black mirrors and cavasses, to being plain white walls just a few hours later. She took all her supplies: the easel, her chair, her paints and brushes. I mean, there was literally nothing left except the overhead lights, which were flickering consistently. She said she'd be glad to finally be out of the studio, partly because the space was starting to feel really constricted. It's not that the space given to students were small either, but I think that her artistic vision had just grown and grown until she finally made the choice to get a bigger space. I wasn't an artist, but I could see that she really had a vision, like there was something inside of her that she wanted to express, and if she couldn't project it somehow, it would be a source of frustration.

Anyway, we borrowed a friend's car, and drove back and forth with her supplies and art pieces. When we had finished unpacking the final car load, she gave us a tour of the building. She went to a fuse-box near the entrance and pulled a level. The place lit up – sort of – as most of the lightbulbs inside had burnt out a while ago. At first glance, I didn't know what she saw in the place – it was large, drafty, and had a thick layer of dust everywhere. The place smelled of piss, and I suspect that the building had been used by the homeless in wintertime, as the building was proof against the elements, if nothing else. The main floor was one giant room, where I guess the majority of the factory's machinery would have been located. Large truck bays were visible at the back. It was all empty now, and no evidence remained of what exactly had been produced or manufactured here. Next, she showed us the upper floor, which was a maze of small offices or storerooms, which reminded me slightly of the oddly-arranged studio section in the Ashbridge Fine Arts building.

"You need to see the basement," she'd said, with a

crooked smile that indicated she's saved it for last.

We followed her back down to the main floor, where she led us to the back of that large central room. In the far corner, there was a dark pit, with a heavy iron staircase that descended into the murk. I could see a dim lightbulb at the bottom of the stairs, and Jade started down, motioning for us to follow.

At the bottom, we found ourselves in a damp basement, which effectively mirrored the large factory space above. The ground was concrete, dirty and stained, and it stank of mold and urine. The floor in the center of the large room had a large iron drainage grill, leading down to the sewer. I thought I saw dog shit (or worse) in the corner, and I shuddered in spite of myself.

"This is perfect," our friend purred, and she rubbed her hands together gleefully.

"It's – ah – it's large," Reagan said, in a voice that echoed the anxiety I felt myself. "Do you think it'll be safe to work here?"

She nodded.

"The owner promised to check in occasionally, and I'll also let campus police know that I'm here. Besides, campus isn't far, and I've got my phone if anything goes wrong."

To be fair, Ashbridge was such a small town that there was practically zero crime, unless you counted the occasional drunken disorderly caused by the college students. Had we been in Boston, I would have objected to the space more strenuously. Besides, Jade was fiercely independent, and while she wasn't foolhardy, she didn't like suggestions that she ever needed help taking care of herself, even when she was sick or injured. So we congratulated her on the site, and admired the sheer size of it – this at least could be done genuinely, as there was not much else to praise.

Over the coming weeks, Jade spent increasing

amounts of time at the factory. In the first week of the project, I think she'd had to do some cleaning. She'd come to the college cafeteria or Trident still smelling of chemical cleaning products or else vinegar. But she made it clear early on that she had no illusions of cleaning the entire factory, which would have been impossible anyway. She refused to tell us much about the installation, except to say that the factory itself was the installation, and that she was working to use the entire space – every room, every crack and crevice – to express the idea that had come to her as a result of reading that insane notebook.

I'm sure that she was sleeping there some nights, and she admitted that she'd purchased a thin camping mattress and blanket so she could take naps when she needed them. She didn't ever seem exhausted or overtired, and she didn't exhibit any signs of wear and tear, except for sometimes being a little more tired than normal, and that happened to her during her intensive weeks in the normal studio anyway. I would say that apart from the fact that she was spending a lot of time off campus, Jade looked really fulfilled, like she had thrown herself completely into her work, and her work was going really phenomenally well. It was nice to see her so in love with her art, because not every artist can actually rejoice in their craft. Even the masters had their moments of deep depression, but that was clearly not the case here.

Jade would occasionally get excited and just burst out with brief vocalizations on the installation. I gathered that it was going to be relatively dim in terms of lighting, but that the lack of lighting was part of the statement. She'd left most of the dust and dirt, but she'd cleaned up the worst of the urine and animal feces. She'd used a LOT of black paint – no surprise there –

and had to bring additional mirrors from the Fine Arts building, which luckily had been no problem. She hinted that she'd actually used human organic materials in places, but she'd clam up as soon as I'd ask what that meant. Her hands had cuts on them frequently, I noticed, so I guessed that she was working with a lot of cutting implements, maybe for fabrics or plastics. I remember her grumbling at one point about the problems of mixing oil with other organics, and when I asked what she meant, she laughed and laughed as though I'd made some absurd joke. Ultimately, she seemed happy and sane and good, and her enthusiasm was contagious – I soon found myself excited about the exhibit, I mean really excited. I didn't even really know what there was to be excited about, but she would come back from the site practically glowing. It was a good month.

That wasn't the only positive thing. Reagan had finally gotten rid of that damned notebook. About the same time that Jade started working at the factory, he'd stopped carrying the notebook. I don't know if he actually got rid of it, or just stopped carrying it, but I stopped seeing it altogether. I asked him about it just once, and he said that it had nothing left to teach him, and that he'd finally overcome his addiction to it. He joked once or twice about creating his own journal, which worried me a little, but that seemed infinitely less noxious than carrying or reading that grimy conspiracy-ridden text that seemed to have possessed him since December. I found him frequently handwriting notes in a sleek black moleskin journal that he'd gotten at the campus bookstore, but honestly, that didn't seem any worse a habit than Facebook. He'd also gotten that big research grant and spent a lot of time planning where he'd travel and who he'd interview. Admittedly, doing a paper on secret societies would mean more time in the archives than actually doing live interviews, but he told

Jade and I both that he was planning to visit a couple of universities in Washington DC and meet with some professors who worked on espionage and covert movements. While there, he'd also consulted the Library of Congress, which had resources that dwarfed anything at Ashbridge, though he'd always be quick to point out that our little college library was excellent, despite its sleepy surroundings.

In general, it felt like a perfect Spring semester. My grades were good, I had even managed to finally get a job on campus, shelving books at the college library, and the best part was that I never had to work mornings, it was only ever evenings. My friends seemed to be doing well in their own pursuits, and by the end of April, I felt like the eeriness of December and January had eased off. Maybe, I reflected, there really was something to that whole "dark half / light half" of the year, which some of the ancient cultures believed in. Truthfully, I didn't really care too much why things were back to normal – I just wanted to believe that it had been a weird winter, and that things were gearing up for a decent end of term, followed by a relaxing summer with easy courses, some vacation time, and that new "Game of Thrones" series that was about to launch on HBO that month.

I had never, ever, been more wrong in all my life.

It was the night of the installation opening. That entire week had been a sort of creative insanity on Jade's part. We hardly saw her at all, and I'm positive that she was fueling herself on coffee and pure manic energy, but somehow she managed to get to her classes, join us for breakfast, and still maintain an air that reminded me of the Cheshire cat. It's not that she was languid or even feline, but rather that she had this constant grin, like she knew something the rest of us didn't. No mystery there, of course, her secret was the giant gallery, the installation, which she'd been guarding so jealously.

Jade had gotten these sleek invitations printed on black cardstock, which read:

INFERIS
74 MAIOR STREET
SATURDAY 16 APRIL
EXHIBITION OPENS AT 11:00PM
FORMAL ATTIRE REQUIRED

Reagan and I praised her for the classy invitations, and she admitted she was proud with how they'd turned out. Arguably, it was a little creepy that she was using the title from the grey journal, but I didn't think it worth mentioning. That little book had definitely impacted her creative energies, there was no questioning that. The late start time encouraged me to take an afternoon nap, but admittedly so did almost anything else related to schoolwork. My only issue was that my shift at the Library didn't end until midnight, and since I had just started the job, it didn't seem smart to knock off early. But Jade didn't mind when I told her, and she said that the installation would be open all night until sunrise anyway, so I could come after midnight and still enjoy the exhibit. I told her I felt badly not being there to help out, but she said that she'd recruited some friends from the Fine Arts program to help curate the installation on opening night, which made me feel a lot better.

The library stayed open all night at Ashbridge, but my shift did end precisely at midnight. I'd actually worn a suit to work, which my co-workers teased me about; this was mainly to save time so I could leave straight from the library to go to the factory, without going home to change. At 11:50pm I called for a taxi, which was waiting to pick me up at midnight. It was only a 15 minute drive to the factory, and I could have walked it, but it would have taken about an hour, and I was conscious that I was arriving late.

When I arrived at the factory, I could see a good number of cars, all of which I'm sure belonged to other students and staff associated with the college. The factory entrance was illuminated by a single halogen bulb, which glowed sullenly in the cool night air. I could see that there were two figures stationed at the entrance next to a table. I paid the taxi driver and stepped out of the cab. As I neared the door, I could see that one attendant was male, the other female, and both were dressed in dark suits and were wearing black theatre masks. I smiled in the darkness – apparently, this was part of the performance aspect of Jade's installation. I could hear music faintly playing from inside the building, and the babble of voices inside.

As I came near the door, I could see that there were shot glasses on the table, filled with a cloudy substance. A dark box was under the table. The female attendant interposed herself.

"Invitation?" she asked, voice muted through the mask.

I reached into my jacket to fish out my black card. I handed it to her.

She studied it for a moment and nodded to her male counterpart. He reached under the table into the box and pulled out a black mask identical to their own. He handed it to me.

"You'll need this."

When I had finished placing the mask over my face, the female attendant handed me one of the shot glasses.

"Drink this."

I did as I was told. The milky fluid was vodka-based for sure, but there was something else in there, something unfamiliar and slightly bitter in there. I winced as it slid down my throat.

"What was that?" I asked.

"Laudanum," the female figure remarked in a nonchalant tone.

Laudanum, I thought, *can she be serious?*

The male attendant opened the door for me, and for a moment it looked almost pitch-black inside. I could hear music playing more clearly now, some sort of droning industrial track was playing, and I could hear voices inside, laughing and talking all at once. The attendant gestured for me to enter, and so I stepped inside.

It was dark inside, but not pitch-black: a bluish-purple haze filtered down from bulbs on either side of the door. Black-light, I noted. The other thing I noticed was that the air was thick with some kind of smoky, pungent incense, and so the very dim light of the black-light bulbs was reduced even more, such that there was no actual illumination, but rather just a general murkiness that one had to struggle to peer through. The murk was so think that I bumped into another guest almost immediately and realized that the darkness would make it hard to see the other guests. I understood next that as the other guests most likely wore dark formal wear with dark masks in a dark space, it was going to be an interesting experience trying to navigate the exhibit. Maybe that was part of the point though – not to be separated from the exhibit, but to be part of it. *Very profound, Jade*, I thought to myself, and smiled. I had been here during the day, and so I knew that I was at the south side of the gigantic main room. Normally speaking, unless Jade had erected walls, it should be fine to walk from one end of the room to the other and not run into anything except other people. I guessed that whatever art she'd installed would be lining the walls, and so I took a turn to the right, and began to move forward, with one hand stretched in front of me to avoid any collisions, and the other hand running along the wall to maintain my bearings.

The music was strange, a dark ambient noise that lacked any coherent beat or rhythm. There were moments where I could hear a voice track laid over it, maybe Jade's, but it was so faint that I couldn't tell who it was or what they were saying.

As I started forward, for a moment my head began to feel strange, almost heavy. I couldn't tell if it was the flavored vodka shot, or the strange incense – which was definitely not just some standard sandalwood packaged in India. The room wasn't exactly spinning, but as I learned on the wall for a moment, it felt almost as though my fingers sank into the concrete. I shook my head to clear it.

Another black-light bulb shone faintly ahead, and I headed towards it. In the dim light I could see that the surface of the wall was covered in oily black paint. I felt the wall more carefully, and the paint seemed both grainy and oily at the same time, almost as through she'd painted in the same thick paste that she'd used to do the original spiral design in her studio on campus. It made me think of tar, given its grainy, muddy texture.

Through the murk, suddenly I could see another masked shape reaching out towards me, and for a moment I thought that I'd come face-to-face with another guest, but then realized that I'd come across one of Jade's mirrors. Around the mirror, now, I could see something else: large white letters, spelling out words that I didn't recognize:

EZZAT SHAMRAT ILU NAMURAT…

As I looked to my left and right at the other visible black-light bulbs, it seemed to me that the white words were clustered around them as well.

Was the point of the exhibit to experience the installation in near blindness? I decided to close my eyes, and focus on *feeling* the wall. I could feel the warp and weft of the substance she'd smeared on the walls. The oily, bizarre texture seemed almost to move under my fingers, like it was strangely alive. I'm not sure if it was the effect of the music, or the incense, or maybe the shot of vodka that they claimed was laudanum, but as my hands explored the wall, I had the most curious sensations in my head. It felt strangely good to be there, like I was discovering some darkly secret pleasure for the first time. Some of the voices around me began to sound less raucous and more coy. There was an alluring, seductive feeling to the black paint.

I moved along the wall, my hands exploring more insistently now. As I did, I passed through several small clusters of guests. They too seemed to be enjoying themselves, some in the company of their fellows, others in the exploration of the exhibit. I could hear people trying to read the gently glowing white names aloud from the wall, the alien syntax awkward in the mouths of English-speakers:

U SHI BARBARAT MARAT ANU

As I moved about the room, I tried to keep track of my surroundings. It was difficult to gage how far I'd come, and how far the four corners of the room would be. I knew that eventually I would come to the stairs leading upwards. Hand over hand, I felt my way along – I was in no hurry, because the sensation of touching and feeling the black walls was becoming almost euphoric. I marveled at Jade's imagination, to have conceived such an exhibit that simultaneously deprived one of their sight, while taunting them with sound and touch. I wondered for a moment if or how I might find the artist to congratulate her, or whether Reagan was in here also, blindly groping his way along some wall or corridor in the building.

Then I saw a blackish bulb ahead of me, and a white arrow pointing upwards. *The stairs*, I recalled, *should be right about here*. I remembered that there was a handrail at about the level of my waist, and so I reached out in that general direction. It took a moment to find it, and I was not keen to race up the dark stairs without it. I wondered for a moment why she hadn't at least allowed proper illumination for the ascending or descending guests, but I supposed it was necessary to maintain the sense of the otherworldly glamor.

With my hand on the rail, I began to make my way upstairs. I could hear the music pulsing louder on the floor above, and also the sounds of voices, muted behind black masks

The scent of the incense was also stronger on the second floor, and there was even less of the black light. I remembered that the entire upper floor was a maze of corridors and small rooms, and I was unsure which direction to choose, and how far I should actually stray from the stairs. I remembered an old rule that when in a labyrinth, it is best to put your hand to the wall, and decide to make all left turns, or all right turns, so as to be able to find the exit, or retrace your steps. So I reached out with my left hand, and began to inch my way forward cautiously.

As I moved through the gloom, I felt another wave of euphoria surge through me. There was something almost alien about the entire experience, a kind of slow ecstasy that was sensual, if not sexual. And as I moved along the corridor, I could hear heavy breathing and groans coming from one of the rooms ahead that suggested that one couple had also found the sensory power of the exhibit to be overwhelming, but in a slightly different way than the installation was affecting me. Even as that thought crossed my mind, I passed several laughing guests who were moving along the corridor in the opposite direction, and one of them stumbled into me in the blinding darkness. I grabbed the wall to steady myself, and with my other hand tried to balance the other party. A female voice apologized, and as she moved to regain her balance, I realized that she was in a state of partial undress. Then as quickly as she had pressed against me, she was moving away. Normally I would have been flustered, or surprised, instead I just smiled indulgently under my black mask, and continue my exploration of the second floor.

I came to a room without sighs or heavy breathing, and ventured inside. There was a single black-light bulb in the ceiling, and it gave just enough light to show that the walls were wall-to-wall mirrors, with symbols and glyphs in white paint on some, and dark spirals on others. As I studied the symbols, I felt a sudden sensation, almost an oozing in my brain, and my legs buckled under me. The music seemed louder, and the voice track seemed to be harsher, more insistent. I still could not make out the words, but there was a definite sense of meaning, almost a cadence.

I must have spent another half an hour exploring the upper floor, but it was hard to gauge the passing of time.

I may have been up there for hours, and still I had not seen my friends. I decided then that I should try the basement, as it was the only part of the installation that I had yet to visit. So I retraced my steps (right turn, right turn, right turn) back to the stairs, and gingerly made my way down in the dark. This time it was I who almost stumbled in the dark, but I managed to keep my balance, and soon found myself on the ground floor.

I remembered that the iron staircase to the basement was not far from the stairs leading up, and so I began to move forward. The installation seemed to be even more crowded now, as guests had continued to arrive after me. Though I did not have far to go, I had to push past other guests more insistently. It was not that I was in any kind of hurry.

As I moved along the walls, the black oily texture feeling more and more welcoming with each moment, I could read more of the white words that had been painted across the black:

SHEPASU ANZU QATASHA LU'ATU

There was something about the names that triggered new spasms of euphoria across my temples, but my stomach seemed to twist at the same time, as though I had swallowed something bitter. Nonplussed, I moved along until I could see the faint outline of the iron staircase descending into the darkness below.

I grasped the handrail, as I did not wish to fall down into that darkness, knowing that the floor beneath was hard concrete. Moving downwards, I could hear the murmur of many voices below, as though the bulk of the guests had descended ahead of me. *What a turnout*, I thought, *Jade must be thrilled*. The droning industrial music seemed to come in pulses now, strange sounds that I couldn't identify as organic or synthetic almost becoming visible patterns in the darkness. I felt completely inebriated, not in the bad, sickened way that comes before vomiting, but in that state that people want to experience at a club, when they're happy and carefree, and buzzing with energy and intensity. The voice track seemed to be coming clearer now, and I could almost make out the words. It had occurred to me then that perhaps the reason I could not understand the speech was that the language was not English. I could make out some phrases which repeated themselves now, but they were nonsense to me: *Lamsashtu, Dimme, Barbarat* seemed the most common, but there were other phrases that seemed to creep into my consciousness.

My feet reached the concrete floor of the basement, and I brushed up against a large group of people. Their backs were to me, and they all seemed to be facing the center of the room. I couldn't see what they were facing, so I began to feel my way gently along the back of the crowd, hoping to find an opening so I could see what my fellow guests were watching. The lights were sparse down here, and the air was oppressive with the incense. In fact, in the depths of the basement, it was so thick that I wondered if all the fumes above ground had originated below, and simply drifted up through whatever ventilation the factory had.

I heard a voice, chanting now in the center of the room. There was no mistaking, it was Jade. She seemed to be saying something again and again, but it was definitely not in English. It sounded like *am ah zay am ah zay dee ay.* There was something about the way she said it that made my stomach twist, violently, but the pleasant feeling in my head got stronger. I felt a powerful compulsion to see what was happening, not just because I was curious, but because I suddenly felt like she was speaking to me, or at least to us as a group.

There was a gap ahead, and I moved forward. I might have been too insistent, because I think I almost knocked over several other guests in order to move through the throng, but the sick, pulsing urge in my head ordered me to move – I didn't even do it consciously, it was like I was sleepwalking at this point.

As I'd seen when I came downstairs, the room was almost entirely dark, with only random blacklights along the walls at very distant intervals. But now that I'd moved somewhat towards the center of the room, I could see that Jade had installed several blacklight bulbs in the low ceiling overhead. The blackish-blue light cast just enough illumination to show that a female figure dressed in a black smock and wearing a black mask was standing in the very center of the room, atop the iron drainage grill that I'd seen on my first visit. The grill must have been a good 10 feet in diameter, and around it, she'd drawn a thick chalk circle. Around that circle there were several smaller circles, and inside those were mason jars, like the ones I'd seen in Reagan's loft. The mason jars each held a blacklight glowstick, which provided just enough illumination to reveal the chalk circles and the strange characters that were curled around them.

The ceiling itself was low, and there was just enough light to see that it was Jade's masterpiece. She had somehow managed to transform the ceiling into a giant black spiral, contained within a great black circle that glistened and seemed to flow, slowly. I'm not even sure how I was able to see the ceiling, because the blacklight would not have illuminated anything so dark. But the ceiling was visible, somehow, and she had managed to craft it such that it seemed to be made up of moving shadows, which shifted and twitched softly in the black un-light of that place.

Looking at the spiral, I thought for a moment that I was going to pass out. That dull, sensual pleasure that I had felt in the rooms upstairs, that intimate glistening sensation as I had groped the walls – it fell away, and as I looked into the rippling black spiral overhead, I felt a genuine ache of longing that defied any sense of reason or explanation I could provide. I wanted to lose myself in that room, to the thing that she'd brought into being on the ceiling. It was utterly perverse, and I wanted so badly to be possessed by it, or possess it, or even just to touch it. But the ceiling was still too far overhead for me to have reached it, and so my hunger for the image remained unsated.

A sharp bleating sound echoed across the room, and I could see now that a second masked figure had appeared behind Jade in the circle. They appeared to be wrestling with a shadow, and as they turned towards me, I could see that the shadow was in fact a black goat, which had been bound by its feet. Jade's face was covered by the mask, but as her chanting continued, I could hear a sense of exaltation in her voice. The throng of people around me swayed, and I understood then that the powerful sense of want, of lust or need for something indescribable was not unique to me, it was common to us all. Students, staff, faculty, we swayed, listening to the droning music, groaning, murmuring, muttering along with it, with her.

DIMME, LAMASHTU, MARAT ANU.

The figure next to her had finally pinned the goat down to the ground, and I could see now the shine of sharp metal in her hand. Jade's masked face surveyed the crowed, and someone in the room began to howl wildly. First one voice, then several, broke into animal noises – savage growling, hissing, even roaring. I was alarmed to find that I was among them, my own throat tightening as I swayed in the darkness, fighting unsuccessfully to suppress a low growl that came from deep in some part of my subconscious mind.

Amid the noise, akin to some terrible anti-Pentecost, Jade fell silent for a moment. She seemed to sway, while the other figure was rigid, almost violent in his or her inaction. Then Jade straightened suddenly, the knife flashed down towards the goat. There was a flash of red, spurting out of the darkness and onto the grate, and Jade screamed.

The sound that came out of her throat was unlike anything a human should have been able to produce. It was like something out of a nightmare – a sound of utter loss, rage, and hatred of all living things. It sounded like something that came from the throat of a dead creature, not a living person. When she screamed, my knees buckled, and that feeling of euphoria swept over me like a tidal wave. The few blacklight bulbs in the room died in unison, and even the glowsticks guttered and failed.

The ceiling writhed violently. The spiral twisted open. My head pulsed one final time, and it was too much. My knees gave out and I fell, my head hitting the concrete, and everything went black.

Sunlight filtered into the factory through the many cracks in the room and filtered down into the basement. I awoke the next morning, surrounded by other sprawling students, my head pounding with the absolute worst hangover I had ever had. I rolled over and vomited bile, then tried to stand again. My stomach heaved again, and I bent over, throwing up more yellow fluid onto the piss-stained concrete flood.

The other guests, now recognizably other students and the odd faculty member, were either rousing in a similar state, or still unconscious. Some had clearly left in the night. I tried to speak to one or two, but they seemed embarrassed to still be there, and I found that my throat was so hoarse I could barely speak. My head hurt so badly that I could hardly remember the events of the night before, much like someone who attends a party and drinks so much that they black out, and wake up in a strange bed, wondering how they survived the night.

Jade. Reagan. White panic stabbed past the fog of memory, and I looked about anxiously for them. The chalk circles were still there on the floor, but the mason jars were shattered, and the glowsticks had rolled away. There was no sign of the dead goat, only black oily stains on the drainage grate where the goat ought to have been. A box cutter had fallen though the grate, and I could see its blade glinting dulling in the sewer pipe below.

The ceiling, however, had changed considerably. The concrete was cracked, damaged even, and I did not remember seeing that damage when Jade had initially shown us the site almost two months earlier. The giant spiral on the ceiling was gone, entirely. I don't mean it was effaced – I mean there was absolutely no trace that it ever existed at all. As my eyes searched the ceiling, I felt a gentle pulse at my temples, a hint of something pleasant that moved under the nigh-unbearable pain of the hangover. It wasn't enough – I bent over and threw up again, my own bile staining my black dress shoes.

I searched the rest of the room, but they weren't there. I ran upstairs, my legs shaking, and I looked around the main factory room. In the light of the sun that now came through the upper windows, I could see that the walls had been covered with the black tarry mixture of her studio. Yet as the incense and gloom had faded, I sensed a loss of vitality to the space. The white words painted over the black seemed almost like amateurish graffiti. I couldn't understand how such a powerful exhibition the night before could be so reduced, almost violated by the daylight.

My body ached, and my stomach heaved again, but I forced myself upstairs to the second floor. I went from room to room, hoarsely calling for Jade and Reagan. As I dreaded, I did find several rooms occupied by students caught in various states of undress. Worse, I knew most of them. But the embarrassment didn't matter – I was desperate to find my friends and make sure that they were okay.

My phone. I remembered that I had brought it with me. My hands shook as I tried to dial their cell phones. Nothing – each of their phones went straight to voicemail, as though they were battery dead or else turned off.

Eventually, when it was obvious that they were no longer on site, I called a taxi and headed back to campus.

Not knowing what else to do, or who I could speak to, I went back and slept. After all, the only thing I knew was that Jade's exhibit had degenerated into some kind of drug-fueled bacchanal, and that I'd passed out. My friends might have left on their own or been somewhere on site. We had all been wearing masks, and so even if they'd stepped over me on the concrete floor, there's no reason that they would have known I was there.

I lay in bed, fitfully dozing, too hungover to fall into

a proper sleep. I didn't know how to treat the throbbing headache, because I didn't feel especially dehydrated – it was more as if centers of my brain had been burned out via the strange mix of sensory overload and sensory derivation that Jade had engineered so seamlessly. I took acetaminophen, which seemed to take the edge off the worst of the "burned out" sensations.

In the afternoon, I tried to call them both again, but their phones remained off. I went to their rooms, to Trident, the library, and even to Jade's empty studio. Finally, though I didn't really want to go there, I called a taxi, and asked to be driven back to the factory.

The door was open, and the building was deserted. The attendants had left, taking with them the table with the masks and shot glasses. The air still smelled of the pungent incense that had enchanted the guests, but the haze had dissipated, and in the light of day, the magic of the installation was dispelled. It was a building of mirrors and paint, creative, but mundane. The otherworldly sense that Jade had conjured into this world had fled, taking with it much (if not all) of the awe which the site was meant to inspire.

Slowly, I made my way around the room, stepping gingerly around puddles of what I guessed to be vomit and bile from other guests, who like me, had lost control of their functions when they'd finally passed out. With the incense gone, the smells of stale piss and mold began to reassert themselves.

I climbed the stairs, and wandered from room to room, calling my friends by name. I heard the occasional skittering sound in one or two rooms, likely from a startled car or rodent. The power had been cut to the blacklight bulbs, or perhaps they'd be deactivated by the main fuse-box. Whatever sensual couplings had taken place in these dark rooms, there was no evidence of it now. In the gloom, it was no longer possible to make out either the darkness of the walls, or the white painted names which I knew were veiled in shadows now.

With a sigh, I returned to the ground floor, and headed towards the iron stairs that would lead me to the basement. The only illumination here was the faint sunlight that filtered down from cracks in the floor above, or through the clotted air-ducts which had piped the incense fumes upwards from the subterranean basement. My footfalls rang heavily on the stairs as I descended below ground.

"Reagan! Jade! Where are you?"

I pulled out my phone and switched on the flashlight app. It helped a good deal, better than I might have thought. The light didn't shine very far, but it had a good arc, and I could definitely see what was ahead of me as I began to search the basement. I started by roaming along the four walls, since it was easiest to keep my bearings that way. More vomit, more piss. Swallowing, I turned my temporary flashlight towards the center of the gaping dark room and headed towards center.

The light of my torch reached the large chalk ring that encircled the drainage grate. Against my better judgement, I shone the light up. The ceiling glistened, black and rippling, as blackish, oil tendrils reached outward from a central point beyond my feeble flashlight. *The central spiral was back.* I swallowed, my head beginning to ache. Had I hallucinated that it had disappeared in the first place? Here in the dark, away from the sunlight, I began to feel uneasy hints of the otherworldly sensations. This time, there was nothing pleasant, nothing sensual. There was only a feeling of being in a place that was wrong in some way, that this space didn't really fit into the basement of a New England factory.

Stubbornly I advanced, having come too far now to turn back. The light fell upon the drainage grate. Then I saw a leg, an arm. Two figures were sprawled atop the grate, lying over the iron bars that lead down to the sewers below. My friends were there, unmoving and unbreathing, their masks gone, their faces pale, almost white.

I shouted in alarm, and almost dropped my phone-turned-flashlight. I set the phone down on the concrete, facing up so that that dim flashlight illuminated the black ceiling. I raced to my friends, almost tripping over myself in the process. I grabbed them, reaching for their faces. They were cold, so cold that I was praying that they were not dead. I felt for Reagan's pulse, placed my head against his chest. I prayed to whatever god might be listening to not let my friends be dead. I couldn't feel or hear anything. My heart was beginning to race faster and faster, and I reached for Jade. She felt like a statue, cold and rigid, as though she'd been frozen for hours. Her eyes had rolled back into her head, the blood vessels had swollen so greatly that her eyes looked black in the gloom, and her facial expression was twisted in surprise. I checked Reagan's face – he showed the same blackish cast to the eyes from the swelling of the blood vessels.

My head pulsed, and I thought for a moment that I was going to faint. That sensation of a "burnt" feeling in my brain had returned, worsened by the panic of finding my friends. I didn't know what to do, but I found myself reaching for the phone. I remember marveling that my phone could get a signal down here, and I know that I called 911, because the ambulance arrived twenty minutes later. The paramedics descended the stairs shouting, and I waved to them with my phone's light. Before I knew it, they were putting Reagan and Jade on stretchers. The ambulance team were asking me questions, but I hardly knew more than they did – I kept telling them over and over that I'd just found them, and that they wouldn't wake up. The paramedics didn't find a pulse, and they began CPR on the spot.

It didn't work. My friends were pronounced dead on arrival. The college officers later told my parents that when I heard this, I became hysterical, shrieking that my friends were just asleep, and that the medics just needed to wake them up. The paramedics had needed to sedate me to get me out of that basement and into the ambulance. It was one of the worst moments of my life.

The autopsies at the hospital showed that they were both deceased of some kind of chemical shock. Blood tests showed that they'd ingested some opiates, but that alone didn't seem to satisfy the coroner. There were extremely high levels of adrenaline, norepinephrine, and cortisol, which were consistent with killing levels of stress. But Jade and Reagan had both been in good health, with no history of stress or anxiety conditions of any kind.

The police had been called the day after the exhibition, and the college administration had used all of its influence to prevent the scandal from being a state-wide affair. The families and police had been called, and various students and faculty were interviewed. I myself was spoken to several times by the detectives and college officers, but it was clear that I had absolutely no idea what had happened. There was no evidence that they'd planned to vanish, and there was no suggestion of foul play. The strangest thing was that the few cogent witnesses all admitted to seeing the same thing – some sort of half-made Greek bacchanal had taken place, followed by the reenactment of a mystery play, and a staged animal sacrifice. However, there were only two bodies, and even the black fluid on the drainage grate could not be identified by the police investigators. It was a great mystery, and it left all parties in a considerable state of distress. Ultimately, it was easiest for the coroner to finally rule that the deaths were the result of a fatal combination of narcotics and alcohol, which the college would later use in a campus-wide initiative for drug awareness. It was a bitter pill to swallow, but what other explanation could I or someone have offered?

I wish the story ended here, but it doesn't.

AFTERMATH.

lasses ended for the semester, and final exams came and went. I lived, slept, ate, and studied with all the passion of a dead man. My friends were dead. For the first time I could recall, I was glad that they hadn't included me in whatever had happened at the installation. But the experience wasn't just at the factory, it had been really something that began at Ashbridge. I couldn't stand the sight of Trident, the Library, or the studio building any more. I had no choice but to stay and finish my degree, but there was a sourness that crept into my heart where the college was concerned. My only remaining wish was to finish my degree and to get the hell out, as quickly as possible. That meant not failing any more courses, so I applied myself with the strength and willpower that remained in me.

I had been present when the police and college security team searched Reagan's room, and of the original grey notebook there was no sign. Reagan's personal notes which seemed related to the installation were confiscated, together with his new black moleskin journal, which the police hoped would have some clues as to what had happened. Whatever they might have found was unknown to us after that, and after the campus campaign about drug awareness, the investigation seemed to dry up. It was a shame for the college to have lost two of its better students, and so it became the dirty laundry that we didn't air in public.

Time may not heal all wounds, but it certainly scabs over the fresh cuts. I kept my job at the library, and tended to work the night shifts, because it occupied me at hours that other students might have been social. No parties or dates for me, just the dullness of shelving books, and tedium of helping people find articles and essays at 2am or 3am, when they were desperate to finish a paper for a morning class. I became almost entirely nocturnal, retiring to bed around 7am, and sleeping until noon. In this way, April became May, May rolled into June, and then summer semester and the August break were upon us. Soon it was the fall semester, and the air began to cool again. The leaves began to change, and the night air became colder and colder. October came, and with it the midterm exams.

Then came November, and the bad dreams started for the first time. As winter neared and the nights grew longer and darker again, my schedule at the library had been moved earlier in the day. The librarian wanted me to work late afternoons when traffic was heavier, as I had actually become a good student library assistant in spite of my nonchalant attitude towards the job. I needed the money, and it worked with my course schedule, so I couldn't really object. My sleep schedule changed accordingly, and so against my antisocial nature, I was free in the evenings to visit other students, and to return to some semblance of a normal college student.

On one particular evening, for reasons I couldn't quite articulate, I forced myself to return to Trident. It was my first time there since Jade and Reagan had been taken from me, and I felt that there was no sense in avoiding best coffee house in town because of some grief not directly associated with the place. So when it had become dark, I dressed in my winter coat, wound my scarf around my neck, and started through the cold night air towards the coffee shop. I dreaded going there alone but staying away had begun to feel awkward. I walked briskly, because it was cold, but also because I wanted to get there (and back) quickly.

Along the way, I looked at the various college buildings and residences. I had to pass by the Fine Arts building, and so I quickened my pace. As I did so, something caught my eye– it looked as though someone had painted a black spiral on the side of the building. I couldn't remember having seen it there during the day and wondered if it was someone's idea of a joke, or if it was just a bad coincidence. I shuddered and walked faster.

I reached Trident, and the matronly owner smiled as she poured my coffee for the first time in months. On the house, she mouthed, and refused to take my money. When I turned to the old familiar table, I found that it was occupied by a small group of new undergraduate students, who were laughing and carrying on. I smiled, in spite of myself, to see that the space was being used by a happy group of friends. I took my coffee to a new table, closer to windows, and began to browse the campus newspaper which I found there.

The cover story was about the college sports team,

and the second and third pages had mostly idle speculation about the new programs that the college might launch for 2015. The fourth page, however, had an article that made my blood run cold: strange, black graffiti was beginning to appear around the college since the end of October and no one had any idea what the source was. The graffiti appeared to be comprised largely of symbols, and the college reporter speculated that it was satanic in nature. The Fine Arts building had suffered the worst, having been vandalized repeatedly, and despite the presence of cameras and a competent security staff, strange blackouts had obscured the identity (or identities) of the artists.

But the most bizarre graffiti had been the very week in which I read the paper, where the lone occupant of one of the college dormitory lofts awoke to find that the room had been rearranged, and someone had scrawled a chalk doorway on the wall of the room. The worst part was that they had done this while he slept in the room, but the door had been dead-bolted from the inside. This caused a real uproar for campus security, and now the student's parents were threatening to sue the college administration.

I finished my coffee, put down the newspaper, and left Trident. *Nothing weird*, I said to myself, *PLEASE, nothing weird. Just let things be normal, I just need normal. Study for class, work the job, finish the degree.* I repeated this mantra the entire walk back to my dormitory. I made it home and managed to avoid looking at the spiral that I was sure was glistening in black paint on the side of the Fine Arts building.

That night the dreams began. I was in the abandoned factory, watching Reagan in the dark basement, carefully etching the large chalk circle around the drainage grate. He was moving slowly and carefully, his face turned down towards the concrete.

"You need to see the big picture," he was saying to me, "you need to see what's happening here. You think that doors only open from one side, but they open from the other side too."

He paused, surveying his work. He moved, his pale face turning to look at me. I could see that his teeth were sharp, and the veins in his eyes were still swollen with dead blood, appearing like two black orbs.

"Don't worry Tom, we're not alone. Can you hear *them*?"

The walls and ceiling around me were rumbling, a distant sound not unlike the movement of icebergs or glaciers sliding against each other, like cold, giant corpses moving in the dark.

I was in the Fine Arts building at night with Jade, who was painting in the dark. She was sopping paint on its white walls with a large brush, so big it was almost a broom, which she would occasionally dip in a large bucket of black resin. Her sleeves were rolled up so the whiteness of her arms was visible, and the blues and blacks of dead blood had pooled in her joints. Yet she painted slowly and gracefully, pausing only to survey her work at intervals. Her back was to me as she painted, and I couldn't see her face. For this I was grateful.

"Do you like it, Tom?" she asked. She moved the brush, and more of the black resin covered the wall.

In the dream, my eyes blurred with tears. Jade moved the brush back and forth, and the black oily resin spread further and further along the walls.

"Poor Tom," she said in a cold voice. "Don't be sad. Do you miss us, Tom?"

I nodded sullenly. Of course I missed them.

"Do you want to see my face now?" she said, her voice sounding far away.

I shook my head. She turned to face me anyway, and

I clapped my hands over my eyes.

Her cold hands closed over mine, and her grip was like ice. She pulled my hands down and forced open my eyes.

She looked pale, just as on the night I found her dead. Her eyes were just black sockets, darker than the oily blackness of the paint. She was grinning her familiar crooked grin, her teeth gleaming oddly white in this dark place.

She pushed my hand against the wall and cold resin moved against it.

"Don't worry, Tom. We're not alone here. You'll see *them* soon enough." She started to force my hand deeper in the wall. The blackness rippled and began to buckle, and my hand sank into the darkness up to my wrist, then my shoulder. She was pushing me from behind, forcing me into the spiraling black maw that now yawned before me.

The dreams came nightly now, and they're getting worse. Sometimes I'm in the factory, sometimes the library, other times at Trident. The cold, grinding noise is always there, and my dead friends are always there. They've always seemed close, but their voices were far away, like they were shouting so I could hear. But now they don't need to shout, they sound like they're just down the hall, out of sight, but closer every day.

I dreamed last night that I found them hunched over a dead carcass in the darkness, their faces down, making cold, wet tearing noises. When I stepped closer, they turned to face me, their mouths wet with the blood of the dead animal.

"We're hungry, Tom," complained Jade.

Reagan turned back to the carcass, and there were more tearing noises. The next morning when I was walking to the cafeteria, I passed a dead dog that had crawled to die in an alley near the campus dumpsters. It looked like it had been run through a meat grinder. I could have sworn for a second that I saw shadows flitting away from the carcass.

That image stayed with me all throughout breakfast, and shortly after I passed out in class, and then awoke in the campus infirmary with a high fever. I was delirious and spent several days passing between one nightmare and the next without relief. The doctors on staff treated me with antibiotics and ordered bedrest for several days – nervous breakdowns were common, especially near exam times. But the delirium did not abate, and so they had me transferred to the larger hospital in Boston where there were better facilities for treating stress disorders. That was probably the luckiest thing that ever happened to me, because after I left Ashbridge, the delirium stopped almost immediately. I had nightmares a few more times, but they seemed to be genuinely just *normal* bad dreams, not eerie séances where I spoke to the cold dead things that took the shape of my friends. My parents asked about whether I'd go back in the spring, but I suggested transferring to a college closer to home in Boston, and they seemed ok with this.

Most days, I just wanted to forget what happened. When I left Ashbridge, I burned my ties to the place – I got off Facebook, I changed my phone number, and my folks even had the administration stop sending me the campus newsletter, because they saw that it upset me so badly. I hoped my friends were genuinely in a better place, but I prefered not to think about it. Wherever they were, they worked hard enough to get there. I just prayed they didn't work hard to get back, and if they did, I hoped they're not still hungry.

FIN

'DATE NIGHT'

tried calling you, but you're not answering your phone. It's probably better this way by email. Look, I know you're still mad, and I'm sorry that I called so late, but I wanted to set the record straight. This will be the last email you ever get from me, I promise. It's probably better that you're not taking my calls, because you'll try to talk me out of leaving.

I know what you're thinking – James is dead, and the guilt is getting to me. That's not it. I mean, that's not all of it, anyway. I know you probably won't believe me but let me explain. I know you blame me for your brother's death, but I swear to you it's not my fault. I loved your brother. Shit, we were going to be married in another three months. I'm sorry, this has all gotten so fucked up. You're my best friend, but you won't even take my calls.

Christ, I don't even know how to tell you about this. *Arrrrghh.*

Ok. You remember about six months ago, James and I had a huge fight, because he thought I was fucking some other guy, and I swore to you it wasn't the case? I wasn't lying, but I didn't tell you the truth, not all of it. I was going through something that I wanted to tell you about, and I just didn't know how to even begin to talk about it with you. But I'll try now, because I don't want to leave with a lie on my conscience.

You know a year ago I started attending the mystic circle meetings at the Occult Shoppe down on King Street. At first James was kind of freaked out, because your family has always been practicing Catholics, but I made him come a few times to see that it wasn't anything like devil worship, and so he calmed down enough that he didn't protest against me going. Most of the weeks it was just like a book club, where we would all read the same book, and then the priestess would lead a discussion about the material. We did rituals once a month, but it was really pretty tame, like calling the quarters and invoking the goddess and the horned god.

Look, I know you never understood why I even went there, but like I tried to tell James, there used to be these voices in my parent's house growing up. Late at night, probably around 2am or 3am when everyone was asleep, I'd wake up and hear people speaking somewhere in the dark. It wasn't my parents. The voices always sounded angry and cold, and it scared me when I heard them. I tried telling my parents and they told me I had a vivid imagination. Years later, when I found out that there was an occult store with people who actually believed in the paranormal, I just wanted to be able to talk. I needed to meet other people who had grown up in creepy houses, or heard voices in the dark at night, and who didn't automatically assume I was insane for believing in the supernatural.

When I visited the Occult Shoppe for the first time, I wasn't sure what I'd find there. When I opened the front door and stepped inside, I could immediately smell incense burning. Just inside the front door to the right, there was a check-out counter with a nice older lady behind the desk, dressed in a green, thick wool sweater. She wore thick reading glasses and was sipping a cup of tea, while reading a magazine with the words 'Wiccan Read' on the cover. She smiled at me as I walked in and turned back to her magazine.

As I looked around, it seemed as though the owners of the Shoppe were serious Harry Potter enthusiasts. For example, there were crystal spheres and obelisks everywhere, all different sizes and shapes. There was a spice rack with different herbs, roots, and antitoxins, ground up and on sale for ridiculous prices. As far as I could tell, you could buy powdered ginger for $5 a bottle at the local grocery store, but I guess that the 'blessing' advertised by the label justified the $15 price tag. There was an actual wand display – I'm not making this shit up. They had some nice looking pewter jewelry on sale, most of which looked fairly geeky, but there were a few pieces with this 4-winged gargoyle that made me feel a little funny when I looked at them. Most of the Occult Shoppe was dominated by books, in fact it would be fair to say that it was a bookstore that happened to sell mystic products on the side. I browsed some of the shelves. Many of the titles had names like 'Calling Down the Moon,' 'Unlocking Your Inner Goddess,' and

'Becoming A Vampire.' I recognized some of the authors by their reputation, like Crowley, Castaneda, and Myatt. The back of the shop had more shelves with more books, with sections labelled 'Tantra', 'Yoga', 'New Age,' and 'Black Arts.' There was also a staircase leading down, with a chain across the top, blocking access. Still, when I peered downstairs, I could see that it was well lit, and that the basement and been turned into some kind of furnished salon. A sign hung from the chain, saying 'Closed – open only for Wiccan Circle Meetings.'

'Can I help you?' a quavering voice asked from behind me.

It was the kindly older lady from the front desk. I told her that I'd come looking for a book about haunted houses. She was really sweet, and she took me to a corner of the bookstore where there was a section labelled 'Paranormal.' There was a lot of books on hauntings, possession, and spiritual infestation. I didn't even know where to start, so she asked if I could be more specific about my study needs. I'm not sure what came over me, but I found myself telling her all about my parent's weird haunted house, and the ugly, cold voices I'd hear at night when I stayed there. She was amazing – she didn't laugh or make fun of me at all. Instead, she picked out two books that she said would help explain some of what could be happening there, and she took me to the talisman display. She hemmed and hawed over a few pewter pieces with a bright blue eye, and an outstretched left hand, but then she selected the 4-winged gargoyle charm and handed it to me. I told her I only had enough money to cover the books, but she told me that she wanted me to have the charm, 'for protection,' she said in a serious tone. I was really touched – I'd expected the storekeeper to be some freaky new-ager, not someone's friendly older auntie.

When we were at the check-out, she asked me if I knew about the Thursday night 'mystic circle' meetings. I obviously didn't, and so she explained that the Shoppe had a weekly series of meetings where they had different occult speakers, authors, and once a month they did group ritual work. She told me that it would be a great place to meet other people who'd had paranormal experiences like my own, and that it could be a place to get answers and do research, if I was interested in finding out more about the unseen world around us. I really liked it there, and I liked the feel of the shop, even if it was a bit cliché, and so I told her I'd like to attend.

That's how I started going to the mystic circle meetings. James didn't like it at all when I told him about it, and I know your mom didn't approve either. But neither of them had grown up in a creepy house, and even if James didn't hear stuff at my parents' house when we'd visit, I still did.

The meetings were a mix of good, bad, and ugly. Some of the speakers were just local weirdos, who'd cobbled together some folklore and superstition, and wanted to make a few dollars selling at the Occult Shoppe and other such places. Other speakers were the sort of light-and-fluffy witches who had obviously watched 'The Craft' too many times, and never could decide if pagan animal sacrifices had been stamped out by bigoted medieval Christians, or if the bigoted medieval Christians had just invented stories that the ancient pagans even did animal sacrifice. Either way, they were clear that medieval Christians sucked, and that animal sacrifice was bad too, because medieval witches were likely vegetarian anyway. I'm dead certain that one of the 'chaos magic' speakers just used his talk to promote his burgeoning trade in magic mushrooms and crystal meth, but he ended up getting into a fight with the owner when he produced a crack pipe and insisted it was entirely holistic, and so that session got cancelled midway through.

The group rituals were a mix of fun and funny. It was clear to me that most of the occultists there had very vivid fantasy lives. A lot of the 'witches' who lead the rituals were aging housewives who needed the mystic circle as some kind of affirmation, and so it often felt like acting in a play instead of doing any real magic. Hell, I didn't know what real magic felt like, but I was sure that the mystic circle wasn't doing it. The 'high priestess' of the circle was Renata, this slightly heavy lady in tight spandex who usually wore a bright orange shirt with the words 'Ye Olde Wicca' in some medieval looking script across the front. Mercifully, she wore a hooded black bathrobe for the rituals. It was never clear to me how she became the high priestess, but she did manage to attend most of the meetings, and she was friendly enough to new people like me.

Midway through my third month attending the circle, there was a speaker who was talking about techniques for finding your spirit guide. People told me that he was a respected author from Louisiana, a professional medium with several books under his belt. For the life of me, I forgot his name almost as soon as I heard it, but I knew that it was Saint-something-or-other. He had a charming Cajun accent, I really liked it when I heard it. Most of the authors we had at the Occult Shoppe dressed as though they had a stage persona – lots of crystals, weird colors, foreign clothing, strange mannerisms – but this guy just seemed normal and down-to-earth. He had a worn, well-tanned face, and wore a dark grey suit and pants. The only odd thing about him, if it could be called odd, was that he attempted to light a thin cigar at the beginning of the talk, only to have Renata tell him that the spirits were 'offended' by tobacco smoke. The Cajun author looked at her as if she had three heads, but then he shrugged and ground out his cigar with a murmured apology.

His talk was absolutely the best I've ever heard, though James would still be alive if I'd never heard it.

'Spirit guides,' the Cajun author said, 'are important for our daily lives. They offer support, they share their wisdom in difficult decisions, and they can protect us from mundane and supernatural threats. We live in a dark world with bad energies all around us, and without the benefit of spirit guides, we're effectively blind. Spirit guides can take many roles – they can be like your parents, your friend, your teacher, even your lover. Spirits are complex entities, and they don't have the same social preconceptions that you and I have, so they adapt themselves to suit your own particular needs at the particular time. Some spirit guides come from nature, like the raven spirit or the wolf, others are the mighty ancestors, powerful ghosts who watch over their family. Others yet come from places outside the natural world, but those cases are very rare.'

He went on to discuss several examples of spirit guides, many of which I forgot afterwards, and he clearly had worked with many different types of spirits throughout his career. As a medium, most of his stories featured different people in distress who'd come to him for help, and their deceased loved ones were usually hovering around, trying to help the living. Sometimes that was the problem, he said, when the dead just couldn't let go, and so they'd get upset and start causing trouble. It was like a child throwing a tantrum – not because it hates the parent, but because it doesn't know how else to communicate its frustration.

Spiritual aid didn't come free, he stressed. Spirits had their own agendas and intentions, and just because a spirit offered to help someone, that didn't mean that it didn't expect to be compensated for its trouble. Spirits had urges and hungers, and they might expect weekly offerings of blood, incense, alcohol, or tobacco. He tried not to smile when he said the last item, but the corners of his mouth twitched anyway.

The Cajun author ended his talk by promoting his most recent book, *Finding Your Spirit Guide*, which he said gave clear instructions on how to attract a guide, communicate with it, and enter into a long-term relationship that satisfied and benefited both the human and spiritual entity. He then offered to sign copies of the book if anyone wanted to get one, and we all applauded him for what had been a really good talk. He smiled and thanked us, and then the store owner guided him to a table at the side of the downstairs room, with a stack of his books, and a pen ready for the signing. A sign on the table advertised the book for $25 a copy.

I didn't have a lot of cash on myethat night but his words about spirits offering protection really rang in my ears. My parents expected me to visit on a monthly basis, and I hated being there at their place. The fear of waking up at night, and hearing those weird, cold voices – I just hated it, and I hated not being able to tell them without sounding crazy. So, I went up to the table and thanked the author for his talk. I gave my $25, and in return I got a signed copy of his book. There was a brief moment, too short to be awkward, where his eyes rested on my chest for a moment. I thought he was checking me out, but then I realized he was looking at the dark spiral pendant I'd worn since my first visit. His mouth opened and closed for a moment, and then he apparently decided not to say whatever he'd been about to say. He thanked me for the purchase, and said he wished me luck in my quest to find my spirit guide.

I went home that night, eager to read his book. It wasn't long, just over 150 pages, and a lot of the book was a collection of different cultural legends or folktales about spirit guides, and the important role that they seemed to play in the lives of different people. A lot of the spirits seemed to be local to Louisiana where he was from, and there was a strong voodoo feel to the book. I liked it from the moment I started reading it. The last chapter of the book, as promised, was a practical section on how to acquire a spirit guide, and the methods for developing a healthy relationship with them. The chapter had a 'warning' paragraph, which said that spirits were not imaginary friends, and that the decision to call on a spirit guide was not something that should be undertaken lightly, because it was bad luck to call them and ignore them. That sounded a lot like a marketing gimmick to me, but then again, my parents creepy house definitely had something wrong with it, so maybe the Cajun really did know his stuff.

The Saturday after the mystic circle meeting, I decided to try the summoning ritual. Your brother flipped out when I told him I was going to try to find my spirit guide, but I told him it was my apartment, and if he didn't like it, he could move back in with his parents. That shut him up for the most part. I really loved James, but seriously, he could be such a whiner sometimes. He must have been pissed though, because he did stay at your parents' place that Saturday and Sunday.

The ritual was simple. The book said that all you needed was (a) some space in your house to do the ritual, (b) a piece of chalk, (c) a black candle, (d) a bowl with some sugar cubes, (e) a needle, and (f) a personal symbol that represented the kind of spirit guide you wanted.

The spell required you to make a 'spirit door,' which was easy enough. You take some chalk and trace a doorway on a wall somewhere in your house or 'shrine' – the book said it could be any size at all, it didn't really matter. There were some words to trace around the door, I had no idea what they meant, but they weren't too hard: *stellam de caelo cecidisse.* Then you draw your personal symbol on the door in chalk. I decided to use the 4-winged shape from my talisman. I think that entire process took me all of five minutes, and I drew my 'doorway' in the bedroom. I used chalk, because I figured I could wash it off afterwards.

For the ritual itself, you sit down across from the door, with the candle, incense, and bowl of sugar cubes placed around you.

You burn some incense in the room, you light the candle, and then you use the pin to prick your thumb. (*The book didn't say which hand to use, but I'm left-handed, so I used my left thumb.*) You squeeze your thumb so that the blood wells up, and then you dribble a few drops onto the sugar cube as an offering to the spirit guide, and you smear a little blood on the top and sides of the spirit door. It makes a pink paste where the blood mixes with the chalk, but that's expected. Finally, there's a short incantation to read over and over again, until (as the book reads) you 'feel something' arrive.

I chanted the phrase over and over:

viens a moi, je t'appelle.
Soit du ciel, soit d'enfer, soit de la terra,
je t'apelle, viens a moi.

It would be nice to say that I chanted, and then I felt this presence come into the room, but the truth is I felt absolutely nothing. I mean, it was exciting doing the ritual, because I'd never tried magic before on my own. I chanted for ten, maybe fifteen minutes, but nothing happened at all. In fact, the candle kept burning out, and I had to relight it three or four times, so evidently, I couldn't even choose a good candle. I gave up when the stupid candle guttered out for the fifth time. I got up from the floor, feeling silly and stupid, and went to go wash the chalk off from my hands. I came back from the sink but didn't know what to do with the spirit door. Maybe it took a while for spirits to arrive? I decided to leave everything where it was – the bloody sugar, the chalk door, the extinct candle – and I figured that since James wasn't likely to come home before Sunday, I could just leave it all there, and clean up later.

With my magic ritual having flopped, I decided to get out of the house for a few hours, since it was still early, just after eleven pm. It occurred to me to head to the local pub for some drinks. There were some decent pubs in the area, but my favorite was this local Irish place just up the street, *The Black Hound*. The atmosphere was pretty decent, and they had live music a couple of nights a week. I didn't have a drop of Celtic blood, but they had Strongbow on tap, and I had a serious weakness for live music. James was more of a stay-at-home kind of guy, so I decided to head over to *The Hound* and see what band was playing that night. It turned out that the music was actually pretty good. The band was some new group called 'Blood of Amergin,' and they were doing some traditional songs like 'Whiskey in the Jar,' 'The Star of County Down,' and they even attempted to do 'Dulaman' in Gaelic, with mixed success but much applause for effort. Being a Saturday night and already late, it was impossible to find a table, but I was able to get seats at the bar itself. I knew the night manager, Deirdre, who seemed friendly, if a bit withdrawn. At first I used to think she was in a bad relationship, because she sometimes came to work with bruises and cuts on her face, but then I found out that she was really into mixed martial arts, or street fighting, something like that. There were two other bartenders working with her, but she smiled when she saw me, and started to pour me a Strongbow. She slid it across the table with a nod, and I leaned against the bannister to listen to the band.

After the second pint, the band seemed to have their groove, and after the third and fourth pints, they sounded even better. I would have gone for a fifth pint, but there was a commotion at the bar – some skinhead sitting next to me was harassing one of the serving girls, and his friends were egging him on. He was drunk and stupid, and he kept trying to grab the girl's behind while she was trying to carry drinks past him. Deirdre came around the bar to stop him, yelling, trying to be heard over the roar of the music, telling him to get out. Then the drunken skinhead moved to shove her away, and then next thing, he was on the ground bleeding from his nose and mouth while Deirdre stood over him with red glinting on white knuckles, frowning.

I felt something wet and warm on my face and realized that a bit of the skinhead's blood had somehow splashed my cheek. It was only a small amount, but it felt gross, and ruined the night for me, so I decided not to have the fourth pint, and to head home instead. I wiped the blood off my cheek with my sleeve, and then I settled my tab and headed outside into the cold December air.

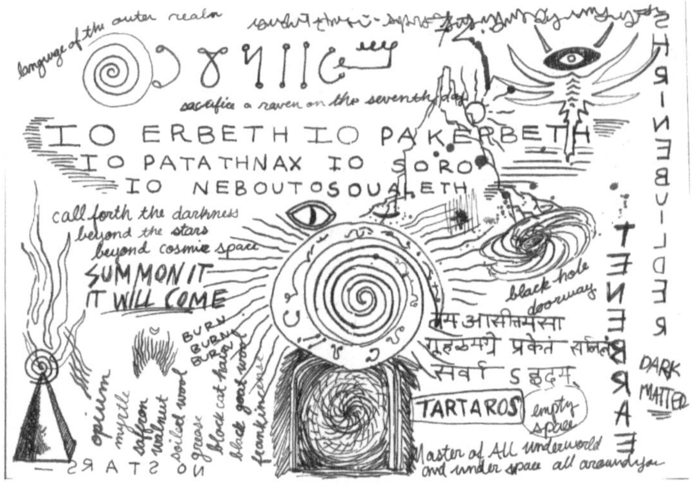

That cider hit me harder than I'd expected, and so I stumbled once or twice on the way home. It wasn't far to my building, though, and so soon I was climbing the stairs, making my way down the corridor to my own apartment. I turned the keys in the lock, and the door opened. *Ahhh*, it was warm – the building had good radiators. I shrugged off my jacket and made my way into the bedroom. James hadn't returned, so he must have been at your parents' place. I pulled off my sweater, shirt and pants, and tumbled into bed. I could see the chalk door in the corner of the room still – I knew James would freak out again if he came home and saw it, but I was too tired to clean it up. It could wait until morning, I decided. I pulled the heavy blankets over my head, and fell into a deep, cider-fueled sleep.

Sometime in the night, James must have come home, and I felt him crawl into bed next to me. I was groggy from sleep and the alcohol, and I murmured in protest when he started nuzzling my neck from behind. He felt warm, and so I was happy for the additional body heat, since I still had the chill from being outside. His nuzzling on my neck got more insistent, and despite the heaviness of the alcohol, I began to realize he was trying to start with me. His breath on my neck felt nice, and his hands had begun to roam me in a meaningful way. One hand cupped my breast, the other was gently reaching between my legs, brushing up against my underwear. Any other night, I would have welcomed the attention, but I was too tired to play with him, and I just wanted to sleep. Undeterred by my lack of response, his hand slipped beneath my panties and he started stroking me. I could feel his erection pushing against me from behind. He was still silent, licking and biting my neck and ears, but I could tell he wasn't planning on stopping.

Normally I would have gotten angry with him, but there was something about the way he moved against me that was exciting, despite the fatigue. I decided to let him have his way – he didn't seem to require much on my part. Besides, his kisses felt good, and the sensations from him slowly stroking me were starting to feel *really* nice. He didn't seem to be in a rush, and I was starting to enjoy his strong, silent act, despite the fatigue. It's not like I was fully awake – I was still half-asleep, but he was making it pleasant enough that sleep no longer seemed to be as pressing as it had been ten minutes earlier.

Somehow he managed to roll me onto my stomach, and I could feel him moving to cover me. His weight pressed me down into the mattress. I could feel him tugging my underwear down to my knees. My head was still spinning from the cider, but not so much that I couldn't feel a rush of excitement as his hardness entered me. There was no ceremony about it, no real romance – my boyfriend just clearly wanted to screw me and didn't seem to realize that I was too drunk to say 'no' or 'let me sleep.' This momentarily flashed into my brain, and I felt a moment of anger at his selfishness. But then he started moving inside me, and there was something just right about the way he moved against me and in me, and I sort of lost track of my anger as he began to fuck me. He felt stronger than normal, a lot stronger, and I began to wonder if he'd had something to drink himself. He pushed into me, again and again, while his teeth closed gently on my neck, biting me gently here and there. Somehow, his hands were still roaming me, reaching between my legs, stroking me, even as he selfishly, silently took his time screwing me, while I really just wanted to sleep. I was drunk, cranky, tired, and starting to really hate him for making me feel really turned on. I was also hoping he'd put on a condom.

My head was spinning now with the alcohol, and for the first time, my stomach twitched. I murmured to him to let me roll over so we could do it in missionary position, but he didn't answer. His pace quickened, and the biting at my neck and shoulders started to get slightly painful. There was a weird, almost vibrating feeling coming from him, like he was shuddering, but not the normal tremors of a guy about to cum. I asked him to move, louder this time. The thrusting was still feeling good, but he was too hard, and it didn't feel like he cared about finding a tempo that worked for me. He continued, oddly silent, not even making any noise when he breathed.

My stomach twitched again, and my head was positively spinning now. Maybe it was better just to let him finish, so he'd leave me alone and let me get back to sleep. So I decided to lie still, like I was playing dead. He continued to grope me, teasing me and biting ever more insistently while he worked between my legs, his hardness pushing into me, again, again, while he shuddered silently atop me.

At some point, he must have climaxed, but I don't remember feeling it. Normally James would go for ten, fifteen minutes, but tonight he had slowly fucked me for nearly an hour. (*Yeah, I'm sorry, I know you don't want to hear this about your own brother.*) But tonight I didn't feel him orgasm. I remember feeling the heaviness of sleep overwhelming me and feeling the sense that he was slowing down. I felt badly, but despite the sexual tension, I was genuinely too tired to stay awake. His sense of urgency passed, and I began to dozs.32e in and out, as he shifted atop me. There was a moment where I felt a wave of sleep pass over me, and there was a sense of satisfaction. I felt him beside me, and it was good.

I awake in the morning to find the bed empty except for me. My panties were down around my knees, and my bra had come off too. James was nowhere to be found. I called him, thinking maybe he'd gone to shower, but there was no reply. I checked the kitchen and the living room, and he wasn't there either. Perplexed, I decided to call his phone, but it went straight to voice mail. I didn't leave a message, figuring that he'd be back soon anyway – he'd probably gone down to the store or something.

My head ached, but the rest of me felt, well, delicious. I was trying to decide whether to berate James for being such a selfish jerk in waking me roughly in the night – or to ask him why we didn't do it like that more often during the day. Probably I would do both, which might lead to another round of sex in the bedroom, if he played his cards right.

Regardless, I decided to clean up the ritual

equipment – there wasn't a lot to do, really, mostly just picking up the candle, and wiping the chalk outline off the wall with a damp cloth. I used a splash of vinegar to get rid of the red stains from the blood, and when I was finished, you couldn't tell that anyone had ever done anything in that corner of the room. The only odd thing was the sugar cubes – I'd definitely dribbled blood onto them, but they seemed only faintly stained, as though the blood had evaporated. The book had said to swallow the cubes after, so I decided to use them in my coffee.

The clock said that it was nearly ten AM, and my stomach was growling. I made some coffee, added the sugar cubes, and poured myself some cereal. My stomach warbled in protest, but I forced myself to eat the cereal and drink the overly sweet coffee.

I spent the morning moping about the apartment, trying to call James, and reading the 'Spirit Guide' book. Probably, in my usual ineptitude, I'd screwed up the ritual, and not managed to attract the attention of my spirit guide. I read and re-read that section of the book about three times, trying to see what had gone wrong. Ultimately, I concluded that I'd done the ritual correctly insofar as the book described it, so maybe my spirit guide was busy doing something else. I figured I could try it again the next weekend, when I had more spare time.

When James got home, he seemed cool and aloof. It totally caught me off guard – I figured he would be sweet and romantic, maybe apologetic, after the night before. Instead, he only asked me if I'd tried my 'stupid ritual' out, and that started a whole fight about my interest in the occult, and the mystic circle, and how his parents were convinced that I was messing around with black magic. I'm sad to admit that I called him some very ugly names and stormed out of the apartment. We never did get to discuss the events of the night before, not because it didn't matter, but really because it never occurred to me until much later that something had gone very wrong in my apartment that weekend.

Two weeks later, I was at work on Monday morning, trying to focus on some report that my boss needed done in order to ready for a meeting with the share-holders later in the day. I was completely over the fight with James, we'd worked things out after a couple days. I'd been secretly hoping for really heated make-up sex, but he clearly hadn't been into it, and so I was left feeling frustrated and angrier than I had been going to bed with him in the first place. I'd had to masturbate while he showered after, mad at myself for having unfair expectations, and mad at him for getting my hopes up and not being able to perform. So here I was, at work, thinking about why my boyfriend was such a fucking beta-male, when I needed to be thinking about the data for the report.

'Jesus Christ,' I groaned, my eyes skimming the numbers on the PC, trying to make sense of which percentage aligned with which line of the report. Normally I liked my job, but I was having a hard time putting my heart into it, today in particular.

Then, I felt something odd. It was as if someone had taken their finger and ran it really gently along the back of my hand. Or maybe even less than that – it more like the sensation you'd get if someone took their index finger and ran it down your wrist and hand, without quite touching you. Like you'd feel the static electricity of their hand almost touching yours, no question, but there wouldn't actually be skin-on-skin. Does that make sense? That's exactly what I felt like, like someone was touching me. I looked around, and I was completely alone in the little office. The door was open, sure, but there was no one else there with me.

I felt it again. This time the pressure lasted longer, and it definitely felt like someone was actually touching me. Clearly, there was no one there, so I started to question if I was experiencing a muscle spasm of some kind. They happened sometimes, but usually that was more like having a throbbing vein. This felt different, strangely, well, electric. Even the light hairs on my arm were standing up, as though I'd gotten a static charge.

Shrugging, I turned back to my work. No time for distractions.

Then, again there came the distinct feeling of someone touching me, but this time on my neck. This was not my imagination, and it was no muscle spasm – it was something touching me. It tickled even, like someone was running a nail along the hairs of my neck, so faintly that I was only just aware of the motion, but not able to dismiss it either.

Jesus. I shivered, my mind racing. Could it be that the ritual to call the spirit guide had worked after all?

My phone rang then, giving me a bit of a start. It was my boss, calling to check on the report, which (of course) I still hadn't gotten done, because I'd been thinking about James, and then the freaky feeling on my skin had distracted me. I assured my boss that I'd get the ritual – I mean the report – done as soon as possible. *Fuck*, I swore internally as I hung up the phone. *Get it together, Mona, get it together*. Biting my lip, I forced my attention back to the Excel sheet. The creepy feeling on my skin did not return again that day, for which I was grateful.

—

It was night, and I was dreaming. I know that I *must* have been dreaming, because I was having really good sex with James in some pitch-dark space. It felt like the darkness around us was fluid, like mist or fog or some kind, and I couldn't really tell how large the space was, because I couldn't really see anything around me. Either the space was small but so dark that I couldn't make out the walls, or else the space was so vast that I couldn't have made out the walls anyway. Sound was muffled – I mean, the space around me didn't sound empty or even quiet, but somehow the moans and animal sounds that we made as we fucked were oddly distorted by the weird shifting atmosphere around us. I didn't care – in my dream, James was an incredible partner. He wasn't so much attentive or caring as he was incredibly empathic – he somehow seemed to anticipate my wants and desires even before I fully understood them myself. I guess that's part of why I thought I was dreaming. It felt like for an hour or more, he'd been chest-to-chest with me in a sort of upright missionary position. His mouth hungrily covered mine with kisses, while his hips worked against mine. His hands – god, it felt like he had ten of them – they were hitting all my erogenous zones, working me into a frenzy. I think I came about five or six times, but there was no real 'downtime' between orgasms – he just kept working me higher and higher from one sexual plateau to the next. The best part about the dream wasn't the feeling of having him inside me, or the kisses, or the way he somehow managed to massage my breasts and my sex, despite what should have been impossible angles for his arms. No, the best part was the sense of utter connection to him, feeling like our union was taking place on some deeper level, maybe not necessarily spiritual exactly, but definitely we were connecting and exchanging on some level that went way beyond the physical act alone. And let me just say, the physical connection was going really, *really* nicely.

There was a moment in there somewhere when I slowly realized that in fact, I wasn't dreaming. Oh, I wasn't entirely awake, but I was definitely in my own bed, in my own room, and the darkness was real, but the shifting shadows were just the usual patterns of the street light bleeding through the leaves of the old oak trees outside our apartment window. I wasn't dreaming of being kissed, James was actually kissing me, and I could feel that I was definitely receiving his considerable attentions in the same sort of upright missionary position I'd been envisioning in my half-sleep state. How we'd gotten into that position was entirely forgotten, but the sex was feeling so genuinely amazing that I honestly didn't care. And that feeling of union – that feeling of raw, primal, connection between us, it was better than the sex itself – it was like for the first time, I thought I was getting a glimpse of what the expression 'two becoming one' is supposed to actually mean, like I could literally feel his heartbeat as my own, and was anxious for him to be enjoying it as much as I was, because I could literally feel his excitement, and knew somehow that he was feeling the same strong urges and feelings that were raging inside me. At that moment, I was so happy that your brother and I were engaged, because this was clearly meant to be on so many more levels than I'd anticipated.

Somewhere in there, I became distracted in thinking about the sex instead of actually doing it. He must have sensed my momentary distraction, because his next few thrusts into me were harder and deeper than those before them, they brushed against my g-spot repeatedly. I knew that the sex had been feeling really good, but all of a sudden I felt the rush of endorphins pouring through me, and I came, hard. The pleasure was so intense, it was likely a tidal wave, pouring over me and driving me under. Everything around me became muted and distant, and I could hear the blood roaring in my ears. I'm sure I was screaming, and my back arched on its own volition – it just felt so good, almost too good. I lost track of James, I was so swept up in the moment, and all I could feel was the incredible sensation of heat, tension, and euphoria that were exploding inside me. It was so intense, for a moment I thought I might faint or get sick. I thought I heard someone calling my name, but I just didn't care.

The lights in the room snapped on, blinding me. James stood in the doorway, looking pale and red-eyed. He was fully dressed, his tie loosened around his neck. His shirt looked damped and stained, as though he'd been wearing it for too long in a hot office. His mouth was open, gaping, and his face at first looked alarmed, and then angry.

What the fuck? I was alone in bed, naked, and I was soaked in sweat. The blankets and bedsheets had fallen onto the floor. I could tell that I was flushed, and my sex was wet and tender. My legs had been open in the missionary position. I struggled to sit up, embarrassed and confused. I could still feel the residual weight of my partner, as if James had just been atop me – but that was impossible, he was standing fully dressed in the doorway. Had I somehow been dreaming?

'What the hell are you doing in here?', he asked in a tense voice, 'Who were you talking to? I heard you from the hallway outside the apartment, I thought you were getting attacked.'

The lights stung my eyes. I winced, covering my face with one hand, trying to focus my thoughts. Between the very real orgasm, the sharp light, and the absence of a male in the bed, my head felt like I'd been hit with a bat. I tried to answer him, but my tongue didn't seem to be able to shape the words.

'I – shit, what are you doing there? What time is it?' I managed to ask.

James snorted. 'It's 2am, I told you I had to work late tonight. I guess you couldn't wait for me to get home, just decided to have a good time by yourself, did you? Fucking selfish… *Jesus Christ,* we haven't fucked in almost a month, Mona, what is wrong with you?' He turned and stalked out of the bedroom.

Hadn't fucked in a month? Was he on drugs? At least once or twice a week we'd fucked in the middle of the night. It had actually become something of a pleasant routine that we pretended wasn't happening by day. I'd have fallen asleep, he'd come to bed in a state of arousal, and he'd take me while I sort of drifted in and out of sleep. I'd wake up and go to work feeling pleasantly satisfied. Maybe he wasn't enjoying it as much as I was? He always seemed satisfied at night, but it's true that by day you wouldn't have known he'd gotten any. I'd intended to make it up to him, but he kept working late, and sometimes he just stayed at his parents' place, which was a lot closer to his office. I'd get home from work, watch tv, and then go to bed alone, and just hope that I'd see him there in the morning before he left for work. I was lucky – my office was a ten minute walk from my apartment, but James worked for an architecture studio on the other side of the city, a good hour away by bus and subway. The job itself had insane hours, and it didn't help that transit took such a long time. It wasn't unusual for him to come home late, sleep a few hours, and be up and gone before I awoke myself. He couldn't seriously be mad at me that we weren't screwing during the day – we were never even home together then.

I got up from the bed with my legs feeling shaky and

weak, and I pulled the bedsheet around me. Hearing him noisily banging around in the kitchen, I went after him. When I reached him, he was pouring milk into a bowl of cereal. He glared at me suspiciously as I stood in the doorway. I was flushed out of embarrassment, not knowing what to even say.

'I guess I was dreaming,' I ventured, 'I didn't mean to upset you. If it helps, I was having this really amazing dream about you making love to me.'

He still looked suspicious, but I could see a slight flush in his cheeks.

'Come on, you were dreaming about Brad Pitt, from the sounds of it,' he retorted.

'Noooo,' I insisted, moving closer to him, 'It was totally you and you were on fire. How about you come back to bed with me, and we pick things up where we left off in my dream?'

He turned his face away when I put my arms around him, but I was undeterred, and gently kissed his cheek. I kissed his neck, his ears, and ran my hand gently down his stomach towards his belt. In a meaningful way, I applied pressure to that area, and felt him tensing. Despite the awkwardness of the way he'd found me, I was pretty sure I could turn this into a positive scenario.

He followed me back to the bedroom, allowing me to slowly pull off his clothes and lure him back into the darkened bedroom. He climbed on top of me, his body hesitant and awkward, anxious to have me. Something felt almost wrong about it, but I knew I couldn't leave him angry and hostile, so I pulled him on top of me, whispering enticements that I didn't actually feel, moaning hollowly when he embraced me, and sighing as he took his pleasure. His love was weak and passionless, and I literally found myself watching the clock.

He lasted all of five minutes, shuddered, and rolled

off of me. He kissed me in the gloom, and then covering himself with the blankets, fell asleep.

Fuck. Now I was the one who was wide awake, while he began to snore. I'd felt deliciously satiated in the weird dream-state, but James' actual attentions just irked me, not so much turning me on as showing me how much better I had hoped my sex life could be. Bad enough that my fiancé couldn't satisfy when I needed it, but worse that I was dreaming about really good sex that he didn't seem able to provide. I'm ashamed to say that I began to have second thoughts about the wedding.

Scratch.

There was a sound from the corner of the room, a dull sound like a fingernail scraping against the wallpaper. I cocked my head to the side, looking curiously into the shadows. We didn't have a cat, so I wondered if there was maybe an insect, like a cockroach or something. The light from the street shone brightly enough that I could see the shadows playing against the wallpaper, but no evidence of any insects, or anything else mobile for that matter.

Scratchhhhh.

The noise came again, faint but certainly audible. I was not imagining it. Curiously, I slipped from the bed and made my way to the wall. I studied the wallpaper but couldn't see anything out of place.

Then I felt it – that odd, tingling feeling across the back of my leg. It was just like I'd felt in the office, but it was sharper somehow, less pleasant, more irritable. I felt like I'd been walked over by an insect with sharp legs. I didn't especially care for it in that moment, and I shuddered despite myself.

The room had gotten very quiet and chilly. I guess that wasn't weird, since we were in early January. Somehow even James' snoring was muted and distant, though he *was* still snoring there in the room. The sound of traffic seemed very far away, and the only sound that seemed not to be dulled was the bitter winter wind whistling through the cracks in the window pane. It wasn't a lot, but the noise seemed louder and more shrill than it had earlier in the evening.

That odd, tingling feeling crossed my forearm, and I slapped at it, like it was a mosquito. A few seconds later, I could feel it on my skin again, insistent. It was really the oddest sensation, and it's hard even to describe it now, but it felt real, tangible, even though I couldn't see what was causing it.

I found myself thinking again: had the ritual worked? Was it my spirit guide, trying tentatively to reveal itself? Had some benevolent protector spirit come, and was it exerting itself to manifest? If so, what should I do? Maybe I could speak to it.

I cleared my throat.

'Are… are you there? Hello?' I ventured, my voice scarcely above a whisper.

James snored on the bed, and the wind whistled dully through the cracks in the window.

Then I felt it again, that gentle scraping feeling, this time across the skin of my left wrist.

Oh my god, I thought, *am I actually talking to my spirit guide?*

'Can you understand me?' I asked in a hopeful tone.

Nothing happened for a moment.

Then, a faint tickle at the base of my neck, a pin-prick of sensation.

Oh shit, oh hell, is this seriously happening? Can this be real?

I tried not to get giddy. You need to understand, I'd done the ritual not really believing that anything would happen. The idea that some external intelligence might be trying to communicate with me was just far and way beyond anything I'd seriously expected to happen. It's not that I didn't believe in magic, but I honestly didn't believe that it would work for me.

Breathe, Mona, I told myself, *breathe.*

'So, ah, I'm glad you're here,' I said in quiet voice, trying not to sound freaked out. 'Are you my spirit guide?'

There was a long pause. I waited for some kind of indication that the spirit (or whatever) was present, but nothing happened.

'Are you still here?' I asked, sounding a little more anxious than I meant it.

There was a sensation on my face, faint, but definitely a presence brushing across my skin.

'So, are you an elemental or fairy?' I asked hesitantly.

Stony silence. I realized that I was holding my breath after the questions, so I had to force myself to breathe.

'Are you a ghost?' I tried instead.

Again, no reaction from the spirit. Maybe it didn't understand me.

As I paused, thinking how to even communicate with my spirit guide, James rolled onto his side, murmuring. He wasn't really very loud, but I felt the bizarre urge to shush him. I didn't, but the air felt colder around me, as though the spirit had disliked the vocal reminder of my partner.

I decided to repeat an earlier question.

'Are you my spirit guide?'

There was silence, as I'd expected. Then suddenly, there was a sharp *CRACK* from the wall. I jumped back in alarm, and James stirred in his sleep. When I looked at the wallpaper, there was now a jagged tear in the drywall, as though the wall had shifted suddenly under its own weight. I felt a strange mix of fear and elation –

this spirit definitely seemed to have the ability to manifest when it wanted to.

Last question.

'Do you have a name?' I asked a bit breathlessly. My heart was still racing from the sharp cracking sound in the wall.

There was a pause, and then I felt something moving in my mouth. It was strange, like some static charge was building up around my tongue. It was by no means unpleasant, but it was still odd, and I shook my head to clear the sensation.

The room felt colder by the minute, and something told me I should get back into bed at that point. I wasn't nervous exactly, but I was getting chilly, and spirit manifestations or not, I was feeling exposed standing naked in the drafty room. I curled up under the blankets and snuggled close to James. Deep asleep, he did not protest or roll away as I worked my way inside his arms. There, in the warmth of his chest, I felt sleepy again. I felt the prickling sensations twice more, gently across my scalp, and they might have continued, but this heavy exhaustion overcame me, and I slept.

I was dreaming. I was dreaming again about sex with James. I don't know what got into me that night, I guess I was frustrated or starved for intimacy, or something like that. I was definitely pissed at him for his inadequate performance before falling asleep, and in my dream, I was really working him hard to make up for it.

In my dream, we were in the weird, dark place, misty and shifting, and the sounds of our voices were oddly dull and distant from one another. He was on the bed or the ground, I didn't care which it was, and I was riding him, rocking back and forth like a maniac. In the dream, I wasn't even myself – I was this other woman almost, a wild, feral creature, muscled and tanned, and with a mane of really wild hair. My nails were longer than normal, and my teeth felt sharper and harder. I don't even know why I remembered that. The funny thing is that I was really enjoying myself – I felt strong and in control, and I felt really, really in control of James. The sex was feeling good, in a raw, angry kind of way. It's not that James was giving me any pleasure – hell, he was so fucking passive, he actually felt kind of sick and weak under me. It made me angry, and so I just fucked him harder – I squeezed him between my thighs, I clawed, I bit, Christ, I bit hard at his neck, his ears. He wouldn't satisfy me, and so I tore at him in a rage. He tried to fend me off, but I was too aroused and too wild. He actually tried to stop me, to interrupt my rhythm. In the dream, I got so pissed that I balled up my first and struck him, once, twice in the face. He was bleeding from his eye and nose. I screamed at him, cursed him, told him to really fuck me or get out of my life.

Mona, he screamed at me, *Mona stop.*

You coward! I raged, *you gutless shit! What's wrong with you, you don't want to fuck me?!*

My hips rocked harder and harder against him, violently working my sex against his. With both hands, I ripped at his face. His skin tore under my nails, and his blood streaked across his face and chest. Perversely, I could finally feel him getting hard inside me.

Mona! He screamed, louder now.

My head started to feel funny.

Mona, wake the fuck up!

I was shaking now – no, I was being shaken.

All at once, the room came into focus. We were in bed together, and James really was beneath me. He was hard, really terribly hard, I could feel his sex inside me almost grotesquely swollen. I was astride him, and I was slick with sweat, breathing hard. *His face* – I breathed in horror – his face was awash in blood and fluid, tears maybe, and his chest was weeping red from open claw marks that cut across him. My fingers stung as I looked at his wounds.

I felt cold, horribly, as though something had crawled inside me and died there and sucked all the heat from me. The worst part is that his swollen organ felt so good inside. Part of me wanted to stay right where I was and just enjoy the sensation, but I knew I had to get off him at once.

'Baby, are you ok?' I gasped, sliding off him, feeling his hardness (*stop it, Mona, stop it*) slipping out of me. I groaned and cursed inwardly. This was really fucked up – *I* was really fucked up. What had I done?

James was looking at me as though I was a monster of some kind. His left eye was visibly swollen, and he seemed to be having trouble breathing.

'You crazy bitch,' he spat at me, 'what the hell is wrong with you?' His one good eye looked wild, as if he expected me to start hitting him again.

'Don't move, I'm going to get some ice from the freezer,' I offered, and ran naked to the kitchen to get a towel and some ice. The heat in the apartment was crap, and my skin had goosebumps from the winter cold that permeated the space. There was no ice in the freezer, but there was a bag of frozen peas, and I figured that would do in a pinch.

Carrying the peas, I made my way back to the bedroom. The cold feeling inside me was starting to subside, masked instead by the heat of shame and embarrassment. James was already sitting up in bed, pulling his clothes on. He wouldn't look at me when I handed him the bag of frozen peas. He put it to his swollen eye and winced at the sudden pain.

'Baby, I'm so sorry,' I started to apologize, 'I don't know what happened. Were we at it for long? I was asleep, I mean I was dreaming of having sex, but I didn't know I was actually on top of you. You have to believe me, I didn't mean to hit you, I'd never hurt you!'

He had pulled on his pants and shirt and was reaching for his shoes. He got up from the bed and grabbed his backpack. He started putting his shoes on, but he paused and cast an accusing glance at me.

'Look, I don't know what kind of games you're playing, or if you took drugs, or alcohol, but I'm not staying here tonight. You're fucking crazy, you know that?'

He started for the door. I tried to grab him, but he threw my hand off.

'James, don't go! It was just a nightmare, come on! You know I love you!'

He stopped and stared at me for a moment in the doorway of the bedroom, and I felt a sudden stab of guilt. The truth is, I wasn't sure that I actually did love him, but that was clearly not the time to tell him.

'Whatever,' he mumbled, 'I'm staying at my parents' place for a couple of days, got a lot of work to do anyway. I'll call you tomorrow.'

I tried to hold him, but he pulled away and headed into the hallway. You know, the sick thing is that as he turned the deadbolt to open the door of the apartment, I was actually glad to see him leaving. For a moment, I felt like he was an intruder in my space, and I was glad to see him go. If he couldn't even get it up unless I was beating him, what the fuck kind of man was he anyway?

Stop it, I berated myself, *stop it, that's your fiancé, that's the man you love. You love him, you LOVE him. Fucking hell, Mona.*

But as you might guess, I felt like I was lying to myself, and whether or not I was in love with him, when the door closed behind him, I felt content with my solitude.

I made my way back to the bedroom. As I slipped under the covers, I didn't even notice the crack in the wall had widened slightly. I made a mental note to inform the superintendent the next morning.

Of course, when I did eventually wake in the morning, feeling rested and beautiful, I entirely forgot to do so.

A few days later, still in January, I was at my desk in the office, papers piled up on all sides around me, and my mind was anywhere but on my job. Emails were also coming in faster than I was able to answer them, and I was just in a bad mood. James hadn't come back to my apartment, and his text messages were polite excuses for not having time to talk. *Was this normal for engagement(?)*, I wondered for the third time that hour. In a way, my distraction at work, my inefficiency and bad mood were really his fault – if he'd just grow the fuck up and act like a man, answer my calls, and come home, we'd get through this momentary glitch in our relationship. Instead, he was acting like a whiney beta-male, and so I felt like I had to carry 'us' by myself. Well, my patience was wearing thin, and my temper was on a very short fuse. If he didn't pick up his fucking phone shortly, he could pack his things and get the hell out of my apartment and my life.

[Shit – I'm sorry I wrote that – I know he was your brother. It's not really me talking, I'm just mad and in strange place.]

Anyway. So I'm in the office, and I'm trying to concentrate, and it starts again. That weird, electric feeling, that gentle touch. The odd thing is that even before I actually felt it, I kind of knew to expect it, like I could feel the presence in the room with me even before it touched me. Is that weird? I guess it's weird. Anyway, there was this half-second where I suddenly realized I wasn't alone, and that by itself made me irritable. It was like someone was watching me through one-way glass – you know that they're there and that they're looking at you, but you can't actually see them or call them on it. Whatever. So I'm wondering what's going to happen, if it's going to touch me, and nothing happens. Just a sense that the room is not empty any more.

'What are you waiting for?' I muttered to the empty air. 'I know you're there. You need an invitation or something? I'm busy here, so do something or get out.'

In retrospect, I have no idea why I was so flippant or short with the entity I was starting to accept as my spirit guide. Definitely, if there was a time that I needed some kind of guardian angel, this was it, but apparently this helpful spirit had done nothing to help me with James, or to keep me from having bad dreams. Pretty ineffective spirit, if you'd asked me then.

Then the touch. Strange, tickling feeling on the back of my neck, almost like a mosquito landing and getting ready to bite – it's not a feeling of pain, but you know it's not going to lead to anything good. I frowned and irritably rubbed at the spot, trying to push the spirit guide away. On some level I knew that this wasn't a good idea – a lot of people would kill for evidence of the spirit world, but I was tired, stressed, and well behind on my work.

Again the touch, this time to the side of my neck,

gentle and oddly soothing this time. But I was in a bad state, and I rubbed at the spot to mute the feeling. It seemed to work – the tingling went away, and in fact the entire office lost that creepy feeling like I was being watched. I actually decided to take a risk and stand up, stretch, and then I walked into the hallway and towards the vending machines to get a soda. Some sugar and caffeine – that seemed like a solid approach to take. A few minutes later I was back at my desk, sipping a cold drink, and shortly afterwards the caffeine began to kick in. Between that and the sugar rush, my mind cleared. I took care of the easy emails, and then a few of the more complex ones. Using the same strategy, I sorted the piles on my desk into 'easy' and 'hard', and by mid-afternoon, I'd managed to turn a really unproductive morning into a decent working day. I was still behind on the larger reports, but it wasn't badly behind, and if I could keep the same momentum up the following day, I'd be caught up and back on track.

So with this in mind, I left the office in good spirits. Maybe when I got home, I could send James a sweet text and entice him to pick up the phone the next time I called. It wasn't unclear that I'd been really irritable, but couples do fight, in fact it's better to fight and learn conflict management before a wedding than to fight for the first time afterwards.

As usual, I took the bus home, transferring once. It was cold, really cold actually, but that wasn't weird for January. It had snowed then rained that week, and of course the snow and slush had turned into hard ice, so the sidewalks were slippery. Despite really good boots, I almost tripped twice – once getting off the busy street, and the second time while heading up the steps of my own building. Yet I kept my footing, as a good Montrealer, and soon I was inside the lobby of my building, shaking the snowflakes off my scarf and coat while I waited for the elevator. My apartment was on the fifth floor, so I guess I could have taken the stairs, but I was a bit tired and frankly grateful to be saved the effort.

The elevator dinged softly as it passed each floor, and then it stopped on the fifth. The doors opened, and I stepped into the hallway and made my way towards my apartment. My fingers were cold and numb, and I fumbled the keys, almost dropping them. I finally got them into the lock of my door, opened it, and stepped inside. As the door opened, I could hear the television set turned on, and my first (happy) thought was that James had come home.

'Jamie?' I called, 'Are you there?'

Silence was my only reply, apart from the white noise of the television. I shrugged – maybe James was resting or in the bathroom, or maybe he'd left it on by accident and stepped out. Anyway, I took off my coat and hung it on the coatrack and walked into the salon. The television screen was black and making this static noise, as if the satellite feed was momentarily offline. I found the remote and tried to turn it off. The television responded sluggishly, as if the remote's batteries needed to be changed. I made a mental note to do this.

I went to use the washroom to freshen up. Not finding James there, I assumed he'd maybe gone to take a nap in the bedroom. I was chilly from the cold, so I turned on the shower and set the water to 'hot,' then stripped out of my clothes. It felt so good to step into the scalding spray. If you don't live in a cold city, you just won't get this, but there's something fantastic about being in the freezing cold, then stepping into a hot bath or hot shower, and just feeling the water washing the chill out of you, and down the drain. I probably showered for a good ten minutes, until I was rosy with the heat, and no longer even remotely cold. Stepping back into the washroom proper, I toweled off and pulled my clothes back on. The mirror was covered in steam, and when I wiped the fog off to see, I wondered if the mirror was stained or something, because for a moment it looked black like the television. It's like I would see the reflection of the light glinting off the mirror's surface, but there was nothing reflecting back at me, like it was just glass over a black surface. I blinked in disbelief, but when I opened my eyes, I was staring at my own reflection. Clearly, I was tired from work, but something about the black mirror made me shiver despite myself. Maybe it was my spirit guide trying to communicate with me? It had been exerting itself more recently, but I wasn't sure what it would be trying to say with that particular gesture.

I stepped out of the bathroom and headed down the hallway towards the bedroom. The light was off in the room, and I called James again, wondering if he was indeed home.

'Jamie?' I called, 'I missed you this week...'

No answer, and as I reached the bedroom, it was pitch black, as though the curtains were drawn shut against the afternoon light. Frowning, I reached for the light switch.

When the lights came on, I shrieked and stumbled backwards out of the bedroom. The blankets and furniture had been torn to shreds, almost as if a wild animal had been caged in there. My clothes had been torn violently out of closet and thrown around the room in disarray, and the door of the closet itself was ripped partially off its hinges. The crack in the wall had widened considerably, as though someone had taken a sledgehammer to it.

Had I been robbed? That was my first thought, but there was nothing of value in the bedroom, and the television and laptop had been left alone in the salon. Steeling my courage, I forced myself to step into the bedroom. Looking around, I could not imagine what had happened.

James. The thought took my breath away, but I had to wonder: was it possible that he'd come home and ripped the place up? The apartment had been locked when I'd gotten home, and the windows were all closed, and nothing valuable was missing. He was the only person besides me with the key. But why would he do it, unless this was some fucked up gesture to get attention, or maybe even to break up with me?

That fucker! I was angry now. I was scared too, but it all made way too much sense. James was a coward – I know that you know it, don't even think to deny it, brother or not! – and he'd been ducking my calls, sending me these short, snippy texts. Did he seriously think that this act of vandalism would impress me?

My hands trembling, I reached for my phone. Some part of my brain was yelling at me to call the police, or call someone, but I was angry and scared, and if I could lash out at him, that would feel good on some level.

HEY JAMES, I texted, *I SAW THAT YOU WERE HOME AND DECIDED TO REDECORATE. FUCK YOU. HOPE YOU TOOK YOUR STUFF HOME, CAUSE YOU'RE NOT STAYING HERE AGAIN, YOU ASS. EVER.*

You're probably wondering what was going through my head, and honestly, I'm not even sure. Sure, I was angry and confused, but there was something else, some kind of fog that was clouding my judgement.

It took me a good half hour to put the room back together, at least as much as I could. It wasn't hard to put the clothes away, but it did take more time to pick up the scraps that used to be the bedsheets and pillowcases, and I needed to get a few garbage bags from the kitchen in order to dispose of those. I did have an extra set of sheets, so I put those on the bed. The closet door wasn't as damaged as I thought – it wasn't so much broken off the hinges as it was 'popped' off, so with some effort and struggle, I was able to force the door back onto the hinges. When the half-hour of cleaning had passed, the only really evident thing was the visible crack in the wall, and even then, it was probably more visible to me since I knew it hadn't been there a month earlier.

Something about the apartment was irritating me – maybe it was too quiet. James hadn't replied to my text, and I didn't feel like spending the evening home reading or watching the [black screen] television. Maybe going to the pub or the library, anything really, just something to get outdoors for a little while and be with other people. That seemed good, healthy even.

I got my wallet and pulled on my coat. Locking the door behind me, I headed for the elevator. Where to go, I wondered. The library was a good choice, but I'd need to take the bus. I didn't feel like coffee; the caffeine would only worsen my bad mood. Perhaps a pint of cider and some live music would be just the thing to calm me down – that seemed good – and so I made my way down the street to *The Black Hound*.

It was only a ten minute walk, albeit over icy sidewalks, but soon the dark black doors of the pub were opening before me, ushering me into the cheery Irish establishment. The smell of ale and clean wooden tables, and the sound of folk music were all incredibly welcoming to me at that moment. I decided that it was nice to be back at the pub, in fact I didn't know why I didn't come more often. It was early still, maybe only 7pm, so I had no problem finding a good table, as the bar was still half-empty. I recognized most of the serving staff, but there was this woman at the bar tonight that was new. She really drew my eye, though for the life of me I could not figure out why – she looked like a vampire, in the sense that she was really, really pale, and had this weird death-like vibe to her, but she moved like an animal in heat. I found myself staring at her a little longer than I ought to have, and I'm not normally into girls, but this one was hot. It's not even that she was especially physically attractive – she was kind of a tomboy even – but there was just this energy to her, like this weird dangerous feeling. I dunno.

Anyway, I was staring at her, and then she suddenly looked at me, and I realized that it was my friend, Deirdre, the boxer who ran the place.

Oh shit, I muttered inwardly, *how did I not recognize her?*

She smiled at me and made her way over to my booth. I smiled back at her, but god help me, I felt my cheeks warming as she made her way across the bar towards me. As she got closer, I realized she was pale, I mean really, really white, like she was sick or something. Her eyes had this weird gleam in them, almost like they were unfocused, and she kept looking past me as though she was expecting to find someone else with me, but of course it was just me at the booth.

Deirdre slid into the seat across from me. She smiled what should have been a warm smile, but there was something off about it, like she wasn't used to smiling and had to force her face to conform to the requisite shape. She did succeed at baring her teeth in an unsettling way.

Still, and hell if I understood why, there was something inexplicable hot about her tonight.

'Hey!' she said, 'Nice to see you tonight. Glad you came in, 'cause it's a quiet night, and usually you're in later when it's loud, so I never get to say hello properly.'

'Yeah, I wanted to get out of the apartment,' I said, 'And besides, I thought maybe I'd get to hear some live music later on.'

Deirdre nodded. 'Yeah, we have a good band on around 9pm, if you're still here. You look thirsty, can I buy you and your handsome friend a drink.' She looked just over my left shoulder, and I swear she bit her lip.

Handsome friend? Was this some kind of a weird pick-up joke I didn't know the punch-line to?

'Haha,' I joked back, 'Sure, me, myself, and I. I get it. You can buy us all a drink.'

Deirdre's eyes unfocused for a moment, like she was having trouble seeing, but she kept smiling. She was flushing, just faintly, but I could see a hint of pink along the white of her cheekbones.

'Awesome, ok I'll be right back.' She stood back up to go.

I watched her go. She was kind of a mystery to me – I mean, it's not that she was unfriendly normally, and she did always make a point of greeting me and other regulars when we came in, but she was something of an introvert. I don't even think she was attractive in a conventional sense – there was a very masculine quality to her, and she tended to wear very unisex styles, so the only thing I really knew about her was that she was strong. I mean, she'd punched out that skinhead without breaking a sweat, and sometimes you'd see her hoisting the kegs around the pub without any help, and they looked monstrously heavy. But tonight, as she moved to the bar, pouring me two pints of cider, and seeing her smile at me (in that weird, dead way) I couldn't help but be drawn to her. Maybe it was her strength, or that cold confidence that just seemed to run through her?

She didn't stay at the booth when she came back. She gave me the two pints, and she pressed her hand against my shoulder. Her grip was cold, but it was strong and pleasant at the same time. I did my best to smile back at her. I kept smiling for the rest of the night, and she kept bringing me pints. The pub got busier, but somehow, she made time for me even when the place was so packed that I couldn't hear her shouting at me. She had to lean closer, her eyes oddly unfocused, looking past me into the shadows of the booth, as if expecting to see me there and not immediately ahead of her. She was trying to tell me something, but the band was so loud that I couldn't hear what, and so I had to shout back at her to speak louder. We must have looked a little funny, both shouting at each other only inches away from the other's face. She put her mouth to my ear, I guess so I'd finally hear her, but to my surprise (and yet not surprise), I felt her teeth close gently on my ear lobe, even as her hand firmly closed on my shoulder. God, she was strong. My hand covered hers and I reached up without thinking, pulling her mouth down to mine, eager to taste her strength and take it for my own. Her mouth, like her hand, was cold, but I didn't care.

I'm not sure how long we stood there for, but she pulled away abruptly in apparent shock, and I thought *Oh Christ, what have I done?* But I shouldn't have worried. She squeezed my shoulder and that cold smile returned to her face, her eyes glinting darkly (*like a shark's dead eyes,* I thought), and then she was gone, back to the bar to continue serving the ever-louder throng of customers.

My dreams that night were feverish, fueled by sexual frustration and way, waaaaay too much apple cider. I dreamed that Deirdre had taken me home, pausing occasionally to pin me against whatever brick surface she could find, so that she could kiss me with her cold lips and teeth. Her tongue would flicker into my mouth, almost unpleasantly dry like sandpaper, but I was so drunk in the dream that I liked it. She helped me up the stairs of my building, into the elevator, and into my apartment. She kept talking to someone else, some tall dark stranger that we'd picked up along the way. In the dream, the three of us tumbled into bed together, Deirdre and the stranger pulling off my clothes. I think my shirt was the last piece of clothing to go, because they were both so intent on getting my pants off. My head was spinning, spinning like a carousel, as they converged on me. One of them was kissing my mouth, while the other worked at my sex. I was wet, so incredibly wet, and it was a dream, so I didn't worry, didn't stress about James coming home and finding me screwing this hot woman with the body of a dancer, and this dark, muscled stranger who alternated between kissing and biting, while I grabbed at his cock in an effort to get him into me so I could really start to enjoy the dream while it lasted.

I forgot about James, forgot about his weakness and his neurosis, and I just went with the current. Somehow then it was me that was the aggressor, me pinning Deirdre down, me who fucked her while the stranger worked at us both, alternating his attentions between us. Deirdre may have been cold, but she had passion, and she bit and clawed at me so hard that dreaming or not, I knew my back and sides were bleeding from her nails. In the dream, we laughed, we tumbled, we panted, we fucked, god, we fucked for *hours*. I came again, and again – I didn't know you could do that in dreams, you know?

Eventually, the sun came up. The light crept in through the cracks in the blinds, and I found myself awake against my will with the sharp pain of a hangover. I rolled over in bed and came face to face with the cold-bartender-with-the-build-of-a-dancer. I almost fell out of bed, covering my mouth to stifle a shriek of surprise. Deirdre was next to me, asleep. She was naked, and I was honestly impressed at her body. It's not that she was curvy, or feminine, or anything like that – she was muscled, like you would imagine an Olympic swimmer would look. Her neck, her shoulders, and her arms looked so strong, like she was made of nothing but bone and hard muscle. It wasn't unattractive – hell, as I looked at her, I had this momentary flash of memory from the previous night, pressed against me, feeling really flushed, feeling an orgasm building while she kissed me. I didn't know what to do – should I wake her up? Should I let her sleep? Fuck, what if James came home and found her there? At least the other was gone, that gorgeous guy that had followed us home, but fuck if I could barely remember his face.

Shaking, I climbed out of the bed and made my way to the washroom. Had the guy even used a condom? I didn't feel anything inside, but that didn't mean much. I turned on the shower and stepped momentarily into the hot spray of water.

The odd thing, the truly odd thing, is that I didn't feel any guilt. I knew that I'd crossed a hard line – I'd definitely cheated on James. No question there. I'd somehow brought home a (gorgeous) guy who I couldn't remember, and an Olympian woman, and they'd both fucked me so hard that I'd passed out. Fine. The creepy part was that I felt okay. Well, actually, no –

I felt amazing. I felt better than I had felt in months. Something about last night had torn something loose inside me, and I could not for the life of me feel any guilt. If anything, and if I was truly honest, my biggest question was whether or not I should go make some coffee for my overnight guest, or whether I should try to find some overtly sensual way to awaken her. *Fuck!* What was wrong with me?

I needn't have bothered with the wondering – as I finished my shower and stepped gingerly into the bathroom, Deirdre ran into me. She looked like a trapped animal – I felt genuinely badly for her for a second – it was obvious she hardly knew where she was. She hung in the hallway as I stood in the bathroom door.

'Hi' I ventured.

'Uhhh, hi? she replied cautiously. She looked uncomfortable.

'About last night,' I began, feeling lame.

Then she lunged at me, and I almost recoiled as she pinned me to the doorway. But then her lips were on mine, just for a moment. I stiffened in surprise, and she pulled back.

'That was a nice night,' she said, and her cold face blushed. 'I need to go, but you should drop by again this week. We can get coffee and hang out. No pressure, ok?'

Did she think I was bi-sexual? Shit. Was I bi-sexual? I wasn't sure anymore.

'Yeah, for sure,' I nodded, 'I'd like that. Coffee this week, for sure.'

I remained there, kind of in shock, and so she smiled briefly, and then a moment later she was gone from the apartment. And I still stood there, curiously feeling around the edges of my mind, fascinated and appalled by the absolute lack of guilt. At some level, sure, I felt like I'd probably done something bad, but on literally every other level, I felt amazing. Hell, I'd brought home *two* attractive strangers (or near-strangers) and fucked them literally until sunrise. How was that not validating on several levels?

But I wasn't a total idiot. I returned to the room and started cleaning. There wasn't a lot to do, but I stripped the bed of the sheets, the pillow-cases, and threw them into the laundry pile. My clothes, still smelling of Deirdre's musk and my own sweat; and I even opened the window to air the room out, which let out all the heat while letting in the bitter winter cold.

The bedroom cleaned of any evidence, I went to the kitchen to make myself some coffee. My head was spinning from the hangover, and the stress of the weirdness of the situation was definitely not making my stomach feel any better. Not trusting myself to eat anything heavy, I made some toast and butter, and had that with the coffee to settle my stomach.

So it was finally Friday, and what a fucking dreadful day it was turning into. Meaningless meetings, boring reports, spread-sheets that seemed to make absolutely no sense – it had been a really numbing week at work, like every day was somehow Monday, repeated over and over again. The only real punctuation was the increasing manifestations of the spirit guide, which seemed to be appearing more and more frequently. My mind should have stayed on my job, but instead it cycled through my problems with James, the insane threesome with Deirdre, and the dreams. Yeah, I was having these re-occurring dreams, the way I'd dreamt about James initially. I'd be in that weird, black misty place, and I'd be having really good sex with a partner. But where initially it had always looked like James, now I couldn't see my partner's face at all. I don't mean that he was faceless, it was more like the light just refused to illuminate him in any meaningful way. The dreams were a welcome distraction from my days of boredom and anxiety, but they weren't satisfying either – I kept waking up feeling the tense frustration of someone who'd been ridden hard, but not allowed to finish the race.

James hadn't replied to my last angry text. I knew I should call him, but I was so angry that he'd trashed the apartment.

I hadn't called Deirdre or stopped by *The Black Hound* to see her. Probably I should have done so, but I just didn't feel up to dealing with the awkwardness of trying to navigate whatever had happened between us. I'd had some day-dreams, flashbacks of that night with her and her friend, but pleasant as they were, I needed to get things sorted out with James before anything else.

It also occurred to me that I should probably make time to attend the Wiccan Circle meetings, but every time I considered going, I was hit by this wave of lethargy. Somehow, seeing Renata and the rest of the coven didn't seem appealing, especially as I was pretty sure that they wouldn't even believe me if I tried to tell them about my spirit guide. No matter. I just needed to get things sorted out with James, and everything else would fall into plan. Except, of course, I didn't really know if I wanted to see James again. He'd trashed the apartment, he'd refused to text me or call me, and frankly, I was just about sick of his high-school drama attitude. Heck, the one thing I didn't miss was his sub-par performance in bed or his consistent whining and bitching. If he wanted to stay away, either at school or with his parents, that was fine by me.

Sorry, I know I shouldn't talk about your brother that way. Besides, he's dead now, and you probably want to know how and why. I'm getting to that, trust me.

I was startled from my grim musings by the tell-tale feeling of the spirit, slowly coiling around me. I could feel its presence more and more clearly with each visit, as if we were somehow developing a resonance. It was funny – I used to find its interruptions at work sort of annoying, like an unwelcome distraction, but in the last week or so, I dunno, I guess we were really *connecting* on some level. Maybe I was learning to accept the spirit guide's presence, and it was somehow strengthened by my increased receptivity. It actually felt kind of pleasant, in some weird way, like it's 'touch' (if that's the word) was both comforting and exciting all at the same time. This might sound kind of weird, but sometimes when it touched me, it felt intimate, like sexually intimate. Was that even possible – I mean, spirits weren't sexual beings were they? I'd always assumed that they were genderless, like sexuality wasn't a part of what they were, or at least if they were sexual, their sexuality would have nothing to do with human physiology. It would be ludicrous to even consider otherwise, unless one engaged in medieval misogynistic Catholic thinking.

But all that rationalizing aside, here I was sitting in my office chair, and I could feel the heavy presence of the spirit coiling around me, like a snake, or a dragon, or something like that, and the contact of it against me was starting to feel really heady. I could swear I could almost smell it, like ozone or something chemical like that, and it was squeezing me. Rather than fighting it, I leaned back into its embrace, and just prayed that no one would walk into the office while the spirit guide was hugging me.

For a few minutes, I enjoyed the strange sensation of having the spirit all around me, sinking into me almost, like I was being saturated by its essence. I could feel its strength, like some magnetic force centering on me, pulsing almost. And while it definitely wasn't going any further than that, that alone was making my heart beat faster, like I was doing something incredibly taboo, and the invisibility of the whole thing was even more delicious – I mean, if someone walked in, all they would see is me leaning back in my chair, and probably a bit flushed in the face, like I'd gotten a dirty text from a friend or something.

Fuck! I was enjoying the strange attention from the spirit, but I needed to work. With a groan, I straightened in my chair and tried to force my mind back to work. I could sense the magnetic strength of the spirit caressing me a few more times, coiling and releasing like a spring, and then eventually it began to dissipate. This gave me mixed relief and disappointment. I did need to get stuff done, but I definitely didn't want the spirit guide to leave. I was enjoying its company far too much…

I finished my work for the day and was stepping off the bus heading back across town to my home. Winter had definitely come to Montreal, and I shivered as I walked quickly down the block towards my building. It wasn't even late, not yet 6pm, but the sun was set already, and the night only made the cold worse. I pulled my coat tighter around me and gritted my teeth. Just a few more steps, and I'd be home. Work had been hell, and I was trying to remember if I had any vodka at home to relax, or if I'd need to risk running into Deirdre at *The Black Hound* if I really wanted to get a drink.

I headed up the steps of the building, and then pushed through the heavy glass doors. A blast of warm air enveloped me as I stepped into the entrance of the building. God, heat, I exalted, finally some warmth! Still I shivered, and I opened the buttons of my heavy winter coat, to let the heat into me properly. I moved towards the elevator and hit the 'up' button. A few seconds later I heard the chime, and the doors opened. I stepped inside and pressed the button for the fifth floor where my apartment was located. The doors closed behind me, and the elevator began to climb.

The lights flicked for a moment, and the elevator buckled gently, but continued its climb. Our building was getting old, and the technology frequently ran into problems. I didn't mind the elevator breaking occasionally, since I didn't mind climbing the stairs, but I definitely didn't want to be inside then that happened.

Then I felt it, the heavy presence of the spirit, in the elevator with me. It hung there in the air, heavy, and strong. I could feel it reaching out for me, and there was nothing gentle or subtle about it. It closed down on me like a shroud, and my knees almost buckled from the weight of it on me. I felt its energy cover me, almost like a second skin, but it was a second skin that was insistent, probing, almost hungry as it moved over me. It moved across my throat and my stomach; it flowed across my sex and down my thighs. It felt really, really pleasant. There was something perversely sensual about the way that the spirit was covering me, like it wanted to possess me in some very direct and intimate way. The thought of letting it *have* me (whatever that meant) made me groan, and for a moment, I suddenly wanted very much to be alone with the spirit in my apartment.

As if on cue, the doors of the elevator opened, and

the light from the hallway poured into the elevator. I hadn't realized how dim the lights were in there until that moment. Moving slowly so that the entity would stay with me, I made my way towards my apartment. The presence of the spirit guide stayed with me, almost like I was wrapped in a heavy cloth. It was tangible – I could literally feel it moving slowly against me. It's hard to explain, because you wouldn't think you could feel something so large moving under your clothes – it wasn't like an insect creeping across my skin, it felt more like I had a body-suit of silk that was slowly twisting against me. It felt good, really, really good.

I made it inside my apartment, and I sagged for a moment against the door. It was dark inside, but I kind of liked it that way, it heightened the somewhat sensual feeling of the spirit guide moving against me. I pulled off my coat and my shoes, and I began to move slowly down the hallway, towards the bedroom, almost on autopilot. I was wearing several layers due to the winter cold, and so it was natural to remove some of them, but I found myself stripping off even my pants and my shirt. I pulled back the covers of the bed and crawled under the sheets.

I felt a moment of panic – somewhere between the door of the bedroom and the bed itself, I'd lost my awareness of the spirit. Maybe the act of shedding the clothes had dislodged it, or discouraged it somehow? I bit my lip – I was feeling aroused now, and I was hoping that the spirit would continue its attentions.

There. There… it had returned. I could feel it, pressing down against me, not like a human lover would, but heavy as if a thick liquid blanket was pouring itself over me. It was hard to describe, but I felt as though my skin was permeable, and the spirit guide wasn't so much resting on top of me, but more like it was insinuating itself into me, from head to foot, like I was being slowly, deliciously invaded. I say 'pleasurably' because it felt incredibly good, like the very cells of my skin and muscles were being caressed on some microscopic level. I definitely, definitely didn't want it to stop.

For the first time, I felt something probing my tongue. The weird thing is that my mouth wasn't open, but I still felt something moving gently inside my mouth. It was like being kissed by a guy, but there was nothing tangible to account for it. But the tip of my tongue was definitely electrified, and I could feel the energy of the spirit guide actually moving. The rest of my body was gripped by something slow and sensual, but this feeling was less static and more active, if that makes any sense.

About the same time, or maybe moments after, I felt something warm and magnetic pushing against my sex. This is the hardest part to explain, but I'll try. It felt like something strong and supple, serpentine maybe, was working its way against me. Not like a guy's dick, which is hard and rigid – this felt more like a plant, or a vine, I dunno, was moving down there, slowly, really slowly entering me. It was so subtle at first that I wondered if I was imagining it altogether, but then my hips started to move instinctively, and I could definitely tell that the spirit guide had a very masculine aspect, even if it wasn't a human aspect exactly. It wasn't deep, it must have been really shallow at first, but it was *happening*. I groaned aloud – I definitely didn't know what the heck was going on here, but it was feeling far, far too good to stop.

The heavy, enveloping feeling began to pulse, like the force of gravity on me started to come in waves. That pressure against my sex, which has initially been soft and subtle, began to undulate now, rippling against me like the ocean waves rippled against the sands of the beach, gently enough, but having a cumulative effect. Without even being really aware that I was doing it, I arched my back slightly, tilting my pelvis upwards to meet the attentions of the spirit that was evidently trying to have intercourse with me.

It flowed against me, again and again, in a slow, almost lazy way. I didn't mind. There was a definite perverse delight in having some invisible entity gradually and slowly making love to me. The darkness of the room was oppressive, and it occurred to me that even if it were visible, I still would not have been able to see whatever covered me.

The soft, silken feeling against my skin began to constrict, and I felt the magnetic, gravity-like sensations increase slightly. I wouldn't call it intense exactly, but I got the distinct impression that my positive reaction to the entity was serving to feed it or encourage it. And definitely, with each pulse, I felt like it was digging into me more and more, like it was insinuating itself into me incrementally. It was the most bizarre sensation, though I would not have traded it for the world at that point. I was definitely being fucked (and fucked nicely) by this shapeless lover, but at the same time, I could literally feel it seeping into my fingers and toes, my arms and legs, my chest. Even my eyes and nose felt strangely (but pleasantly) invaded. I didn't feel like it had any reproductive agenda whatsoever, but I did feel like it wanted to be inside me and maybe not leave, like if we continued coupling, it might become a part of me. I don't even know why I thought that, but the thought was definitely in my conscious mind.

I probably should have resisted, and a few months earlier I would have. Instead, I just lay back and tried to surrender to it. The thought of becoming part of this thing, or having it be part of me, was suddenly more erotic than any fantasy I'd ever had. I didn't want to be fucked, I wanted to be possessed, taken, overridden, and to have my spirit guide as a permanent passenger.

No more foreplay, I whispered mentally, show me what you can do.

There was a moment when the spirit slowed for just a fraction of a second, like it was gathering its strength, and then I felt it bare down on me. It pushed down so hard that for a second it was difficult to even breathe. I swear I could hear the mattress groan in complaint as the entity pushed against me, against my sex, my mouth, my skin, my eyes. And I could really feel it, furiously surging against my skin, hungrily burrowing into me. There was nothing seductive, it was palpable hunger. It didn't hurt, in fact, it felt good – I would have cried out, but I lacked the air to do it. My muscles began to tremble and shake, and my eyes rolled back into my head. I could hear a roaring in my ears, and the blood was rushing to my head. My legs began to tremble violently, and my arms shook. Full body orgasm, my mind whispered, this is what it feels like.

Then my skin stopped being a barrier, and my lover surged into me. There was a strange, elastic feeling as the monster filled the hollow, empty places inside me, like the pit of my stomach, in the hollow of my sex, in the space right between my eyes. I gasped, and my back arched in surprise. It hurt, but only for a moment. It also felt wonderful. I felt, *fuck*, I felt complete. I felt full to bursting. For a split second, I thought I heard the front door open, and a voice calling my name. But the roaring in my ears grew louder and louder, and then I blacked out.

Later, when I awoke, we were on the floor in the living room, and I was curled up naked like a cat on the rug. We stretched, feeling like a woman who has just had incredibly good sex. I suppose in some way, that was correct. When we woke up, we felt delightfully, incredibly wicked. You're probably expecting me to use another word, but 'wicked' is the only word I can think of that properly captures how we felt at that moment. If I had to make a list of words, I would say that we awoke feeling cherished, vindictive, angry, sexy, possessed (I mean owned), and enhanced. Yes, definitely enhanced. We felt wicked too, mostly that.

I stepped carelessly over the body of your brother, your fucking, asshole brother, who had dared to interrupt us. He'd walked into the room right at the wrong time, and he'd started yelling at us. I should have locked the deadbolt, some pathetic part of me had whimpered, but we ignored that part. We ignored James and got up, wandering into the living room, hungry for food. James kept following me, prattling, whining like some puppy mewling for attention. I tried to ignore him, thinking that he'd eventually just leave, and allow us to go back to sleep. He knew something was wrong – he wouldn't meet my gaze when I started at him, like he could sense the other one inside us. I mean me, inside me. He was stupid, though, and he'd tried to lay hands on us, and even shake us, like we were his property. I don't like people touching my things, and so I had taken his face between my hands and squeezed him until he stopped making those annoying noises. When he stopped making the noises, I twisted his neck hard, just to be thorough. The snapping sound was audible, and very gratifying. After I pulled his body out of the kitchen and back into the hallway, I finished getting food. We were so hungry.

Then I went back into the room to get dressed. I understood that I would need to go somewhere else, so we took our wallet and some clothes that would keep this body warm. It was funny – it was only now that I could see the spirit door, and the spiral, painted on the wall. Oh, I'd washed it off, but I wasn't seeing it with my eyes. My mind momentarily flashed to Deirdre, and I considered going to see her. Perhaps. Perhaps not. We would need to see.

Some part of me understood that you would want to know why James is lying dead inside my apartment, and so I took the time to write this email. I hope you understand that it's his fault, really. He should never have come back, or yelled, or touched us. Anyway, we're really doing your family a favor – he was a weakling anyway, and he would never have done as a husband. I was crazy ever to have thought otherwise.

You would do well to delete this after you read it. As

I said, I feel no guilt for what happened, but you have been a good friend, and I wanted you to understand why James had to die. I'm sorry if his loss causes you grief. You see? It's not my fault that he had to die. He just lacked the basic survival instincts to stay the hell away. He shouldn't have touched my things. We don't like to share.

We're going now. Don't try to find me, and don't worry about me. I'm fine. Beside, I'm not alone.

We'll never be alone again.

FIN

CHAKRAS

hen the new Yoga Center opened in my neighborhood in early November, everyone on my block received a voucher for a free day pass with unlimited classes. I checked out their website, which turned out to be both informative and pretty user friendly. It showed a good variety of programs that were on offer during the course of the week, and also had short bios for the different instructors who would be teaching there. The Center listed classes in ashtanga, hatha, and kundalini yoga, as well as courses in mindfulness, meditation, and Pilates. The center even had introductory classes in Sanskrit and Indian astrology (jyotisha), which seemed a little advanced for my tastes, but would likely appeal to some of the more serious yoga practitioners in the region. It even offered a class in "Ayurvedic Cooking" which looked really interesting, but it happened to be on a night that I had to work late.

Unfortunately, as I checked the schedule of classes against my work schedule, I realized that I couldn't attend any of the yoga classes that seemed most interesting. I'd been working for several years at *The Black Hound*, our local Irish pub, and had just been promoted to assistant manager, which meant working almost exclusively evenings and nights. Unfortunately, this was when the Center had scheduled most of its best courses. This made perfect sense, as most of the sports and fitness clubs in my area tended to operate outside of the regular business hours, much like my bar.

Still, I wanted to take advantage of the free coupon, so I called the Center up, and the instructor who answered the phone said that there was a Shava Yoga course being taught on Saturday afternoons at 2pm. I'd never heard of Shava Yoga, but the instructor explained that it was basically a form of kundalini yoga, with strong emphasis on the chakras or energy centers along the spine. He used the phrase "serious health benefits" about four times in a row, and so I decided I'd use my free pass for that particular class. Even aside from the schedule, I tended to have chronic back issues from carrying the heavy kegs of Guinness and Strongbow, and so it seemed like a good potential fit. The instructor said just to wear comfortable clothes, and that yoga mats would be provided on site.

I showed up the next Saturday for the class, wearing my usual gym gear: loose cotton pants, tank-top, and hooded sweatshirt. The Yoga center occupied the upper three floors of a commercial building, and it took me a few minutes to find the door leading to the stairs up. When I got to the top of the stairs, there was an open door to an antechamber area, where there were small storage shelves for people to stash their shoes, backpacks, and other belongings. Some upscale futons were next to the shelves, and there was a newly painted reception desk, where two red-haired young women in yoga pants were speaking to a young staff-person who seemed to be the guy on the phone I'd spoken with earlier. From the looks of them, they were probably twins. They were asking about the very same course I'd hoped to attend, and he was telling them that the class would be starting in about fifteen minutes. He indicated the corridor, which lead past the desk and said that they were welcome to wait inside the studio until the instructor arrived. The women put their shoes and coats in two of the storage shelves and left the reception area to head in the direction of the studio room.

I waited until they had moved past the reception desk, and then approached the attendant. I presented my free coupon, and he welcomed me to the Yoga Center, and asked if I have any questions. He seemed to be a very pleasant guy, with a cheerful demeanor, and genuinely willingly to help me get settled in. I told him that we'd spoken on the phone earlier, and that I'd overheard him tell the two girls that the class was just down the hallway. He nodded and said I could join the class, and that yoga mats were available in the studio if I needed to borrow one (which I did). I thanked him and headed down the hallway.

The building had obviously not been built as a yoga center, but the contractors had done a good job of converting the space into its new incarnation. The walls of the place still smelled of paint, but the center was clean and well lit. The studio was the main room on this floor of the building, and one didn't have to move very far past the reception desk to walk into the studio room itself.

The room was large, and probably could have held seventy or eighty people comfortably. Three of the walls had large windows that gave a decent view of the neighborhood, and allowed a lot of sunlight into the space, which gave it a very healthy feel. There were already about twenty people there for the class, most of them being in their twenties or thirties. I recognized a few of them as familiar faces from the neighborhood. At the head of the class, there was a low cushion, which looked to be reserved for the yoga instructor, who had yet to arrive.

I took a yoga mat from a pile near the side of the room and looked around to decide where best to sit. One of the two girls who'd been in the reception area smiled shyly at me and waved, so I waved back and moved to take the place next to her.

"Hi, can I sit here?" I asked, smiling.

"Sure," she replied. "Saw you coming in behind us. You work or live nearby?" she asked.

"Yeah, I work just across the street at *The Black Hound*."

"The Irish place?" she asked.

I nodded.

"I'm Deirdre," I said, extending my hand.

"Carrie," she answered, shaking mine in turn.

"Nice to meet you," she smiled. "So, you ever take yoga before?"

"No," I admitted, "my first class ever. You?"

"Yes," she nodded, "I took a few months of some basic Hatha Yoga last year at a place downtown, but it took too long back and forth, and I wanted something closer to home. I was really happy when the Yoga Center opened, it's a lot easier to get here from my place."

I nodded. I'd had the same issue with finding a good

place to do boxing, since all the good gyms were downtown, and with my apartment and workplace being a good ways from downtown, it was harder and harder to find time to commute in order to be able to train. I was in good shape from working at the bar, but I liked boxing a lot, both the competitive part of the sport, as well as the discipline of the training. I'm not a juicer, but I do have a temper, and it feels good hitting people – there, I said it.

A flicker of shadow crossed my field of vision, and a dark-haired woman walked to the front of the room and took the low cushioned seat. She looked to be about the same age as me, somewhere in her late twenties, though she had that serene ageless look that one tends to find in people engaged in serious spiritual practices. She was dressed in a dark grey tracksuit, with a black t-shirt overtop. The instructor folded her legs under her in the lotus position, and brought her palms together. Her graze lowered momentarily as she inclined slightly towards the class.

"*Namaste*," she said in a gentle voice. "I'm Leigh, and I'll be your yoga instructor for this class."

She rested her hands gracefully on her thighs, and looked around the room, taking in the twenty of us.

"Since today is our first session together, I want to tell you a little bit about myself, and more importantly, about Shava yoga. We'll go over the basic theory of the system, the primary benefits of its practice, and then we'll begin with the introductory exercises."

She rocked back and forth slowly, side to side, as if settling her hips deeper into the cushion. She pursed her lips for a moment, looking around the room at everyone and no-one in particular.

"So I'll start with myself. I've been a Yoga Center member for almost ten years, and I've been in the Instructor Training Program for three years. I've taught both Ashtanga Yoga, and Hatha Yoga before, but this is my first time teaching Shava Yoga, and I've been practicing it as my primary *sadhana* or style for four years. Ummm, what else …. I'm originally from New York, and now I live here in Montreal. I like cats, bicycling, books, and I'm kind of a yoga fanatic."

We all laughed. She smiled broadly.

"I teach yoga because I genuinely believe that it's a powerful spiritual system that doesn't rely on external beings or energies. Yoga is about you, and it means taking responsibility for your body, your mind, and your spirit. Yoga gives me a focus that I found extremely helpful in my day-to-day life and career. My partner is also a Yoga Center instructor, and we kind of think of this organization as our extended family. I hope that you enjoy your time at Yoga Center, and my job is to help you feel welcome, and to provide a safe space for you to explore your physical and spiritual body, and to gain a sense of inner harmony and power. Does this all sound good so far?"

There was a positive murmur around the room. Lee smiled again and brushed a strand of dark hair out of her eyes.

"So this course is 'Introduction to Shava Yoga.' If you've studied yoga before, that's great, but you don't need to have ever studied yoga before. I'm going to assume absolute beginner level across the board, so don't worry if you don't know which end of the yoga mat is up."

There was more laughter. She kept a great poker face, but she seemed to have a nice sense of humor.

"Let's start with the basics: what is Shava Yoga? Even if you've taken classes at another yoga studio, you're not likely to have heard about it before. Well, *shava* is the Sanskrit word for "corpse" or "dead body," and *yoga* means "that which connects mind, body, and spirit." So *shava yoga* is literally "Corpse Yoga."

Someone in the front row of the class shifted uncomfortably. Leigh nodded and smiled in some kind of embarrassed way.

"I know, it sounds creepy, right? Like yoga for the undead."

We all laughed, a little nervously. Leigh paused for a moment, and then continued.

"Most yoga systems take for granted that you are already good or complete in some way, but you're disconnected. Like your body doesn't talk to your head, or your spirit, or your heart. So most systems of yoga are trying to get your body to connect to your spirit, usually through disciplining and exercising the body as a meditation aid."

Leigh shifted slightly on her cushion.

"So if you took Hatha Yoga or Ashtanga Yoga with me or another instructor, we'd be stretching, bending, turning, working on making the body a better vessel for the spirit, and working on a greater sense of internal connectedness."

A few people around the classroom were nodding in a knowing way. Evidently this was common knowledge.

"Now other types of yoga, like Kundalini Yoga, or Laya Yoga, or Kriya Yoga, they work on the energy of the body, especially the *shakti* or power of the body that is seated in the spine. This power or biological energy, if you prefer, runs along the central vertical corridor of the body, and it gathers at these centers, which we call *chakras* or wheels."

She placed her left hand at the level of her groin, and moved it upwards, pausing at waist, her solar plexus, heart, throat, forehead, and touching the top of her head.

"Now most systems of yoga that deal with the chakras are based on the premise that the energy that's there is positive and healthy. They help you to guide the flow of energy through the chakras, which naturally diffuse your energy into your various natural powers, like intelligence, creativity, insight, and the urge for enlightenment. In theory, this is good for you, and leads you to become a better, more functional version of yourself."

"Of course, that approach is really only valid if you're happy being *you*. If you're already in a good place in life, you like your body, your job, wherever you live, you have good health – then you can definitely try the standard Kundalini practices and expect good results."

She looked pensive for a moment.

"On a personal note, I got into Shava Yoga because my own yoga instructor suggested that the usual yogas weren't working for me. I mean, yoga definitely got me in shape, and the meditation did wonders for my day-to-day mental focus, but I always felt like I was missing something. Like other people were doing less advanced practices than me, and they were getting better benefits on a psychological or spiritual level, and it was really frustrating."

"So my teacher finally suggested that maybe the problem wasn't with the yoga, it was with *me*. I believe now that I got into yoga to change who and what I was, and not in order to make friends with myself. I was looking for serious spiritual growth. I also wanted to get rid of neuroses and other mental garbage that had accrued over my relatively short life."

She shifted again, warming to her topic.

"So ultimately my instructor encouraged me to attend this intensive winter retreat in northern Quebec, and the focus was Shava Yoga. I loved it, because it completely redefined how I saw yoga, and how I saw myself, my mind, and my body. So let's see if I can explain it clearly, like we learned at the retreat."

She smiled.

"Shava Yoga is corpse yoga, and there are five fundamental principles of the system. Let's go over these now."

"The first principle: as the Buddha said, *life is suffering*. As long as we live, we experience destructive, negative emotions like hate, greed, fear, and self-doubt."

"The second principle: *the cause of suffering is life itself*. Life, channeled through the chakras, manifests as our ego. The ego causes us to experience lust, hunger, envy, and aggression. Instead of letting us focus on the real external truths, the chakras serve as our innate spiritual jailers, keeping us trapped inside the prison of the body. The chakras promote our sense of self, even promising moksha or enlightenment, but you can see that it's a selfish dream. You become enlightened, but you're still *you*. You become an idealized version of yourself, but you're still trapped in your body, with no thought of the afterlife. If you do think of the afterlife, you're trapped in life again, which leads to more aggression, more hate, more suffering."

"The third principle: *death is inevitable* – we're born with death built into us, and we spend most of our lives preparing for death, which is our natural, permanent state. The instinct for death is our escape hatch, our own real protection from the suffering of life. Most people unfortunately don't even confront their mortality until it's too late, and they're sick or dying, usually in a mental state of fear and anguish."

"The fourth principle: *death leads to freedom from life and its suffering*. Death is not just the absence of life, it is a state of emptiness and bliss. In death, there is no life to cause suffering, no ego to cause negative feelings, no chemicals or hormones to cause stress and anxiety. Death is greater than life, because where life is competitive and isolating, all things are connected by death and through the eventual loss of the ego."

"Finally, the fifth principle: *By embracing our inner corpse, we can be free of suffering*. Through guided instruction and with practice, we can learn to eject the spiritual energy from the chakras, much like bad fuel can be ejected from a reactor. Through mediation, the Shava Yogi or "corpse practitioner" can learn to reverse the current of the chakras, so that they become centers of death energy, rather than life. This process has to be done slowly, in order to avoid system shock. However, if done carefully, it can lead to real healing from mental and physical sickness and bring about a state of permanent focus and confidence that is really out of this world."

Leigh beamed.

"Wow, great! I remembered all five! First time for everything, I guess."

We laughed, and a few people applauded in a light-hearted way. The young instructor chuckled herself.

"Look, I know that it sounds really different than other systems of yoga. But the system is based on ancient tantric principles, and I can honestly tell you from my own experience that it's made a ton of difference for me. Before I started practicing Shava Yoga, I struggled with migraines and chronic insomnia, and I also struggled with serious anger issues, which manifested in problems with my coworkers and family members. Traditional Yoga helped me to feel in shape and flexible, but I was still mad and afraid all the time."

She frowned at the obviously bitter memories.

"However, after three months of practicing Shava Yoga, the insomnia was gone, and I felt much more aware of how my chakras were inhibiting my personal growth and success. After six months of practice, I no longer needed any medication for the migraines, and all the mental or psychic garbage felt like it had just been washed away. The Shava Yoga had provided serious relief, and I felt confident and strong – really strong – for the first time in my life.

"So the question is how to actually *do* this. How do you reverse your chakra energy, so that you can experience the spiritual benefits of death while still being physically alive? The answer is through corpse yoga, Shava Yoga. If you decide that you like the basic system as I've outlined and choose to stay in the class, we're going to spend the next seven months working on each of our seven chakras in sequence, in order to awaken your spiritual death state."

As Leigh was speaking, for a moment I found myself wondering why I was taking this particular yoga class. On the one hand, Leigh seemed really smart and really competent. But on the other hand, this was all kind of more *spiritual* than I'd been expecting. I'd always understood yoga to be stretching, weird poses, and some meditation too. Stretching I was comfortable with – heck, I even liked it, I did it often. I stretched at the gym all the time, but I often felt stiff during the day, so I figured yoga might help me to work out the soreness that I got from sparring practice or from moving heavy kegs up from the cellar in the pub. When the guy at the reception desk had told me that there was some kind of serious health benefits, I'd assumed it was going to be like the yoga I'd seen on television or on the internet. Still, I'd come this far, so I figured I should at least see how the yoga actually worked.

Leigh looked around the class. We all must have all looked interested, because she straightened up slightly on her cushion and stretched briefly.

"Okay, so before we start the initial exercise, we're

going to briefly identify the seven chakras, and just get a sense of where in the body they are, and what the life-processes they're responsible for. We're going to start from the bottom, because life and death energy flow upwards from below."

She touched her hand gently to her groin area.

"First, the **root chakra** is located at the base of the spine, in the coccyx area, or near the tip of the spine, if you like. It is the center of our most primal urges, and it controls the instincts related to security, lust, sensuality, and sexuality. Tantric tradition says that you can visualize it as a red energy sphere, and it's mantra (or power-sound) is "*lam*." Don't worry about mantras right now, I'll explain more about them later on."

She moved her hand to the waist region.

"Second, you have the **sacral chakra**, which is located at the sacrum or pelvic section of the spine. The sacral chakra controls instincts related to relationships, base emotions, addictions, violence, creativity, and reproduction. You can visualize it as a white energy sphere, and its mantra is "*vam*.""

I wondered to myself exactly how much this chakra stuff was real. It was all well and good that Leigh had done the retreat and gotten a bit hung-up on her ex-partner, but I was having a hard time believing that the tip of the spine, or the pelvis actually could have any control over mental processes like the need for security, or addictions, or anything that was obviously controlled by the brain.

Leigh moved her hand up to the level of her stomach.

"Third, you have the **solar plexus chakra** located along the spine at the level of the solar plexus. This chakra controls processes related to digestion, complex emotions, personal power, fear, anxiety, opinions, and contemplation. Definitely one to get control of! Tradition says that we can visualize it as a yellow energy sphere, and its mantra or power-sound is *"ram."*

Her hand moved up to her heart.

"Fourth, we have the **heart chakra**, which is located along the spine at the heart's level. The heart chakra governs complex emotions, compassion, love, equilibrium, rejection and well-being. It also controls the immune system, or at least helps regulate health. We can imagine it as a green energy sphere, and its power-sound is *"yam."*

An older, grizzled man near the back of the class cleared his throat noisily.

"I could definitely use some of the immune system benefits, so can we just start with that one?" he inquired humorously.

Everyone chuckled at that. Leigh smiled but shook her head.

"No, we need to do them in sequence, but I promise that they all have health benefits. No question there."

Next, she touched two fingers to her throat.

"Fifth, we have the **throat chakra**, which is located at the level of the throat. The throat charka governs the powers of communication, expression, thoughts related to any tasks or processes like those, and security on a spiritual or mental level. Tradition says that we can imagine it as a blue energy sphere, and its mantra is *"ham"*.

One of the younger males in class on my far left raised his hand. He was pale and looked to be in his early twenties. He wore plain black t-shirt and jeans and had extensive tattoos on his arms and neck. I thought he was kind of attractive in a gothic sort of way, but a bit too thin for my liking. Jade saw his raised arm and nodded in his direction.

"I just wanted to ask if the throat chakra controls the

creative processes? I'm asking because I do online professional writing and web-design part-time, and I'm taking this class because someone told me that it could help me to be a better writer," he said in a curious tone.

Leigh pursed her lips thoughtfully.

"Gosh, well it's kind of a partial 'yes'? Technically, the sacral chakra controls the creative impulse," and she touched her waist again, "but the throat chakra controls the expression of that artistic vision. You could think of it like dreamers versus artists. Dreamers have very active sacral chakras, which causes lots of creativity, but sometimes they have weaker throat chakras, which means that they can't express their visions easily. Artists, though, have strong sacral and throat chakras, which produces creativity and the power to share their vision with other people. Does that make sense?"

The guy in black nodded. Leigh smiled back at him.

Next, she pressed her index finger to the center of her forehead.

"Sixth, we have the **third eye chakra**, which is located at the point of the "third eye" in the forehead. It mediates between the higher and lower self, and governs the consciousness, as well as the higher mental processes, as well as intuition. Some associate it with the pineal gland. Tradition says that we can imagine it as an indigo energy sphere, and its mantra is "*om*.""

Her hand came to rest on the top of her head.

"Seventh, finally, is the **crown chakra**, located above the head, or at the crown of the head. It governs the state of pure consciousness, physical death, psychic unity, meditation and occult powers. Obviously, it is going to be important for our work. We can envision it as a purple energy sphere, and its mantra is secret."

The guy in black raised his hand again, and Leigh turned to face him, gesturing in his direction.

"Ok, so when you say occult powers, what do you mean exactly?" he asked curiously.

Leigh considered.

"So, a lot of people get caught up on the word 'powers,' but technically in yoga we considered all of the senses and mental processes as 'powers.' Sight, hearing, touch, logic, foresight are all examples of innate powers that everyone has. Does that make sense?"

The guy in black nodded.

"Good," said Leigh, "so yoga also holds that there are other powers that are innate to humans that we don't use, and that you need to learn how to unlock. So the crown chakra is traditionally the doorway to unlocking those powers. Or, sometimes once you begin to activate the crown chakra, you begin to develop certain abilities and insights spontaneously."

She paused, looking suddenly very serious.

"Um, also, if you take this class and learn to levitate, definitely teach me that trick. I still haven't managed to get the hovering thing down yet."

Everyone laughed aloud at that.

Leigh grinned at her own joke, and then folded her hand again on her lap.

"Now that's a basic overview of the chakras, and if you look into most Asian systems of medicine and healing, you'll see that chakras are pretty much a universal concept. Some people understand them as a literal node of energy in the spine, and others think that they're more figurative. At this stage of the practice, it doesn't matter whether we accept them as literal or metaphorical. What matters is that we accept the chakras as a representation of very real energies that run through the human body."

She paused for a few moments, allowing us to digest this information, and then she continued.

"So before we jump into the practices, we need to

review the potential risks of this particular practice."

Risks in yoga, I thought, *is she serious?*

A few of us must have made a strange face, because she smiled shyly, and gestured in an abstract way.

"So when I say 'risks,' I don't mean that Shava Yoga is dangerous, but like any kind of exercise, you need to do it properly to avoid injury. Like, if I were introducing you to swimming, or running, or weight-lifting, we'd need to discuss stretching and the dangers of over-exertion, because you can really hurt yourself doing those sports if you're careless."

Well, sure, when you put it that way, it did make sense.

Leigh continued. She looked like she was thinking how best to articulate something tricky.

"With some kinds of yoga, like Ashtanga, you'd need to actually worry about tearing muscles. Shava Yoga really only has two primary asanas or positions, and they're deliberately very simple, so even an injured person can practice them. There's no direct risk of physical injury in Shava Yoga. Instead, we need to be careful of the mental and energetic side-effects that the practice can generate.

"When we first begin any new sport or practice, it's expected that we'll experience some minor discomfort. You can get aches or pains as muscles begin to stretch and grow – and that's actually a positive sign. In Shava Yoga, at first we're working to expel the ego-centric energies of the body beginning with the root chakra. So on a physical level, it usually feels weird, because all this energy that your body insists is part of you needs to be expelled."

One of the students in the front row raised his hand.

"Um, but if something occurs naturally in the body, why would you want to get rid of it? I'm having a tough time with that point."

Leigh nodded thoughtfully.

"Yeah, that's a totally valid question. I think the best analogy to use is that humans produce a lot of stuff that we need to release or can choose to release. Everyone has to go to the bathroom, for example, that's universal. If you don't go to the bathroom, like if you try to retain your urine, you can really hurt yourself. A different example: the phlegm in your chest when you have a cough – you can swallow it, or you can cough it up and expel it. Both are possible but expelling it will make you heal faster. Or, last but not least, the sexual fluids – no one *needs* to expel those to live, but.... anyway, you get my point."

Everyone chuckled, and she smiled again shyly.

"So the chakra energy is like those fluids that the body produces, and in Shava Yoga we work to expel those energies because we think it's ultimately better to be rid of them. But that being said, we can't leave the chakras hollow, because they'll just fill up again, just like the venom glands of a snake. So instead, we need to fill them with the death energy, corpse energy, which is actually all around us, and you can learn to absorb and integrate through constant practice.

"Now like I was saying before, the act of expelling that bad life energy and absorbing the death energy is going to feel strange at first. The actual physical space can feel slightly uncomfortable, and it's normal to experience an ache in the region of the chakra that you're working on. So if you feel discomfort during the meditation practice or right after, it's a good sign, but if you don't, that's also fine.

"So the chakras are located along the spine, but each one has unique powers or themes, and when we engage with each particular chakra from month to month, we're definitely going to feel some physical or psychological sensations, and these can be mild or intense, it's different for everyone. Let me give an example from this upcoming week. We're going to start with the root chakra, which we noted already is located around the base of the spine. So that chakra helps to regulate or inspire our instincts that are related to really basic urges, especially the urge for sensuality – what feels good, smells good, tastes good, looks good, all that kind of stuff. It also controls our sexual urges, and the instinct for safety and security."

She looked thoughtful for a moment.

"Let me give a personal example of how that chakra affected me at first. So I mentioned that I was at this retreat in Quebec, it was cold and dark because it was winter. There were thirty-five of us, all studying Shava Yoga together. So the first two days, I felt this dull ache at the base of my spine, and it wasn't painful, just kind of there. Then on the third day, I just woke up kind of, umm, frustrated? I'd just left a bad relationship at the time, but for the rest of that entire week, I really struggled to focus because I was *really* missing intimacy with my ex-partner. Like, it was bad. And they'd made us give up our cell phones for the retreat, so I couldn't even call him, which was probably a good thing."

She blushed, and I smiled – I think pretty much everyone had experienced what she was getting at.

"Anyway, the danger there was that I might have left the retreat, or I could have tried to get into bed with another yoga student – for sure, there was some of that happening at the retreat. Both ideas crossed my mind a few times, but instead I just focused on the yoga. I managed to cope, and ultimately it taught me how much that particular chakra had been responsible for my natural drive in a way that I'd taken for granted. The best thing about the practice, after that, was being able to be in control of my urges, instead of being controlled. By embracing my inner corpse, I became able to completely suppress (or redirect) my basic urges when they become a distraction. It's really just that simple."

She stretched her arms briefly and craned her neck. Then she surveyed the class with a critical eye.

"Ok, so enough about me, are you ready to try this out yourselves?"

There was a chorus of affirmations from the classroom.

Leigh straightened slightly on her cushion.

"First, I want to invite everyone to sit upright, with your legs folded, either in a natural pose, or lotus, or whatever is comfortable. Your back shouldn't be rigid, but your head should be held high, and your spine should be upward-rising, like a vine growing upwards. Hands can be on your knees or folded together on your lap like mine."

She waited while the assembled class shifted into position, some quicker than others, likely based on prior yoga instruction or lack thereof (in my case).

"Good, and this is a great way to start, because a lot of yoga exercises are done in a seated position, and especially so for Shava Yoga."

She paused for a moment, waiting for a few stragglers to finish sitting upright.

"So this is the basic position that you'll be using on a daily basis for the practice. Now I want you to feel the very tip of your spine, which you can feel if you shift slightly on your cushion. Go again and wiggle your hips against the cushion, just for a moment, so you can feel it inside you."

I wiggled my hips, and as she said, I could feel the tip of my spine as I shifted my weight.

"Great. So now that you are aware of the base of the spine, I want you to visualize a sphere of energy there, with a reddish tinge. Everyone has one, you just need to become aware of yours. Even if you don't sense it, just concentrate on the *image* of the chakra"

I tried to visualize the reddish sphere that she was describing, and it was a bit of a challenge. I'd never been a really creative or visual person, I was more of a hands-on type. But I could feel the base of my spine against the cushion, so I imagined the red sphere of energy that she wanted us to see.

"You might not feel the chakra right away but be confident that it is there. It's the same with your heart – it's there, working, whether or not you are aware of it. Visualize the chakra's essence surrounding the base of the spine. Feel its energy pulsing with your heartbeat. It's warm, and it feels full of vitality. See its redness, feel the gentle heat that radiates outwards from the chakra."

As she spoke, I began to actually *feel* something, like a gentle energy that did seem to rest at the base of my spine. It was a positive moment in the practice, and it encouraged me to concentrate.

Leigh paused for several minutes, allowing us to concentrate on the initial visualization. Then she shifted slightly, speaking in a gentle but assured tone.

"Now, you need to visualize the red essence of the chakra descending down into the earth. The earth feels dark and hungry, and it naturally wants to absorb the chakra's light. We need to discharge the light of the chakra into the darkness of the earth, because it's the safest place for it to go, we don't want that vital energy to be dispersed back into the air where it will hurt people."

I tried hard to imagine what she was saying. I imagined the earth beneath me like a dark cave, empty and hungry. I imagined myself contracting the chakra, forcing the red light to bleed down into the earth – it was a somewhat menstrual image for me, and I wondered momentarily how the guys in class were visualizing the same process. Strangely, the visualization seemed to resonate, and I started to feel a gentle ache at the base of my spine, as I imagined the vital energies descending down into the black cave in the earth.

Leigh spoke again, her voice soft and assertive at the same time.

"You're doing really well, I can sense the vitality being expelled into the darkness."

She paused for another few moments. It might have been two or three minutes, it was hard to tell.

"Good, so now we're going to begin to reverse the polarity of the chakra. So first, visualize the last of the red light fading away into the darkness of the earth below."

This, I found I was able to do without much trouble.

"Now, visualize that darkness in the earth reaching upwards towards us. Imagine the black energy entering your chakra, filling it with dark matter. No more red, all black. Now the chakra is black, there's no light at all, it's draining away all that red light. Bring the darkness into your root chakra. Hold it in, let it sit inside you, let it integrate into you – make it part of your system."

Well, I endeavored to do this. I could already imagine the darkness of the earth below me, into which I'd sent the red light of the root chakra. I tried to feel that darkness, which the instructor was describing, and I imagined it rising upward, slowly drifting like smoke up into the base of my spine.

There was a moment in the exercise where I actually could feel what Leigh was describing. At first I hadn't felt anything, but then I started to get this cold feeling, almost a tightening of the muscles in that area. I started to feel very tender, almost bruised, but I kept on with the exercise. I continued to visualize the chakra as a dark sphere, with that unnatural black light filling the hollow space left behind by the chakra's red light. It was difficult to maintain the image consistently, and I'd never done any visualization or meditation exercises before. I was no stranger to strain or exertion – there's tons of that in boxing – but that was a different kind of exercise.

Then, for some reason, the new, blackened energy of the chakra began to move. I guess the original red light was sort of static, like a thick fluid that had settled into place, but the new darkness felt more like dark water, and it was swirling around. I was sitting still, without moving, but I could feel this liquid sensation of fluid flowing in a circular fashion, like water swirling around in a cup. I started to feel a little dizzy.

At the front of the class, Leigh continued to coach us.

"You guys are doing really well. Continue the visualization for just a few more minutes. Vital essence *out* on your exhalation, corpse energy *in* on your inhalation. Dark essence in, vital essence out. You're purging all those urges, all those compulsions. You can feel the vitality toxins seeping out of the body, and the corpse energy flowing back into you. Feel the chakra vibrate with the dark essence, feel the dark matter inside of you. You can feed it your urges, your neuroses, your sickness. It's part of you now, it's there to stay. There is no longer 'you' and the 'darkness' – it's part of you now. It has become the chakra. Feel the darkness as part of you. Feel yourself become the corpse."

She had a very hypnotic voice – I could listen to her for hours.

Yet the class was nearly over. Leigh shifted slightly in the instructor's cushion. She spoke again, her voice once again normal, the voice of a friend, not a teacher.

"Ok, bring your attention back to me," Leigh said, "You can relax your mind and let go of the visualization."

I relaxed. A kind of spasm shook me as I pulled away from the black chakra and turned my concentration back to the external world around me. I could hear other students around me exhaling, as though they'd been deep in concentration.

Leigh was beaming at us. She had a slight flush to her face, like some people get when they're under pressure in public.

"Wow, you guys did great! I can really feel the shift in the room's resonance, can you feel it too?"

You know, oddly enough, I could feel exactly what she was referring to in the space around us. The room felt cooler, like a cloud had passed over the sun. The base of my spine continued to tingle in that weird, cold way, and I was a little bit sore. I squirmed in my seat – and looking around, I wasn't the only one.

Leigh noticed me moving, and a few others around me. She put on her serious instructor face again.

"Ok, so for the rest of the week, you should make time to do this every morning or every night. My own instructor says that it's best to do right before sunrise, or well after sunset. Sort of like yoga for vampires."

We laughed. It felt good to laugh, and I felt relaxed and fresh from doing the practice with my classmates.

Leigh smiled again.

"I know it sounds funny, but the corpse practice really is most effective in the darker hours. You can do it during the day, but personally I find that it causes headaches and distraction. Your mileage may vary, try it yourself and see what works best for your own schedule. I'm an early riser, so I like to do it before sunrise, that's when I'm awake and rested."

She rolled her shoulders and craned her neck again.

"It's good to begin with a minimum ten minutes of practice a day and try to increase that by about five minutes weekly. Eventually, after two or three months, we're looking at a stable daily practice of 30-40 minutes a day."

She looked serious again.

"Now here's the safety warning that I mentioned earlier. This initial practice is simple and it's not difficult to do, but it's important not to overdo it. Don't go home and do this for an hour a day. And please, don't go home and try it for several hours. The chakras need time to adjust and heal from the stretching and pulling we're doing to them, and like any muscle or ligament, they are vulnerable to exhaustion and trauma. The practice begins little by little, so just ten minutes, fifteen minutes at most for the first week. Next week, we'll increase to the ten-to-twenty minute range. Remember, it's worlds better to have a really focused and productive ten-minute meditation than a bad half-hour."

Leigh paused, looking around the class.

"Any questions?" she asked.

A woman in the front row put up her hand. She was rather stout but had somehow managed to squeeze herself into a super tight spandex yoga pants, with a bright orange shirt that said "Ye Olde Wicca" in large Old English font. She also seemed (to me) to be wearing a lot of crystals for someone coming to a yoga class.

Leigh saw her and gestured in her direction.

"I really like incense," began the woman, "and I like to burn it when I'm meditating on the gods. Can I burn incense during this practice?"

Leigh nodded affirmatively.

"You don't have to do so," she answered, "but if you feel that the incense helps to create a positive space for your spiritual practice, absolutely. And I should add, it's good to establish a dedicated space for spiritual practice, like a corner of your apartment, a large closet, even a dedicated shrine room if you have the space."

The lady in the "Ye Olde Wicca" shirt was nodding in a very knowing way.

"Any more questions?" Leigh asked us all.

As it turned out, there weren't any.

"Ok, great!" she said. "So classes are Saturday afternoons, but you can find me here most evenings leading some of the other courses, and if you have any questions, the front desk has business cards with my name and contact information."

She folded her palms in our direction, and I saw that the other students were making a similar gesture, so I did the same.

"*Namaste*," said Leigh softly, and we repeated the phrase. She smiled, and stood to go, and we all did likewise.

That was my first yoga class ever, and I loved it. It was different from sparring, but I really liked it. On the way out, I stopped at the desk and got Leigh's card. I also signed up for the course, which by itself didn't have any cost, though it did require me to get a monthly membership at Yoga Center. Still, the monthly cost was less than I expected, and I figured that I could take an extra shift or two to cover the additional expense. I also bought a black yoga mat, and then feeling whimsical, I bought an incense burner and some sandalwood cones. "Ye Olde Wicca" seemed a bit of a flake, but I did like the idea of making a dedicated space in my apartment, and maybe the incense would help. I paid the receptionist for the membership and the merchandise, got my shoes from the storage shelves, and headed home.

NOVEMBER. ROOT CHAKRA

After the first class, I went home to my small apartment, and tried to decide where I could set up space for yoga. I've always been a very active person, but most of my exercise is from lifting and carrying heavy materials at work, jogging, or training at the gym. Having space at home to train had never been possible, because I was renting such a tiny apartment. Still, if the only real issue was to have a corner of the apartment in which to rest my black mat, I figured that I could use the corner nearest to the one window, which was empty at present, except for a plant that I'd been slowly killing in spite of my best intentions. So the plant went into the hallway, and the yoga mat took its place. I unpacked the incense burner and cones from my backpack and set them on the bookshelf nearest to my newly designated yoga corner. While the space certainly didn't look like a shrine, it did have the makings of a dedicated practice space, and that felt like a good beginning to long-term practice.

I had to work that evening, and the yoga hadn't been a very tiring experience, so I decided to go for a run for an hour. I was already dressed for exercise, so it made sense. I've always been a habitual runner, doing anywhere from thirty minutes to an hour daily. I headed back outside and decided to do the shorter route. Turning right, I began to run, my route taking me past the local bakery where I could smell fresh bread cooking, past the corner store, and past *The Black Hound*, the pub where I'd be working in a few hours. It felt good to run – always does – especially because it was a predictable feeling. The yoga session hadn't been predictable, and it was more spiritual than I'd expected, so it felt good to do something earthy like running.

The funny thing though, was that even as I ran along the sidewalk, weaving in and out of the way of other pedestrians and parked bicycles, I could still feel the dull ache of the chakra meditation. It was an odd place, the base of the spine, and I wasn't routinely aware of it, even when sitting. But now as I was moving over the concrete, my heart beginning to pound and my blood rushed as I moved faster and faster, I was aware of the chakra area, almost like I'd been bruised there. It didn't hurt, but it felt sort of gingerly, if that makes sense, and when I'd leap up or down a curb, I could feel the jolt there. Then again, I'd been stiff and sore after almost every boxing session, so I decided to take it as a positive sign that the yoga wasn't just some psycho-somatic hypnosis, and if I could actually feel some soreness after the practice, then it must genuinely have helped exercise some of the tissues down there. That was a good thought.

I finished my run, and headed home to shower. I stripped off my damp clothes, leaving them in a pile on the floor, and stepped into the bathroom. My apartment was tiny, and the heating was crap, but the shower had great water pressure, and that was definitely a bonus. The hot water always felt good after a workout, and the aching feeling from the initial yoga session seemed to wash away with the water. As the water spiraled down the shower drain, though, I had momentary flashes to the session where Leigh was telling us to channel our life essence down into the earth. She was a good teacher, I thought, and I figured I could probably learn a lot from her in the coming months.

The November air felt colder after the hot shower, so I dried off quickly and got dressed. The pub would be really warm, but the air outside would be cold, so I layered up accordingly: black jeans, black turtleneck, a thick sweater that I could peel off once I got to *The Black Hound*, and my coat. Putting my wallet and keys into my pocket, I stepped into the hallway and pulled my door closed behind me. Time to go to work.

—

Routines were something that I found extremely helpful, so I tried to maintain the same schedule daily, as much as my work allowed. Managing *The Hound* tended to be evenings and nights, so I had days to myself. Since I worked late most nights and didn't get to bed until 5am, on a typical day I'd wake up around noon. I'd make some coffee, eat a light breakfast, and then head to the gym to train for an hour or two. Afterwards, I'd do shopping and errands, see friends, and then have an hour or two at home before heading to *The Hound* to start my shift. It was a simple life, and I really liked it for the most part.

Now, I needed to figure out when to do the yoga practice. At first, I figured I'd do it as soon as I woke up, but Leigh had said that it was really best to do it while it was dark out. I couldn't do it at sunset, because I was usually heading to work then. If I wanted to follow Leigh's advice and do the practice while it was still nighttime, it made sense to do it as soon as I got home from work, so usually around 4am. That didn't seem too bad to me, and I usually found that I needed some activity to help unwind after my shift. Often, I would watch some downloaded movies on my laptop, or read a book, so yoga seemed like a nice alternative. I wasn't a big reader, and I suspected that staring at the laptop monitor before bed wasn't exactly helping me to sleep, so I decided from now on, I'd practice yoga as soon as I got home from work.

For better or worse, I've always been an all-or-nothing person, so I decided to start my Shava Yoga that first Saturday night after work, and I did get into a good routine immediately. Like I planned, right after work was the perfect time to practice. I'd come home tired, frustrated, moody, or any mix of the above, and the yoga practice was just the thing to get me into the right headspace so that I could sleep. At first, it was difficult to do the practice apart from the class, but I found that each session got progressively easier. My second class on the following Saturday was even better than the first, probably because I'd been practicing daily. After Leigh's introductory session, I was half expecting to wake up with hot flashes, or the urge to take an attractive stranger home from the pub – but absolutely none of that happened.

The same cannot necessarily be said for the others in my yoga class. On the third class, later in November, I noticed that one of the red-haired twins had gotten together with the pale guy in black. It wasn't obvious in the classroom, but I'd seen them come in to *The Black Hound* together one evening, and she'd been all over him after a few drinks. Later I learned that his name was David, and hers was Alesha (her twin was Alice). At the yoga studio, they were holding hands in the reception area when I came in for class, and they set up their yoga mats next to each other, so I guess they'd gotten together. *Good for them*, I figured, at least they had a hobby in common.

Leigh also noticed the two of them in class, and I think she had to stifle a laugh when she saw them covertly pawing each other after class in the reception area. It wasn't so much that they were being overly inappropriate, it was more the fact that Leigh had gone out of the way to spell out that the root chakra had a certain influence on the libido and judging from the way that the two of them were carrying on at the pub, they didn't give the impression that their connection had to do with their mutual love of cinema. Just saying.

In my case, though, while the yoga practice didn't have any effect on my sensuality or paranoia, it did produce a definite sense of rawness at the base of my spine. It's kind of hard to explain, but Leigh described the sense of bad energies draining into the earth, and after the second week of the practice, I really began to feel that I'd gotten rid of a lot of bad stuff. In fact, in retrospect, I think that where Leigh, or Dave and Alesha might have gotten sex-crazed (even if briefly), I think the practice had the reverse effect on me. It's not that I stopped noticing when hot guys were in the pub, but I definitely became a lot more immune to male charm during that particular phase of the practice. It's like the chakra practice had made me, I dunno, *colder (?)* somehow. Like it had shunted some of my emotions away, or at least some of my hungers. I guess I was really getting in touch with my inner corpse, but it was kind of freaking me out. So I asked Leigh about this after the third class, but she told me it was completely normal, and that the chakras can have a wide range of side-effects, depending on the natural energies of the yogi (or yoga practitioner). In fact, she said that my state of being – that coldness I described to her – was actually the desired result of the practice.

"If you think about it," she said, "being in a state of arousal is fun, but it's not helpful. Being dead to your sex drive, that's real freedom. What you were able to do in a matter of weeks is the very thing that most of the class will take several months to learn, so you should be happy."

When she put it like that, I was actually quite happy. Who wouldn't be? It's nice to be told that you're a natural, after all. If the instructor said I was making progress, that was plenty enough for me, and so I just relaxed in to the cold strength that had begun to wrap around me like a cocoon, gradually and subtly alienating me from my own physical hungers.

DECEMBER

The month of December came, and the nights were getting colder and longer, and the people of Montreal were braced for winter. The pub was really busy, and we'd actually had to fire someone for petty theft, which meant I was stuck doing a few extra shifts a week. Still, I was able to maintain my training schedule at the gym pretty regularly, and the Saturday classes at Yoga Center and the daily yoga practice were starting to feel like part of my weekly routine.

It was the first Saturday of the month, and time for Shava Yoga at the center. I was starting to get to know the names of the other people in class. Alesha and Alice were the red-headed twins, David was the goth boyfriend of Alesha, and "Ye Olde Wicca" was actually named Renata. The older gentleman who'd spoken up in the first session was Andy. I didn't see any of them much outside of the class, but it was still a friendly enough group. I found out that Andy had chronic arthritis and had tried other types of yoga but found them too strenuous. Renata had heard that Shava Yoga was the new big thing in alternative healing and was sure it would increase her psychic abilities. David just seemed to like the "corpse" aspect of "corpse yoga." In retrospect, I never did figure out exactly why the twins were in class, but they seemed friendly, so it didn't make much difference to me.

Leigh, I learned, had been with Yoga Center for several years, but she only did it part-time, her main job was a research librarian at Mount Royal University, which was downtown. She was also teaching the Ashtanga Yoga class on Tuesdays and Thursdays, and if I'd not been working most nights, I might have thought about trying that out. From what I was hearing, it was kind of like intensive strength training, and you used your own body in place of weights for strength training. Leigh usually wore long sleeves and loose pants for the Shava Yoga class, but there was one day where she came in wearing a tank-top, and she was probably as muscled as I was – and between the boxing and lifting tanks at work, I'd always had really good muscle tone.

I was seated in the second row of class, and Leigh was beginning to introduce us to the second of the seven chakras.

She smiled and greeted us with the traditional folded palms.

"*Namaste*, everyone. Great to see you. Ok, so today we're going to move up one level, so that we're activating the **sacral chakra**. Now just to remind you, this chakra is located at the sacrum or pelvic section of the spine. Now you might be surprised to learn that this chakra controls a lot of very important aspects of our lives. It helps regulate our relationships, simple emotions, reproduction, and our creative energies. It is also connected to the cycles of addiction and violence, so it can be great if you struggle with those but working with it can also aggravate those areas."

Renata ("Ye Olde Wicca") was still wearing unfortunately tight spandex that was several sizes too small. Whatever her issues, courage or common sense were not among them. She raised her hand.

"I've been using a lot of pot recently, and I'm starting to think I should cut back. Will working on this chakra help?"

Leigh tried hard not to smile, with limited success.

"Well, in the long run, definitely. In the short term, it's probably going to make it harder to quit, if that's what you're hoping for."

Renata looked a bit nonplussed, but didn't respond further, so Leigh continued.

"First, we're going to activate the root chakra, just like in previous sessions. Focus on your breath and remember to expel any life energy on the exhalation, and to absorb dark essence on the inhalation. Great, very good. Just maintain that image for several minutes first, and remember that we're transforming the chakra into a permanent mass of shadow energy. It's light, cool, and calming. Slight pain is good, it's the life energy being expelled."

We meditated in this way for several minutes. This was very familiar from the previous classes. When Leigh felt that we were ready to proceed, she continued the guided meditation.

"Now much like the root chakra, we're going to imagine that the sacral chakra is filled with negative, egocentric white light, and that we need to reject and expel that light. We can channel it down, deep into the earth beneath us. As we inhale, we're bringing the dark matter of the universe into our chakra, filling it with that natural dark energy that's already all around us. We're taking it in, absorbing it. Let that emptiness sit inside you, scouring away the white residue. We're slowly, gently awakening our own corpse nature, allowing the bad karmas of organic life to be dissolved into the black nothingness that's gathering around and inside the chakra."

God, I could actually feel the sensation of coldness wrapping itself around my spine near the pelvis. The region started to throb, aching in a dull way that had become almost familiar from the root chakra meditations. For a moment, I had this image of my blackened root chakra sending out tendrils to invade the sacral chakra above it, wrapping around like the filaments of a black spider web. I could see the chakra darkening, the light guttering as the black filaments strangled the ego-centered karmas out of it, like wringing droplets of blood out of a soaking bandage.

Leigh's voice rang out at the front of the room.

"Visualize your addictions, your anger, your ego, all just filtering down into the earth. That dark matter is replacing those energies, eating away those aspects that have been hurting you for so long. You can feel the ache as the chakra re-aligns, opening itself to your corpse nature. You're filling yourself with death energy, killing the chakra, so that you're truly alive. You're welcoming death inside yourself, so that you're stronger, healthier, more resilient."

Oddly, I actually was feeling tougher during this particular session. My back was aching as she was describing the death essence, but there was something, I dunno, hypnotic about the way Leigh guided the class, that made me feel like I could really see what she was saying. She made you believe that you could do it, and so you could. It was literally that simple.

Yet in spite of Leigh's voice guiding us, pushing us ahead, I found my mind straying back to the bar. It had been a really tough week, and two of my staff members had been screwing around on their shifts, showing up late, and otherwise not pulling their weight. I'd been forced to pick up the slack, staying later and doing more of their jobs than I was really comfortable with doing. Several times I'd already told them to shape the hell up, or else I'd hire someone else to do the job.

"You guys are doing great. Just feel that aggression, that passion, draining down, flowing away like dirty water after a shower. You feel cool, as your natural corpse nature takes hold," Leigh intoned.

Well, I did not *feel* great, and my aggression did not feel better. I did not feel cool or collected like a dead body should feel - I felt tired and pissed off with my staff and was starting to wonder how to get them to understand that they needed to start seriously doing the job, or else I'd have to show them the door.

Mechanically, I completed the rest of the class. I barely heard Leigh's voice, coaching us through the remaining movements. I mean, I did everything she told us to do, but my mind was just elsewhere. Breathe in, breathe out. Be a corpse. Jesus, whatever.

Soon class was done. I numbly folded my palms at the end and muttered *namaste* with the rest of the class. As we were leaving, Leigh gave each of us her new business card. It was essentially the same as the previous card, except that this one had Leigh's phone number.

"Now if you guys have a yoga emergency, you know how to reach me," she joked, smiling at us through her thick black glasses. We all laughed with her. She was a good teacher, and it pissed me off that I hadn't been very attentive that session. I promised her (silently) that I'd try harder at the next class.

—

That Saturday, I was supposed to be off, and I'd planned to hit the gym and do some sparring. You can imagine how fucking pissed off I was when the owner called to tell me that one of the idiot servers had called in sick. I patiently tried to explain to him that this was the server's third weekend in a row being "sick" and maybe it was time to take action to ensure a more constant level of staff commitment. The manager told me I needed to relax, and I almost hung up on him. Asshole, I thought, he was only being patient because he didn't have to clean the shitty washrooms when the staff blew off their shifts – that delightful job fell to me.

So instead of beating the shit out of a punching bag at the gym, I found myself at *The Hound*, pouring pints and smiling a fake smile at the usual regulars. My smile, at least, felt corpse-like and taunt, stretching unnaturally as I tried to keep up a cheerful demeanor. I felt cold and hot at the same time, my cheeks burning as I grinned and joked with the patrons and clients, brushing aside the odd newbie who tried to get my phone number. I didn't blame them for trying. I made a point of dressing to look good, and the hours at the gym gave me a physique that appealed to a lot of guys (and some girls), but I never mixed work with pleasure. Even if a guy was hot, he was a client, and so I just smiled, poured the pints, and tried to make people feel welcome, even if I myself wanted to strangle anyone who asked for beer. Most of the night was ok, admittedly. We were trying out a new band, "Blood of Amergin", and they were playing pretty well, a bit loud for my taste, but the patrons seemed to enjoy their first couple of sets. Things were pretty decent for the most part. But – and it pains me to admit it – around midnight, there was an incident.

There was a girl who came in sometimes, not exactly a regular, but someone I knew to see. Her name was Mona, or Monica or something like that. Anyway, she was there that night with these two other friends. It's kind of weird – I didn't get a good look at them, because it was a really busy night. It's kind of like I saw her with a male friend, and I remember thinking that he was *really* attractive, which was not normal for me for me to think when I was working. When I turned to serve them, the guy must have disappeared into the crowd, because she was just there by herself. There was a loud skinhead next to her who was getting rowdy, meaning he was getting to the point where we'd have to stop serving him. It was busy, and I can't swear that I really saw what was going on, but out of the corner of my eye it looked like the skinhead was getting grabby. It happened sometimes – people got drunk, they got fast hands, they had to be cut off. As the manager of the bar, you had to be careful – you wanted to keep your staff safe (at all costs), but you also don't want to needlessly kick someone to the curb, because when they sobered up, YOU become the hard-ass who disrespected them, and they'll tell their friends, and that eats into revenues. So I try to keep "incidents" to a minimum, because it was better for business all around.

The skinhead had other ideas. He grabbed one of the servers twice, despite being told to keep his hands to himself. I found myself yelling at him across the bar that he was on his last warning, but he just didn't fucking listen. That girl, Mona, seemed oblivious to his advances, but that didn't seem to deter him. Fucker kept reaching. I don't remember actually crossing the bar, but I know that I must have closed the distance. I tried to tell the skinhead to back off, but he didn't seem to hear me over the roar of the band. He was practically leaning over Mona's shoulder, and I could see her frowning and trying to get away from the guy. I was shouting now, trying to be heard over the roaring of applause as the band ended a number, but the skinhead couldn't hear me. I finally had to put my hand on his shoulder to get his attention. He didn't seem to feel it, so I grabbed his jacket and started to haul him off of Mona. Maybe I startled him, or maybe he was just drunk, but the fucker turned towards me faster than I would have expected. His face was a mix of anger and confusion, and maybe he thought I was some jealous girlfriend or something.

But then he tried to shove me, and that's when something inside me just, well, just kind of happened.

If I had to explain it, it was like when he started to shove me, time seemed to slow to a crawl around me. I was pissed, I mean I was really fucking mad. I was mad at the skinhead, mad at the noise, and mad that I didn't seem to have any control over my emotions despite several weeks of yoga. But it's not like I was conscious of my emotional state, I just want you to understand that in that precise moment, I was several shades of pissed off. And this fucker, this stupid asshole was making my night worse by forcing me to act the part of the heavy, which I hated doing, and he just wouldn't leave this poor girl alone, and no one else seemed to give a damn. So he's reaching towards me, and time seems to have slowed to a crawl, and I'm not even aware that I've bent sideways, so that the force of his arms pushes past me. I don't really remember hammering his face with a hard right hook, and I also don't remember the feeling of strength in my hips as I pivoted back, my other first smashing into his face with a vicious left cross. I don't remember because it was instinct and practice, but I can hit really, *really* hard when I'm motivated to do so. I don't really remember his jaw slamming shut, jarring his teeth and breaking his nose, or the look of shock on his face. I do, however, remember seeing the skinhead on the ground, and feeling his warm red blood on my white knuckles. I do remember seeing him at my feet, cradling his face, and wondering if he was crying like a fucking baby, and I remember seeing mixed looks around the room: shock from Mona, surprise from some skinheads in the crowd, and but mostly looks of approval from the other customers nearby. I remember feeling an empty contempt for him, wondering if he'd have the guts to get up and fight me. I looked across the bar to see my staff, but instead caught sight of my own reflection in the mirror – my face was frozen in this weird rictus grin, I looked, well, happy in an angry, sick way. When I looked down, he was crawling away, cradling his jaw, and apparently determined not to look back and risk (I guess) another punch or two from the psychotic manager on duty.

But what kind of scared me most in all of this, was the feeling of absolute confidence, the weird sense of cold, zen-like calm that came over me, washing away the anger, and leaving me feeling like I had just plunged into an ice-cold bath. I didn't regret hitting him, or breaking his bones, or protecting a client – that was my job, for crying out loud. What was weird was the icy sense of emptiness that followed in the wake of the assault, the sense of numbness and total control. Was it shock? I'd been in shock before after a car accident, and it sure hadn't felt like this. I wondered about my state of mind, as I headed back around the other side of the bar. Other patrons, oblivious to the brief attack, began ordering drinks, and I found myself pouring pints of beer with a continued sense of absolute deadness, a sense of queer, cold strength and purpose moving through me for the rest of the night.

When the night shift was over, and the pub was closed, I made my way home. Usually I felt wary on the short walk back to my building, but instead I felt kind of dead inside. I don't mean that I was depressed – it was more like this cold strength had slipped underneath my skin and into my innards, and I felt strangely aware and yet apart from myself so that I was watching as I experienced this bizarre state of mind.

I reached my apartment and stepped inside. I stripped off my clothes and got into the shower. The water was scalding hot, hotter than I would normally like it, but the cold feeling was creeping me out, and I sort of hoped that sheer exterior temperature would help me to feel "normal" again. The water felt good, and it did help wash away some of the negative tension that had been stored up in my hands and wrists. My knuckles were still white, I noticed. The water felt good on my back and my hips, and I finished showering feeling slightly more normal. I pulled on my thick gym clothes, which doubled as pajamas, and slipped under the covers of my bed. I hoped to sleep, but sleep didn't seem to want to come for me.

"Calm down," Leigh said to me reassuringly, sipping her tall green tea. "Walk me through this. I'm sure you're ok, just tell me what happened."

It was the next morning. I hadn't slept all night, and I was starting to feel a bit freaked out at the cold, empty feeling that wouldn't go away. So I'd called her using the number on her card, and she'd very kindly offered to meet me for coffee. So we were sitting at this coffee house named 'Trident' that had just opened next door to the pub, and across from Yoga Center.

I should have felt tired, or manic, or something like that from the sleep deprivation, but I didn't feel anything like that at all. I just felt "normal," but something was off. It was like something had torn loose inside me, and I was starting to feel like a spectator in my own head.

I tried to explain what had happened. I told Leigh about the prior evening, about the skinhead harassing some poor female client, and how I'd tried to defuse the situation. I told her how the guy had tried to shake me off, to shove me away, and how I'd momentarily turned into a psycho rage monster, smashing the guy's face into a bloody mess. Then, worse, the sense of coldness, that feeling of absolute zero, the emotional black hole that I'd fallen into. I guess I felt that I should have felt freaked out, but didn't, and that itself was kind of alarming.

Leigh didn't seem worried or upset at all. She seemed happy for me.

"This is excellent," she enthused, "you're making such incredible progress. Don't you see? This is the whole point, the meditation and the yoga sadhana, you've been trying to awaken your latent corpse nature, and you – hell – you did it! I'm so proud of you."

I must have been hearing her wrong.

"But I punched a guy out, I really fucked him up," I protested, "where's the serenity in that?"

Leigh shook her head impatiently.

"No, you can never control life, that's not practical or even desirable. Look, you've been doing the practice for weeks, and then you were thrust into a bad circumstance. Somehow, that crisis must have served as a catalyst, and instead of freaking out, you asserted your inner corpse nature, and rejected the natural chakra fight-or-flight reaction. I'm so proud of you! You should be proud too!"

I wanted to believe her, but I felt so weird, so distant.

"Look, I did what I had to do, it was my job," I hesitantly explained, "and I'd do it again if I had to, but I'm trying to tell you that I feel like I've fallen into some kind of emotional black hole."

"No," Leigh argued, "the black hole has been there for weeks, ever since you committed to the practice. YOU are the black hole, and the whole point of Shava Yoga is to get you to understand that and accept it, so you can start to make serious spiritual or psychological progress."

"I feel cold," I complained dully.

"No, you *are* the cold, you're just starting to feel it. Would you rather be feeling rage or guilt or fear for defending a customer?"

She had a point, I had to confess. I nodded slowly.

We finished our drinks in relative silence. There wasn't much else to say. She told me to call anytime if I needed to talk, and I thanked her for making time to see me. I know it wasn't the usual part of a yoga instructor's job, after all. I tried to make small talk about the class, but Leigh drained her mug and got up, saying she needed to run some errands. She left in a hurry, and I decided to hit the gym to burn off some of the confusion. Training, at least, was clean and clear.

APRIL

I'm having this dream. I know that I must be dreaming, because I never feel this good when I'm awake. In the dream, I'm underwater. It's dark here, and there's hardly any light, maybe no light at all, except faint glimmers far away. The water tastes bitter and cold, but I don't mind. I must be deep underwater, because the pressure around me feels like it must be crushing, but it doesn't hurt at all. In fact, I'm not even sure where my body is, I can't see anything at all, so maybe I am the water.

Somehow I slide forward, without effort, like an eel moving through the mire. Half-formed shapes brush past me, but I don't pay them any mind. I think there are other things in the water down here, dead things like me, but that doesn't bother me. After all, we're all dead here. I have no idea how I'm moving around down here, but it feels natural, and the flow of water around me (or through me?) is soothing. The only thing that bothers me is the sense of disorientation, like I can't seem to remember who I am. Down here, there's really no "me" or "I", it's more like us, you know, us, the dead shapes (*shavas*, haha) moving around together. No anger, no sadness, just a coolness, a calm, a dead calm. I realize that it's not that I'm alone, or that there are other people down here, it's more like one cold, fluid collective, slowly moving and changing, moving endlessly like the bitter tides of a black ocean.

Open your eyes, says a familiar voice.

I don't want to stop the dream, so I plunge deeper, deeper into the dead water, trying to burrow down in the depths of the water - but of course, the ocean is endlessness, there are no depths (really) to hide in.

"Open your eyes," says the voice again. It's Leigh, speaking more insistently now.

But I resist the urge to open my eyes. Slivers of light, bright at first, stings my eyes through my lids. I remember now: I'm not dreaming. I'm in the Yoga Centre, sitting on my practice mat, surrounded by my classmates. Leigh is seated at the head of the class, her eyes moving around the room with her usual clinical detachment. I feel a dull ache in my forehead, not quite a throbbing, but an ache. I feel cold, but that's become my normal mode of being.

The light feels hateful to me, and so I dive deeper into the black water. Leigh's voice persists, but it seems muted, further away as I tunnel down into the murk. I'm not even sure how I'm moving – I feel like I have arms and legs somehow, but logically (*who cares*, whispers a cold voice inside) I can't be moving through actual motion. Is the water real? It sure feels real – it feels cold and wet, and thick. There's a strange bitter taste to it, when it passes my lips, but it feels good on my skin as I glide down deeper and deeper. My forehead continues to ache, but oddly, I'm starting to enjoy the pain.

Ahead of me, I feel – *or see? Is there sight here? –* something enormous, like the outline of an enormous gateway. I will myself to pass through it.

Deirdre! I hear someone saying my name. It sounds like they're shouting, but the voice is so far away that I can pretty much ignore it. There's some turbulence, like someone is trying to find me in the water, but I'm too quick for them. I reach out towards the gateway and find myself already sliding past it. I can feel it rather than see it. When I slip through the cold stone archway, my body seems to shudder, and the voice calling my name suddenly goes silent.

My feet touch the ground. I'm still underwater, and it's dark here, but somehow I can see what's around me.

Well, I guess it's not sight – it's pitch black still – but I have this sense that I'm somewhere very cold and deep, and there's this maze that seems to stretch out around me. I can feel its walls reach up around me on all sides, and the texture of the walls is like some weird oily stone, almost like obsidian or hematite. I don't mind the cold, though, and I feel pretty good about being here. No distractions. No anger. No stupid gym, no bar, no music, just mostly the strange droning sound of the dead ocean around me.

So I start to wander the maze, lazily tracing my hands along the stone walls. There's no rush to go anywhere, and besides, I don't have anywhere to go back to. I think maybe I've been here for a while, like a few weeks or months or something. It's ok, because this is a nice place to be when you're dead like me.

Distant voices reach my ears, like the sound of people shrieking. *CALL 911! OH MY GOD, IS SHE STILL BREATHING? DEIRDRE, FOR CHRISTS SAKE, SNAP OUT OF IT!*

I ignore the voices. Stupid living people, such a waste of energy. Better to be dead like me. (The dead black ocean around me chortles and warbles its agreement.) Everything seems so muted here, so washed of color.

Then I turn a corner and find some other dead people in the maze. There's a guy and a girl, and they look like they just got here. Their hands seem to be dripping black paint. I've never met them, but I can tell – I mean, feel – that they have black chakras too. Well, maybe not quite, not exactly like me, but they belong here, like I do. It's good, because living things don't last long down here. (*How do you even know that*, some small part of me screams.)

Hi, I say, *Are you dead too?*

Yes, says the girl, *and we made it here. The Black City.*

The guy nods slowly. *Irkalla,* he says, *or Abzu, if you prefer Sumerian to Akkadian.*

Or Inferis, I remark in a dull voice. I have no idea how I know that, but as soon as I say it, I realize it's true. The guy nods sagely.

I'm Jade, says the girl. She's tracing a black spiral on the wall of the maze. She gestures at her friend. This is Reagan.

My name was Deirdre, but no one uses names down here, I remind.

Of course, Reagan nods, almost apologetically.

The ocean droning gets louder around us.

Shall we go to the heart of the maze? I suggest. *I want to see the darkness at the center of it all.*

Jade finishes tracing the spiral on the wall, and now I'm starting to wonder where the black paint came from. I guess it doesn't matter – dead things don't need paint. Her spiral has teeth and tendrils reaching out of it. I like the design, but it makes my crown-chakra burn when I stare at it.

We wander together for a while. The dead, black water flows slowly all around us. Once in a while something larger and much less human glides past us overhead, making strange keening noises. I would say it sounds like a whale, except the noise is all wrong, like it's been played backward through a machine.

There's a cold light above us, like some pale, distant star shining hatefully down into the maze. We all stop to stare at it for a while, and oddly, I find myself praying to it for guidance.

That's Ninib, says Reagan, *or Shani, or Saturn, if you prefer its other names. It's the only star that shines in the underworld.*

I find it very peaceful to watch that cold distant star, comforting even, but we need to get to the center of the maze. So we keep walking, or swimming, or whatever it is that you can call this slow, fluid movement along the floor of the black ocean. I find myself thinking that this can't actually be the floor of the Abyss, it must be more of a gigantic platform. (*Yes*, agrees Jade.) And I realize then that the dead don't need to speak, it's all communication by thought.

Then we hear it, altogether. There's a sound in the distance, a noise I can hardly begin to describe. At first I think it's just that constant droning, and droning is there, but this is different. It's as if dead animals and people were all trying to still speak through dry vocal cords, or dead insects were still chittering. There's something metallic about it, almost like a machine, almost like black radio static. (*Exactly*, exclaims Regan.) The static hisses in my head, and when it hits me, I can feel my chakras beginning to shake, like glass or metal when a particular sound makes it vibrate. That sound pulls you in when you hear it – even without me consciously willing myself forward, I find myself moving through the maze towards it.

Then the static begins to make sense, I can hear a chorus of voices all chittering and hissing and speaking, all at once, in languages I didn't know in life, but which make perfect sense now. *COME CLOSER* seems to be the dominant message. *CONVERGE. BECOME WHOLE.* Images of tendrils, and teeth, and liquid darkness that pre-dates the divide between life and death slithers into my mind. Forcefully. Part of me, the smallest, weakest part of me, the fucking human part, tries to run when it hears those voices, but I'm not a weakling. I silence my humanity and quicken my pace.

The maze ends suddenly, and we find ourselves at its heart. If I described the center of the maze as a chamber, it wouldn't do it justice. It's more like the corridor of the maze ends, and you're suddenly looking onto a vast space, which is fenced in by the maze itself. I can see the edges of the maze where they are close to me, but they recede in the murk as they get further away.

The black radio static is a roar now, raging like a storm, or more like an earthquake. At this close range, it's not that you just hear it, it's more like you're being shaken by the waves of black water that ripple outwards from the core of the storm. The water that flows here is different, thicker, more bitter than salty. It's almost like amniotic fluid, and I could feel it washing over me, slipping past my skin and behind my eyes. And I can't even begin to describe it visually. I'm no good with words, but you have to hear this. It was like – fuck – like at first it seemed like this immense, blackish emptiness, just there at the core of the maze. It hurt what was left of my dead eyes, like it refused to let them see it. So I shut my eyes and willed myself to see it clearly, and I could feel my third-eye chakra grow so cold that it hurt, it really hurt. But I could see better now. It wasn't so much an emptiness as it was like an enormous, dome-shaped *rift* in space, like some terrible mistake that had violated the laws of physics. The black ocean flowed into the dome and then out of it, and there were other shapes drifting in and out along with the water. Inside the edges of the rift you could see flickers of movement, sharp edges and wrong angles, and teeth, so many teeth. Grinding, crushing, crushing sounds, but also screams and shrieks and howls. I wanted to say it seemed alive, but it had this horrible corpse-like quality to it, like some ancient dead thing that just didn't care to acknowledge the difference between life and death. It was like a ravenous, dark storm cloud, and its hunger was tangible, though, like you could feel it deliberately pulling everything around it – even us – closer and closer. In fact, in the time I'd been studying it, I could see that we'd gotten closer and closer to the blackness. Now it was evident that it wasn't so much a dome as it was an immense sphere, which descended deep into the labyrinth. Even looking at it spatially produced a sense of sickening vertigo, just because of the sheer immensity of the rift, sort of like seeing a huge iceberg, and knowing that you're only just seeing the tip of something that's mostly underwater. I guess it was like that – seeing this terrible black rip in the fabric of the black ocean and knowing that the maze wasn't so much around it, as it was on top of it.

It's like a black hole, intoned Reagan, *the sun in the underworld.* The *portal to the Abyss, the mouth of the void, the doorway to true chaos. It has so many names.*

Even as we drifted closer, I could feel its essence quicken under my skin, as bits and tatters of it wormed through the water around us. At this range – no more than 100 feet, I could see that its surface rippled and vibrated like thick molasses. It's hard to describe sight in such a lightless place, but this darkness in front of us made the dead maze seem almost bright by contrast. Tendrils reached out to the three of us, wrapping around us, pulling us closer. Where the darkness brushed against me, it was so cold that it burned the skin. I was dead anyway, but I could still feel the frost spreading inside my veins and bones. Then I was there, at the threshold of existence, where being and non-being stop having any meaning, and then I crossed over.

OH!

It's hard to put into words what happens next. On the one hand, it hurt. It really, *really* fucking hurt. I could feel thousands of teeth sawing through me, cold slivers of nothingness and frozen claws pulling apart my skin, flaying me layer by layer from the inside out. The blackness poured into my mouth, my eyes, my ears, into every vulnerable part of me, and started replacing the skin and sinew as it went. It's like the Abyss was devouring me and vomiting its own un-substance into the empty space as it chewed, replacing my reality with its own counter-narrative. I felt memories being probed, discarded, and re-written. My own life story flashed before its million unseeing eyes, and I realized how pathetic and useless I was in the grand scheme of things. Maybe that's what hurt the most. But there was a pleasant, almost sensual feeling as the process went on – because I was being rebuilt, or fixed, or remade. I was aware of new sensations in my hands and feet, I could see with new eyes, and whatever black jelly replaced my brain could hear the black radio static so much more clearly. I could see hundreds, thousands of other beings inside the Abyss, and they were simultaneously all connected, like one massive, writhing colony, and yet still individual, if that makes any sense. Even me, I was now part of it – an extension of something so much bigger. The pain stopped, and I just felt this feverish euphoria, as my own consciousness opened up and allowed a greater mind to assert control.

Wake up, a voice said.

My heart chakra pulsed. I could feel pressure in my chest, like someone punching me again and again.

WAKE UP, DEIRDRE, crackles the black radio static. The Abyss itself is speaking to me. Its voice isn't asking me, it is ordering me, and I am compelled to obey.

"*Wake up Deirdre*," whispers Leigh, and I can hear the black radio static hidden in her voice. I am surprised

I have never heard her speak that way before. Or maybe I just never listened clearly.

I'm lying on the floor in the yoga studio, my classmates crowded around. There are paramedics leaning over me, working to intubate my arm with an I-V of some kind. I can see that one of them holds defibrillator paddles – did they just shock me? My t-shirt has been rolled up, and my skin burns slightly.

I notice two things right away. First, I can see that none of these people have any real substance to them – they're all pathetic and weak, sacks of meat and blood and emotion that serve no real purpose. *I can't wait to get away from them, or maybe to hurt them in some way later on*, the black radio static, the void radio, chitters in the back of my mind. I'm startled by this new range of thinking, but it's very comforting to hear that the Abyss is still with me.

But the other thing I notice is Leigh herself. When I look at her face, I can see the blackness behind her eyes, I can see the oily black water moving sluggishly under her skin, I can hear the black radio static hissing with each breath. *Oh. I never knew*, I think, *how could I not see it before?* And I realize how patient she's been, how hard it must have been for her to act human, to be human, to talk, and eat, and drink, and laugh. Will it be hard for me, I wonder?

Don't worry, she says through the void radio, *it will get easier*.

"You were dead," exhales a large woman in a tight spandex 'Ye Olde Wicca' t-shirt. Renata, I remember, her name is Renata. "Christ on a stick, they just said you were dead!" She looks like she's turning purple.

Yesssss, hisses the static. The void radio crackles and flares in my head. So many instructions to follow – I hardly know what to do.

"I'm fine," says a quiet voice, and I realize with a

start that I'm the one speaking. But it's not me, not consciously. Then I feel myself starting to sit up, to fend off the shocked paramedics, who now have to explain to Leigh and my classmates how they could have misdiagnosed my condition. I pull out the I-V and get to my feet. "I think I fainted," says the cold force using my vocal cords.

"But your heart was stopped cold," protests one of the paramedics. "You weren't breathing!"

"Nonsense," snorts Leigh, interposing herself between them and me. "Look, you're clearly trying to help, but it's obvious my friend just fainted from exhaustion."

"Yoga *is* exhausting," agrees Ye Olde Wicca, and I have to try not to laugh.

The paramedics obviously don't want to leave yet, but I certainly look fine, and honestly, I have never felt better in my life. (*Ha, what irony*, says the black jelly in my head.) Leigh shepherds them to the door of the studio, and I follow. She's still speaking, reassuring them that I'm fine.

"We're good here. If she relapses, I promise I'll drive her to the hospital myself," she says, in her usual calm voice. They do go, and then it's just us and the class.

I'm able to re-join the class, and we take our seats on the mat. I think Leigh wants to show everyone that everything is fine. We finish the session with shavaasana, the corpse pose, and Leigh does a brief guided meditation on the chakras, and you know, it feels really good. I can feel the black ocean flooding up each of my chakras, rising from my pelvis to my chest, my throat, my forehead, and the black static builds to a roar as my crown chakra floods with the black seawater from below. Pure bliss. Dead calm. Find your inner corpse.

Class ends. My friends leave, and I lag behind to speak with Leigh. There's so much to discuss.

We sit in silence facing each other in the studio. If you were to watch us, you'd think we weren't speaking at all. But the black radio static in our heads chitters, and crackles, and hisses. For an hour or two, I can see her own journey towards the maze, towards the Abyss. I can see what she's doing now, how she's helping create the conditions so that others can touch the Abyss, can get ripped apart and stitched back together, alloyed by its purity, rebuilt into weapons against the cosmos.

How can I help? I ask her. Leigh has so many ideas, so many answers. It's so exciting to listen to her, to really hear her for the first time. She tells me that others are trying to help people to find the black city. She mentions a special book, some talismans, an artist somewhere who creates contagious Abyssal horrors, and others. *But you need to find your own way to express the Abyss,* she insists. *You were chosen for a reason.*

Maybe I'll go start hurting people, I say half-in-jest, because I do like hitting people.

Sure, she agrees, and she's not joking at all. *That would be great. Whatever the black static tells you, just do that.*

And that's the end of class. We don't hug, or even shake hands. I just thank her out loud, in case anyone living is listening, put on my coat, and step outside into the cool night air. It's almost 10pm as I'm heading home from the studio, watching cars, people, animals. The city looks mostly the same, but now I see a little differently. A weird vagrant in an alley leers at me and makes a strange gesture downward, as if to say, "I know, I know!" then he turns and shuffles away. His shadow remains behind a moment longer, then turns to follow him, and I smile.

My head buzzes like a machine now, or maybe more

like a hive, it's hard to say. I'm suddenly thinking I should go to the bar and see if there are some drunks that I can provoke and then kill in self-defense. That idea tastes good in my mouth, and so I change direction and head to *The Black Hound*. As I move towards the bar, I can actually feel the darkness moving under my skin, the cold slivers of the void that have been stitched into my sinews and riveted into my hands and feet. My dark chakras are pulsing quietly, almost gently, and I'm having to fight down a smile at the thrill that anticipated violence gives me. I've never wanted to hurt someone so badly. *Soon*, says the static. The bar is just ahead. I can hear loud, drunken shouts, and I can smell the stupidity. The black static in my head begins to purr like a great cat, like it can smell blood ready to be spilled.

As soon as I enter the bar, some pig makes the fatal mistake of leering at me. My lips peel back in a snarl, and I begin to move towards him. *YES*, crackles the black static. *Smile, fucker…*

FIN.

Other HellBound Books Titles
Available at:
www.hellboundbookspublishing.com

Down by the Sea, and Other Tales of Dark Destiny

"The closest in originality to Books of Blood I've read in many a year..."
James H Longmore

This exceptional collection or spine-chillers follows the inevitable path travelled towards truth or justice, whether their own, or from the universe at large:

A tough teen meets his match in an elderly woman who has been ridding the neighborhood of its thugs, one by one.
A repeat drunk driver is cursed to spend the rest of his days trapped behind the wheel.
A pregnant teen murders her parents and devises a gruesome nativity scene.
A woman uncovers a preacher's deadly solution to ridding the world of evildoers.
A serial killer looks to reunite with his estranged mother.
The little things you think you see can lead to crippling paranoia, but a little self-surgery can take care of your troublesome eyes.
A young woman discovers her family's fate is to sacrifice themselves to horrific mermaids.
An anxious gardener murders his nosy neighbor to keep the secret about his chemically-enhanced prize rose garden.
A woman is afraid of the dark because it will release the beast that lives inside her.
A woman tries hypnotherapy for childhood trauma and learns her abuser is now her doctor.
A woman tries to forget the murders of her baby and husband by ignoring the proof in the back seat of her car.
Satan seeks revenge on the woman who spurned him by forcing her to give birth to him.
A dying woman returns to her childhood home and encounters the ghosts of her enslaved ancestors.

Blood and Kisses

"Think of what late greats James Herbert and Richard Laymon may have given birth to had they ever collaborated"
Richard Chizmar

Welcome to the long awaited collection from the writer of horror novels 'Pede and Tenebrion; a foreword by Richard Chizmar (co-author of Gwendy's Button Box and author of A Long December),18 short stories, 5 flash fiction and even a poem - all skin-crawling, soul-shredding tales of terror, of the darkest things that skulk amongst the night's inky shadows, and of the everyday gone horribly awry.

The Captivating Flames of Madness

This book's title comes from the reality that - like a moth to the flame - we're all just one event, mishap, or decision away from things that could change our lives forever.

What would you do if fate led you astray into a grim world where you encountered vengeful ghosts, homicidal maniacs, ancient gods, apocalyptic nightmares, dark magic, deadly space aliens, and more?
If you dare, why not find out?
Read for yourself the twenty-two gloriously provocative tales that dwell within this book - but be warned, some of my dear readers have experienced lasting nightmares...

Psychological Breakdown

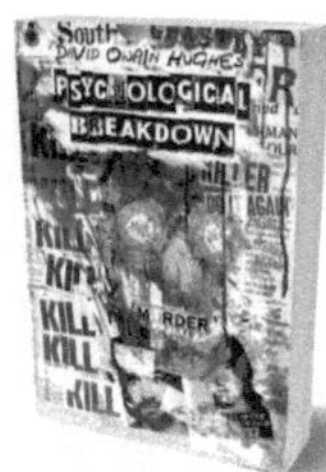

Within this tome lies eighteen tales of mind-bending terror, as Hughes delves into the human psyche and dishes out stories of what becomes of the broken minded, spirited and downright irked.

Part these blood-drenched pages at your own peril, for you will find diseased minds geared towards revenge and bloody chaos, with a few twists, turns and surprises thrown in for good, fucked-up measures.

Keep the lights on!

Graveyard Girls

Female authors + Horror = something spectacularly terrifying!

A delicious collection of horrific tales and darkest poetry from the cream of the crop, all lovingly compiled by the incomparable Gerri R Gray! Nestling between the covers of this formidable tome are twenty-five of the very best lady authors writing on the horror scene today!

These tales of terror are guaranteed to chill your very soul and awaken you in the dead of the night with fear-sweat clinging to your every pore and your heart pounding hard and heavy in your labored breast…

Jane Grey

**A HellBound Books LLC
Publication**

http://www.hellboundbookspublishing.com

Printed in the United States of America

9 781948 318389